BEHAVING BADLY

Mark had not gone in to the house. He was standing on the top step in an oddly uncertain position, as if about to rush back to the car.

'Rebecca,' he said, as she reached him. 'Rebecca, this is Bridget. Bridget, my . . . Bridget, this is Rebecca.'

'How do you do,' said Rebecca politely. Mark's first wife looked quite pleasant she thought, a little stodgy but not without humour. A bit old for Mark, she'd have thought.

'Perhaps we could come in,' said Rebecca.

Bridget moved politely out of the way. 'I like the changes you've made,' she said. 'I had no idea.'

'You have a new dress,' Mark said stupidly.

Bridget said, 'You will need to know. I have moved in. My things are in the spare room, the one next to the stairs. And my car's in the garage. You hadn't clicked the padlock firmly. You always were wickedly careless about locking up.'

Mark shouted, 'What the hell do you mean, your things are in the spare room?'

'I told you, I've moved in. I've moved back.'

Behaving Badly

CATHERINE HEATH

SPHERE BOOKS LIMITED
London and Sydney

First published in Great Britain by
Jonathan Cape Ltd 1984
Copyright © 1984 by Catherine Heath
Published by Sphere Books Ltd 1985
30–32 Gray's Inn Road, London WC1X 8JL

TRADE
MARK

Printed and bound in Great Britain by
Cox & Wyman Ltd, Reading

To
Dorothy and Winifred
Marshall

ABOUT SIX, ONE wet Friday evening in March, Bridget Mayor was preparing for her first (and as it was to turn out her only) visit to the Apostolic Church of the Children of Sinai, where she wrongly thought her vicar had urged her to go as part of the ecumenical services in the district. It would have made little difference if she had found the right meeting place, the Chapel of the Tribes of Israel, since no one else in the tiny congregation had taken him seriously, and Bridget herself was but dutifully filling in an evening of her life. It had been a bad day for her; the passport photographs she had collected that morning from the slit of a kiosk in Streatham High Street had revealed to her that she had the face of a horse.

At fifty-odd, Bridget had a large number of kind, elusive, and successful friends, a too-small flat, slim hips but thick ankles, and a sad obsession with sexual loss. Some such disjointed list of characteristics came to her mind whenever she thought of herself. They remained pieces of a disparate jigsaw; she did not feel that this new discovery, her similarity to a horse, would help create a more integrated picture.

> 'The footbone's connected to the ankle bone,
> The ankle bone's connected to the legbone'

she would sing as she finished ironing the sheets (using up the cotton ones of her married days). But her bones did not connect; she sang it as an elegy, and quietly, so as to disturb nobody: not her neighbours, not her sister in New Zealand, not her ex-husband, not her irritating and aging ex-mother-in-law, not, especially, her daughter, her Phyllida, who was dangling her pretty bare feet in the streams of London's wilderness.

She did not take herself very seriously, she did not allow herself to do so. One must behave. And in any case she had had a mild contempt for herself ever since Mark had left her. 'Well,' she had said brightly to her friends, to too many friends for dignity she now thought, but dignity was a sad virtue, though recently the one most within her grasp, 'I could hardly make a big production of it, you know. I mean, when he said our life was boring and suburban and middle-aged, I could see what he meant. I hadn't any idea, no idea at all, that shows how insensitive I'd become. And then when he told me, about how he'd spent the night with some girl called Rebecca, all I could think of was the fact I'd bought turbot for supper, and you know how one can hardly ever get it these days, and when we were young and people could get it, none of us could afford it. And Mark did like it so, and I was going to do Hollandaise sauce, and I thought, oh dear, our lovely dinner's going to be quite wasted. So when he told me about this girl I just said, oh, yes, I see. Oh, thank you for telling me. And that was all and we ate the turbot and do you know I quite enjoyed it. It wasn't till the next day it dawned on me and I simply stopped eating. But that night all I could think of was cooking the turbot properly. So I mean, there's no point in putting on a tragic act. It stands to reason that nobody, nobody that greedy has much dignity to stand on. "What did you think, Mrs Mayor, when your husband told you he was in love with another woman?" I thought about turbot.'

All this was a long time ago. Only Frieda Mayor, her ex-mother-in-law (who had not been told Bridget's turbot story) behaved still as if there were a cause for grief. Or rather for resentment. She was a woman given to resentment.

AS BRIDGET PREPARED to visit the Church of the Children of Sinai, Frieda Mayor, in Hampstead, poured out a second cup of coffee for her friend and watched disapprovingly as Trudy spooned sugar generously in.

'You are too heavy, already, Trudy. At your age, you should be careful of your heart.'

'My family is well built naturally,' said Trudy, smoothing her skirt complacently over her well cushioned legs, looking down affectionately at her swelling bosom.

'So German a characteristic,' said Frieda, 'so outmoded.'

But Trudy was enjoying the apple strudel and was in any case too good-tempered to rise easily to Frieda's bait.

'You are too thin, Frieda. You do not look after yourself properly. Are you still cooking a good meal every day?'

'Every day. A good midday dinner, and a good tea too, such as you have just eaten. In my own little kitchen.' She nodded towards the end of the converted attic in which they sat; this was unkind of her, for Trudy Goldberg had to share a kitchen with her daughter-in-law, and the two women did not get on.

'In my own little kitchen,' she repeated, in case Trudy had missed the point.

'I think you grow thinner.'

'It is worry.'

'Ah, of course, worry.'

'You would not know.'

'I have my worries,' said Trudy. 'What woman does not?'

'I eat my meals but it is the bread of sorrow, the bread of sorrow,' said Frieda. 'With every mouthful I say to myself, who is cooking for my little grand-daughter? Who is watching over her? How is she surviving in this great and ugly city?'

9

Trudy eyed the apple strudel and decided regretfully not to have a third slice.

'Phyllida at least has a job,' she pointed out. 'She can eat.'

'A job? A job? A girl with her brains, her looks, her intelligence, employers should be begging her to come and work for them. She has a job, yes . . . But Trudy, a job is not all. I think of her, without her father's protection, without her mother's advice, without her loving grandmother's wise guidance, and when I eat I think of her living on yoghurt and brown bread and I cannot swallow. I cannot swallow.'

'With grief,' agreed Trudy. 'I too . . . '

'With anger,' said Frieda. 'Anger. I sit and I hear that Rebecca below where my poor outcast Phyllida should be, in my Phyllida's bedroom, typing. I hear that woman typing. She calls it her study. My son, Phyllida's father, *he* calls it her study. I spit upon that woman. I curse her in the dead of night. I weep for my little lost Phyllida, my only grandchild, Mark's only child.'

'She is not lost,' said Trudy. 'She is at the Duke of Cornwall Mansions.'

'She is lost in spirit. English is a metaphorical language. It is why there are so many poets. You would not know, you did not finish your education.'

'Stepmothers,' said Trudy, to protect herself. 'Obviously, stepmothers . . . a problem forever.' She took the third piece of strudel after all for if poor Frieda was not going to eat it . . . She had an unusual flight of fancy. 'People get lost so easily. I sometimes think of all of us here in this road, you, and Trix, and Beatrice and Margriet . . . I wonder does anyone know we're here – still here, I mean, after all that . . . ' She looked back at the unmentionable years of the dictators. 'Still here . . . I mean, who would notice if we vanished?'

'Our children would notice. They would grieve . . . ' said Frieda uncertainly. 'My little Phyllida would notice,' she added more surely. 'Poor little Phyllida.'

POOR LITTLE PHYLLIDA was lying on her back on the carpet at the very moment when her grandmother had put the still untouched apple strudel on the table and her mother had begun to get ready for her ecumenical outing. She was waiting for someone to bring her a drink.

'There's no sherry,' said Jonathan despondently.

They all turned on Serafina. It was her week to provision the flat.

'Well,' she said, 'I forgot. Anyway I'm going teetotal. The Scarsdale diet says no alcohol. Anyway . . . '

The large room in the flat Phyllida shared with Giles, Jonathan and Serafina, overlooked Battersea Park. Beyond that, unheeded, lay the Thames. No one in the room could have told you what the state of the tide was on that particular night, or any other night come to that. The Thames was but a barrier to be crossed, the bridges were more constantly and imaginatively a part of their lives than the river below. To Phyllida and Giles and Serafina and Jonathan the Thames was that on the other side of which lay Chelsea.

'I'm moving into a flat in the Duke of Cornwall Mansions,' Phyllida had told her friends a year earlier. 'Battersea of course, but only just across the bridge from Chelsea.'

Sprawling unmodernised at the end of the third floor, the flat lay behind a cliff-face of dark red brick which was shadowed with projections, columns, curlicues of tile leaping irrationally across from balcony to window arch. The windows, large though they were, gave no indication of transparency or fragility: in shadow they were black and opaque, like iron shutters. When the sun caught them at sunset they glinted ominously. The building looked like a fortress doodled by a mad baron.

11

The flats themselves were large, inconvenient, faintly grubby in high corners. Retired artillery officers had sallied forth to their clubs from them; widows had shared homes with poorer colonial-service sisters and entertained every Thursday afternoon. Comfortably-off people had been comfortable in them; the aging boringly respectable middle classes had kept up appearances.

Now their grandchildren, even their great-grandchildren, had taken over. The rent of these highly desirable and largely unmodernised homes was high; the running costs, the rates, were unmanageable on a single income. The impoverished and undaunted young had taken over, five, six or even eight to a flat. Several incomes were needed to run one.

'Really, Serafina,' said Giles now, running his fingers gently through his thick, well-cut, freshly washed fair hair, so that it fell exactly as before, 'don't you think it looks a little bad to go teetotal at this point in the month? Not last week, when I was provisioning, oh no. Not next week, when it's Phyllida. This week. Well, I shall claim 60p back from the drinks fund. Hand it over.'

Serafina, lying on the sofa, envying Giles his hair, his looks, his elegance, shook her head.

'Cat got your tongue?' he asked, not unkindly. 'Come on, give me two quid and I'll go and get a bottle.' They all had to watch money, yet refused to let their constant anxieties affect their frivolity. They were adept at charming bank managers, manipulating credit cards and, if necessary, walking to work or sleeping on a friend's floor.

'Haven't you been out all day?' asked Jonathan. He thought she might quite well have spent the whole day stretched out on the sofa, she looked so limp. They all worried about Serafina; little conversations about her took place in the kitchen late at night. She never noticed their concern. She was in a way a burden on them but they accepted her needs, sad only that they could do so little for her.

Serafina said nothing. She stared at the ceiling. She had been to work, of course she had. She wondered uneasily if he had expected her not to go. She herself woke up every morning terrified that she might be unable to make it. It was all right for them working in accountancy firms and solicitors' offices and art galleries, meeting each other for gossipy lunches in City wine bars. She worked in a comprehensive school in Stockwell. None of them had even seen it.

After a bit she said, 'I went to Safeways, of course.' Then the telephone rang and she sat up. 'If it's mummy, I'm not here.' So although the telephone was next to her it was Giles who stretched out a hand and lifted the receiver. It was not Serafina's mother but Phyllida's.

'Oh, hallo, Mrs Mayor, how are you?' He raised his eyebrows in enquiry of Phyllida but she shook her head vigorously. She was always terrified that Bridget's world would collapse; she ran away from the pain which, because she loved her mother yet could do nothing to help her, became unbearable. She tried to shut her eyes to Bridget's existence. Later she might repent and summon up the courage to phone back. 'No,' said Giles, 'I'm awfully sorry, Phyllida isn't here. It's Giles speaking. No, I've no idea, no idea at all. She didn't say. Can I take a message, perhaps, Mrs Mayor?' Despite her determination not to bother Phyllida with her problems, Bridget was apt to talk more than she had intended. Bridget's voice came across more and more urgently. Phyllida found herself trying to listen.

Eventually Giles hung up. 'No, no message,' he said. 'Just to tell you that she didn't get that extra teaching she'd expected for next term but not to worry because she didn't really want it as the syllabus was so dull. Or something. She said it was all for the best really.'

'You ought to introduce Phyllida's mother to Serafina's mother. They could keep each other company in the long winter nights.' Jonathan's parents lived in Switzerland and were easily forgotten.

'They'd hate each other,' said Serafina. 'They're so busy being splendid, each in her own way, that they couldn't bear it. And Mrs Mayor wouldn't know what my mother was on about . . .'

'I should have spoken to her, I suppose,' said Phyllida sadly. She was a kind girl at heart. Could her mother really have enjoyed that week in Gloucestershire with an old schoolfriend which had been her last holiday? And this year it was to be Brittany . . . 'How does a week in St Malo, on your own, in July, grab you?' she asked.

'One could pretend it was Blackpool and be ever so working class with all the Frenchy families and eat chips on the sand,' said Jonathan, 'and give way to lewd urges and get the English a bad name.'

'Or be decadent and live on oysters and refuse to look at the sea and be pointed out, sitting outside a café over absinthe, as the mad English poet,' added Giles, 'but only if one liked oysters, of course.'

'All the same, it isn't really you, my poppet, is it? Surely you can do better than that on your salary?' Jonathan had never discovered what Phyllida was earning, and had a nasty suspicion that it might be more than he was.

'Oh it's not me. But mummy seems to think it might be her. I think it was the first thing she found that she could afford. I really ought to phone her and try to stop it. I should have taken that call.'

'I don't see why.' Serafina was quite clear about the limitations of her own strength. 'I shan't speak to mine if she rings up. I went down to see her last Sunday, that ought to do.'

'Went down,' said Jonathan. 'Went down! Heavens, she lives in Cheam, not Cheddar or Cheltenham.'

'We can't all have parents in super Switzerland.' Serafina shut her eyes, as if to shut out Jonathan's golden tan, Giles's golden hair. It was not done to get sexually involved with your flatmates: well, not in this flat. Other flats, other mores. London was populated by small tribes, tolerant of each other's eccentricities and barbarisms . . .

'Are you all in for supper?' she asked. 'As I'm cook.'

'Oh, good, you're not off food as well as alcohol,' said Jonathan.

'I *forgot* the sherry. Do stop going on about it so. It can't possibly matter that much.'

'Don't bully her,' said Phyllida. 'You can see she's tired. I'll go to the shops if it's too much for you.' She was a dark girl, lively, given to exaggerated clowning gestures in an attempt to give her slight clumsiness an air of deliberate self-mockery, for she was tall and had never learned to manage her height. Yet in most ways she was self-assured, confident, eager for experience. 'Yes, we're all in. There's only the four of us till we decide whether to replace Simon. And we've none of us signed out. I looked.'

'That doesn't mean anything. Everyone forgets. It's not a good system.'

'Too like college,' agreed Giles. 'Never bother myself. But yes, we all seem to be eating in tonight.'

'We're *never* all in,' Serafina repeated. And it was true: theatres and evening classes, bars and discos, sexual adventures and the National Film Theatre swallowed them separately each night. 'It's positively middle-aged, all of us sitting round as if we were going to play bridge.' She remembered her mother's bridge squabbles and felt frightened.

'But *you're* nearly always in, after all,' Giles pointed out.

'I go to parties too, you know.'

'Still . . . '

'And I don't want to stay at home so much, I have to. I've got all that homework to mark, and handouts to prepare. I just can't fit a social life in, not with this job.' She was on the verge of tears; it was as if her youth was slipping away

15

unused. She brought work home, she came in exhausted from fighting to control a class of fifteen-year-olds.

'Just to keep them in their seats,' she had once said to Phyllida. Now she said, 'I shall go out next week. I shall go to Benjie's even if the exams don't get marked.'

'Why don't you leave?'

'I shall, I shall. I shall look for another job.'

Giles went sulkily out to get the drink. Phyllida blew him a kiss and said, 'Why don't you take *The Times Ed* or something, Serafina?'

For Serafina neither applied for jobs nor, in spite of her longings, ventured often into the brilliant London night. She would watch Phyllida arrive home from the City solicitors in her neat woollen dress, and see her sally out in a tight-fitting silky jersey, and often fail to hear her return. She saw Giles go out, racing down the stairs in tightly fitting jeans, or an extravagant suit. Jonathan too would come back from his merchant bank only to leave as soon as possible, though he, at least, was often bound for evening classes before he wandered into Stringfellows or the Embassy. He was studying for exams with strange initials.

'It's Friday,' said Serafina now, 'and last night was your Poly night, but I'm sure you didn't go. You left too late.' She sounded accusing. 'You keep cutting lectures, you'll never pass.' And I am growing to sound like a real school teacher, she thought, sadly, instead of a girl doing the work as fill-in before life starts in all its awaited glory.

'That course is over. It's exams this week, daytime only. I told you. I told you last week it was exams, and you said "Poor Jonathan" in that voice of yours.'

'What voice?'

'Your mother-imitation voice, I suppose. Just shows how deep it goes. You'd make rotten mothers, you and Phyllida.'

'Probably,' said Phyllida. 'Most people do seem to. And rottener fathers.'

Serafina did not want to pursue this. 'Well then,' she said, 'four of us for supper.'

'I ought to have spoken to mother,' said Phyllida, remembering the phone call.

THE SMOOTHNESS, THE coolness of these young men, thought Bridget, hanging up, aware of having been condescended to by Giles, aware that she found her daughter's friends enchanting but not quite real. It was as if Phyllida had retreated to the social life of the thirties . . . not that mixed flats of course . . . but the courtesy, the delight in formality and style, the extravagance of their clothes and their food . . . where did it come from, this assumption that they at least would survive the unemployment and violence and betrayal of the world about her? The first time she had met Giles had been at a party: he was mixing a wine cup. It looked pretty, frosted, with strawberries floating in it. 'Be careful though,' he'd warned her, conspiratorially, as if she needed protection, as if she were precious, not in the least as if she were a fifty-year-old suburban matron, 'it's got vodka. Bottles of it. Elegant but lethal, this drink.'

'Like you.'

'What?'

'Like you. Elegant but lethal.' He had been pleased, and she had been pleased to please him.

All Phyllida's friends seemed to her like that. Except perhaps that rather pathetic Serafina.

She was pleased that Phyllida had not been in. It was no part of her conscious wish to burden her daughter. She was going out tonight largely so that she could manufacture some interesting story for Phyllida, should Phyllida ask. She went cheerfully out to her little Renault, but as she felt in her handbag for the car keys she came across the strip of cardboard she had thrust inside the bag that morning. She did not need to look at it, she remembered only too clearly the severe hair, the jolly shining spectacles, the heavy aging face, the terrible quadrupled image. I do not look like that, thought Bridget, accurately as it happened, opening the car door, turning on the ignition. Oh, passport photographs, she said, carrying on her eternal conversation with herself, slow and controlled in manner, as if she were two people (but which two?), passport photographs have nothing to do with it, and after all you are fifty and not, though your daughter's friends are so good to you and ask you to their dinner parties, and though you are with such initiative learning to skate (though this was but a plan for next winter) and though you have dreams which lead to tears on waking to no caressing hand, not the thirty you feel. What do you expect?

Thirty is not even your own choice, she jeered at herself, waiting for a gap in the traffic so that she could turn on to the main road.

Her mother, waking from the snorting fretful sleep of the very old, chair-bound and arthritic, with the loose lips of Parkinsonism upon her, had said, as if at the tail-end of a long and intimate conversation, 'But you see, Bridget love, inside I still feel thirty.' Bridget too still felt thirty. It did seem to be the definitive age. She would take the photos to her next coffee morning, disinfect the horror, show them round. 'Aren't they dreadful?' she would ask.

'Oh, dreadful, dreadful,' everyone would agree.

Dreadful, dreadful, she thought. The word rang in her head.

Yes, dreadful. It was the most intense feeling she could remember. The word echoed so loudly in her head that it took her a moment after the first hymn had started to realise that the word was not entirely her own creation.

All round her the world spun with it. She began to listen,

emerging from the daze with which she had parked the car, walked here, seated herself.

> Dread the steps of Gabriel
> Archangel
> Gabriel
> But she did the bidding of the Lord.

A great wail of delight and pleasure filled the church. The singers paused at the top of the ski-slope, gazed down, and took off on a winding rhythmic triumphant race down the slope of music.

> Oh, she did the bidding of the Lord
> (tambourines clashed, drums beat)
> When Gabriel brought the word
> And she did the bidding of the Lord.
> Dread the voice of Isaiah . . .

The hymn wound its way through the terror and awe of God until everyone was swaying as the rhythm bade them and then suddenly it was over. The pastor of the Apostolic Church looked down from the pulpit and said, 'Ay-men.'

'Ay-men, brothers and sisters, ay-men.'

'Ay-men,' said the congregation back, nodding at him. There was a rustle as of the Holy Ghost breathing or the wind in trees, or of a hundred Marks and Spencer's nylon petticoats rubbing against corsets and stockings and satin. It sank into silence and the Church was ready for its Sabbath Vigil Prayer Meeting. Bridget, sitting in an inconspicuous sideseat (but of course and inevitably conspicuous, so that the pastor's eyes rested on her a moment, puzzled and concerned), thought how envious Father Long would have been of such an intensity of listening. She thought that after all the Holy Ghost might as well speak through nylon petticoats as through a dove. She had spent years waiting for him to speak in the politely mournful tones of the Anglican clergy.

'Ay-men, brothers and sisters,' repeated the pastor

approvingly. 'And she did the bidding of the Lord.' He was a good preacher. It was a long time since Bridget had heard a sermon so openly based on the Bible; there was the reassuring feeling of a man who had worked at his subject, who assumed his audience knew as much as he did, yet were demanding edification. The textual references came thick and fast, outraging Bridget's historical awareness of the importance of context and the proper use of textual evidence, yet leading to a kind of pleasure in the ingenuity of the cross-referencing and to a hope that new relationships of thought might be revealed. After a little the pastor's theme developed into a close analysis of what obedience to the will of God might be. She grew afraid of the negatives of the Ten Commandments. She forced herself to listen but found herself distracted by the more energetic responsiveness of those around her. Everyone had produced Bibles; as the pastor, a good-looking slim man, perhaps forty, a man of stillness broken by sudden half-completed gestures, a man with a short black beard outlining his already black face, recited the textual references, the congregation riffled through its Bibles. The woman next to Bridget looked unsurely towards her from time to time. After a bit she said quietly, 'If you'd care to borrow my book, sister, I could share my man's.' Bridget accepted the handsomely bound book being tentatively presented to her. She was not the only white person in the room. Indeed she might not have had the confidence to enter the church, even in her mist of depression, had she not seen half a dozen white people making towards the door. But she was one of a very small minority; the expected support from her own suburban church three miles away was not there, and she had realised, once irrevocably in her seat, that the others were already well known to everyone in the church, or rather in the room, for the church was but a converted double-fronted shop in a South London street. The road was part of a one-way system, so that buses and cars raced by continuously; Bridget had found it hard to park.

She accepted the Bible for fear of rebuffing her neighbour, but it was unwelcome. It turned the sermon into a test of skill: she had been hoping for one moment for the voice of God and here she was engaged in some form of competitive parlour game, and one at which she was so embarrassingly bad as well. Her neighbours leapt from Micah to Galatians while she was still leafing through Ezekiel. She could keep up when the texts were drawn from Genesis or Revelations; she could find her way through the four gospels in order as they lay; she knew that Samuel and Kings were somewhere near the beginning and that Corinthians was somewhere near the end. And then the preacher (D. O. Johnson with several strange letters after his name, according to the noticeboard outside the church) had a penchant for minor prophets of whom she had rarely if ever heard, Malachi and Habbakuk for example. She resorted to hunting for what seemed to her a reasonable time and then looking pleased as if she had found the place. All this distracted her from the sermon. After a while her neighbour – a kindly woman in shell-pink spectacles and an exactly toning suit, a woman with some air of authority – leant over, removed the Bible, opened it near the beginning and pointed to the legend at the top of the page: 'The names of the Books of the Old and New Testaments alphabetically arranged.'

This helped although it felt a little like cheating. Bridget could see everyone else turning to the correct place in the Bible each time. And then suddenly the sermon was over and the pastor was praying. Nobody knelt. People bowed their heads. People stood. People prayed aloud, an old man in the front row, a woman just behind Bridget. People were praying aloud now in several parts of the room, simultaneously chanting their separate appeals to heaven. Nobody seemed to regain his seat, once up: gradually the whole congregation, it seemed to Bridget, was rising to its feet. She was panic-stricken, unsure what to do. The woman in shell-pink stood up and called out, very loudly, raising her hands high in the air so that the jacket of her suit strained at its stitches, screamed, 'Oh my son. Oh, Errol. Oh, my lovely son, my son.' Tears were streaming down her face. She stood there crying, and Bridget sat there, with the handsome Bible on her knee, and understood nothing. But the piano had begun, voices were beginning to sing, one by one people sat down and ten neatly dressed young men and women were grouped round the piano, singing. One man only, the old man in the front row, still stood, still shouted his prayer to the white plaster ceiling. Bridget's neighbour, placidly sitting, tear marks on her cheeks, said apologetically to Bridget, 'That old man, that Wordsworth Martin, he went to Atlanta once, he heard speaking in tongues. Poor old man, he hopes every week he'll be blest with speaking in tongues.'

The pastor, still in the pulpit, leant down and said, 'Sit down, Wordsworth now. Listen to your grand-daughter singing.'

The old man paused, shook his head, shouted again. A pretty girl left the choir and put an arm round him. He quietened down. Neighbours grasped his hands. He sat down. The girl, his grand-daughter presumably, kissed him and went back to the piano. She was about the same age as Phyllida. It seemed impossible they lived in the same city.

The service came to an end after the singing, ended with an odd familiarity. 'And now may the peace of God . . . '

'Ay-men.'

'Ay-men,' echoed Bridget. She had now to extricate herself from this church, to escape from this whitewashed cavern, with its old boarded floor from which dust had risen all evening in a soft cloud, settling on the stickily shining woodwork so that the pulpit, lovingly polished as it was, was now dulled. A child, following his parents towards the entrance, pulled his finger across the wood, stretching his arm up high to do so, leaving a bright snail's trail behind him. Lights were being turned off. Everyone was moving. The doors were open and she saw that it was very dark outside. The pastor was standing at the door, shaking everyone by the hand, talking to each one. She stood up and walked towards the door. People were watching her. She felt the pastor's eyes upon her with a certain unease. She stood out, white in a black congregation, and then too, in so close and familiar a group (for people were calling across to each other, 'You seen Rosie lately?' and 'Eddie, Eddie, you give our Johnny a lift, will you?'), any stranger must arouse curiosity.

He gripped her hand. 'Your first visit, I think?'

'Yes.' She would say no more. She recalled the middle-aged, long-jawed face of her photograph. She had a right to privacy.

He held her hand still. 'Why did you come, sister?'

She had a plausible explanation ready. She would say that so many of the teenagers she now taught were girls from the black churches of Croydon and Addington, girls who knew their Bibles, who quoted texts, who recognised (amazing grace) Biblical references in literature, that she had felt it her duty as a teacher to discover more of their background. She should have thought it her duty, she felt. Or she could tell the truth about the ecumenical movement, or the greater truth about constructing a life and filling one's evenings. But before she said anything he continued, What, I ask myself, is a nice lady like you doing in a converted shop in a run-down district listening to the word of God being preached by . . . The elders ask me, are you a social worker, are you perhaps a policewoman, are you just curious?'

She said nothing.

'What do you want of us, sister?' he asked.

She shook her head.

'Shall we see you again?'

'I think not.' People were pressing around them. He

dropped her hand. 'Goodbye, sister. God bless you.'

'It was a mistake,' she said. And this was true too. 'A mistake to come. I'm sorry.' She realised it was unease, not anger, about her. She had spoiled the refuge. She had brought into the hall with her something they wanted to shut out. What it was she could hardly say. She had no longer any image of herself, apart from the passport photographs in her handbag. 'A mistake. I was going somewhere else – to another church. Near by. I forgot the name.'

'A mistake?' he said. 'But now your visit is part of you. God will make it a part of your life and you must accept what he does. You cannot undo it. We are a part of your history now and you are a part of ours. You must live with it. God bless you . . . ' He handed her a tract or pamphlet; she thrust it into her bag. 'Ay-men,' said several voices about her. 'God bless you sister.' The cries followed her down the street.

She was shaking when she reached the car. She sat for a moment wishing she had a cigarette, wishing she still smoked. Then she saw two young men, really boys, walking towards her; she could see them only dimly in the lamplight. They stopped by her car, one each side. She wound down the window, still off-guard. The one on her side said, 'Piss off.' Then he stretched out his hand to her car radio aerial to snap it.

'You dare,' she called, her years of teaching teenagers coming to her rescue, her voice professionally hard. He dropped his hand and they ran off. He was only about fourteen, she thought. She was sad. People should not feel such hate; she dared not allow herself to feel it. She drove off. It was such an interesting evening, she told herself as she drove home, uncertain to whom she was speaking. One of her friends or Phyllida would hear the story one day, reduced to an amusing tale, omitting the hostile teenagers, reduced to another example of Bridget's splendid resourcefulness in filling her life with interest.

But to think of it, all these churches . . . her thoughts flowed more freely as she neared home. 'I had no idea,' she admitted to herself, accusing herself of blindness because self-accusation came easily these days, 'no idea at all . . . all these private cellular lives must be going on all over London. I can't imagine Father Long even noticing it.' Structures of theological thought were producing strange landscapes throughout England, she supposed. And poor Father Long was so easily terrified by the new and the strange. And then Giles . . . She suddenly had an extraordinarily funny picture of Giles talking to the pastor about the prophecies of Ezekiel over his elegant and lethal wine cup.

The map of London disintegrated, swirled round in a dizzying kaleidoscopic pattern, fell in fragments on the floor of her mind.

She turned into her own road. 'Who are the Children of Sinai?' she wondered. 'Who are the Apostolic Brethren? Who are the Congregation of the Pillar of Fire?' All these groups believing and acting according to their own faiths and moralities, she thought to herself, half liberated by the idea, half confused.

She got out of the car intoxicated for a moment by the excitement of her fading vision of a London transformed by strange and innocent faiths. She was sure they were innocent. And now she shut the door of her flat and looked hopefully at the clock, but it stood at only 9.30, too soon for bed, and the flat was silent about her. 'That's another day filled, though,' she said aloud. 'I have managed,' she thought. 'I have behaved well. I have killed another day.'

'Oh, my son, Errol,' the woman had cried.

What had happened to her lost son that she wept for him and struck down the hands of those who would comfort her and felt no shame at her grief and violence?

'Oh, my son, Errol.'

'Oh, my husband, Mark.'

MARK MAYOR HAD originally been named Cecil. When Mark's parents had arrived from Austria, they determined to become fully anglicised in every detail. Their eager readings in English history had revealed to them the existence of the Cecil family, long-established, powerful, central to English society. Over the years the Mayors' intellectual comprehension of the English nation and English attitudes grew steadily more profound and better documented than that of most born Englishmen, but some linguistic subtleties escaped them. They never perceived, for example, the profound gulf between Cecil as a surname and Cecil as a Christian name.

Their only child renamed himself within a term of starting at the local infant school. He was not one to suffer under unnecessary handicaps. As Frieda grew older her resentment at her son's rejection of her first gift grew. She constantly referred to it. Tonight, as Trudy munched the last piece of strudel, Frieda changed the conversation from her grief over Phyllida and her hatred of her new daughter-in-law, Rebecca, to the central concern of her life, her son.

'So what is wrong, Trudy, I ask you, with Cecil?' The evening was following its usual course. 'I said to his father, God bless him, I said, Cecil is a good name. Oscar Wilde, a classic author after all, a stylistic genius central to English comedy –'

'I have heard of Oscar Wilde.' Echoes remained in Frieda Mayor's conversation of the urgent need to educate each other felt by her and her husband in their novice English days. She was still apt to press information on her hearers at every point.

'Oscar Wilde found nothing wrong with the name of Cecily for his heroine. And Cecil is a masculine equivalent. I said to his father, what is good enough for a Master of English Prose is not good enough for our son? So what is it he wants then?'

'Mark is a pleasant enough name.'

'Oh there is nothing wrong with Mark. But it was not the name we chose. And there is St Cecilia too, the patron saint of music. Dryden wrote his Ode . . .'

'I do know.'

'Such a lovely poem.'

'Is Mark musical?'

'Not in the least. You know, Trudy, I am not religious, not at all, not superstitious at all but I can't help wondering . . . it is so *odd* that he is not musical, with his grandfather in the Vienna Philharmonic, and me singing, do you remember, in the Golders Green Townswomen's Guild Choir. But if you turn round and as good as tell St Cecilia that her name is vulgar, well . . .'

'Did he . . .' Trudy did not bother to complete the sentence. She was not listening. She was waiting for a chance to ask why Rebecca and Mark hadn't arrived home yet. She had been waiting for the sound of the car, of the front door, with some impatience.

'It was his own name he said was vulgar. But the parallel stands. How sharper than a serpent's tooth it is . . .'

'To have a thankless child.'

'*Lear.*'

The two old women glared at each other for a moment, unsure who had trumped the trick. It was dark outside; the London winter still lay heavy on the road. The house below was silent. The street too was quiet: children had long returned from school in the one or two houses in which children still lived, but it was too early for many people to be returning from work.

Frieda Mayor got slowly up and went to draw the curtain. Across the road someone pulled a blind down. 'Arnie van

27

Blijven's in,' said Mrs Mayor. She looked down at the road, but her window was too high to allow her to see the lighted windows, mostly on the ground floor, by which she could have checked on the presence of those other women who had been washed up on this foreign shore.

'Trix is back. She came back yesterday,' said Trudy.

'They didn't keep her in?'

'With beds so short?'

'So . . . Does Arnie know Trix is back? She and Trix are such friends . . .' or at least, come from the same town, she thought. 'And Trix's sister in Arnhem, does she know?'

'Trix's daughter said not to phone her. It would only worry her, she said. She might want to come and see her.'

The old women nodded to each other. Trix's daughter would not want her aunt to look after as well as her mother. They expected no more of her, nor of any of those dutiful and diligent children in whose houses they had come so helplessly to rest.

The road, which only twenty or thirty years earlier – less even than that, only a dozen years ago – had echoed with children's voices, was now filled with old women, widows most of them, many of them from Europe. It was nice for her mother, an occasional daughter might say, that Mary's mother was Hungarian too . . . a coffee party might be arranged. But mainly the householders, sunk in their own problems, scarcely realised the secondary population of the road, tucked away in their attics and spare rooms, and occasionally, when stair climbing became a problem, given a grudgingly adapted dining-room. They ignored them, as one assumes the Romans ignored the parallel population of slaves.

The women, separated by language (Jennifer's mother was Dutch, Joanne's mother-in-law Greek, Maria's mother Spanish), eyed each other suspiciously, watching for clues as to social status, freezing against someone who spoke of bribing officials or who failed to provide pastry forks, and yet over the years forming uneasy alliances in the need to create some sense of a society, albeit one so far removed from that envisaged in some distant German or Italian town seventy years ago. Each bed-sitting room held a different country but a shared history. The road was a splintered jigsaw of Europe. The old women looked inward and backward: they watched the goings and comings, they remembered the past.

'It is sad to see them so rootless,' Rebecca had said to Mark one Sunday morning.

'A world war . . . ' He shrugged. 'And then, to be old, to have no context.' He could never sort out all these old women, never recognise which was which. It frightened him to know that they watched him so closely, to realise from his mother that they had observed every detail of his private disaster, of the crumbling of his first marriage, of his daughter's refusal to return home.

'It is sad that the war destroyed so many lives,' said Rebecca to her mother-in-law. 'And left so many rootless.'

'People are not plants. I am not a rhododendron.'

Rebecca did not flinch. She was a self-confident woman and saw no need to placate Frieda. She said, 'But to lose one's past.'

'We must not cling to the past,' said Frieda. 'It is gone. We are made to adapt.'

'Quite,' said Rebecca, moving neatly from generalities to their personal situation.

Mrs Mayor recalled this conversation as she drew the curtains. Arnie van Blijven had not adapted. Frieda shut her out, she shut out Trix, two doors down the North London road, she shut them all out. She said, 'Mark is late home. And he is going out tonight. To a publisher's party. He knows such interesting people.'

'I suppose his wife being a journalist . . .'

'Rebecca . . . that one . . . if you call her his wife. If you call her a journalist, come to that. Knitting patterns. Abortions.' Trudy was looking in her handbag.

'I found such a startling article by her. My daughter-in-law found it for me in *Cosmopolitan*. Here, I cut it out. But I expect you have seen it.'

'No. She said something, I did not bother . . . What is it called?'

' "The Death of Jealousy".'

'The death of . . . ?'

'Jealousy.'

'And she calls that journalism? When you think of the newspapers of our day . . . the political commentators. The specialist knowledge. I remember a friend of mine, a fellow student, he joined the *Frankfurter Zeitung*, and years later I saw an article of his on the significance of the changing economic structure in Ruthenia, four columns of close print and every word an education. And now such nonsense as the death of jealousy. She is not a journalist. That is not journalism.'

Trudy had been hearing noises all through this speech. The front door had shut. They were two flights up, too far for her to have heard the key in the door and the squeak of its opening; but the cheerful sound arising from Mark and Rebecca's return from their respective jobs had reached her. A man's steps were climbing the stairs, presumably Mark's. She must go, for Frieda would want her son to herself, but she was a little in love with Mark, and would allow herself a short conversation.

'I must go,' she said, to reassure Frieda. 'It is growing late, they will be home soon and I must have the potatoes peeled.'

Mark came in. He was a good-looking man. Frieda's face softened. In his presence her sharply critical attitude modified. She still longed to mother him, still refrained as she had done when he was twelve, for boys must stand on their own feet. It was a conscious effort not to say, as he greeted Trudy, as he sat down, 'Have you remembered you're going out later? Wouldn't it be a good idea to have an hour on your bed?'

For he looked a little tired. She looked consideringly at his face, so illogically that of an English intellectual, a mixture of shrewdness, self-indulgence, and indefensible innocence.

'I must go, Mark,' said Trudy, holding 'The Death of Jealousy' out to him. 'Look,' she said, 'I have your wife's article here.'

'His wife,' said Frieda, with scorn. She pitched her voice low enough for Mark to be able to pretend not to hear. Trudy left, embarrassed, clutching the cutting.

'I saw Phyllida today.' Mark offered this news to his mother hopefully: she was always pleased to hear of her grand-daughter. And he wanted to talk about Phyllida, whom he loved.

'She is seeing you again?'

'We met . . . she gets off at the bus stop outside my office, I find.' His daughter had been too poised actually to cut him. She had offered him her hand and said it was always pleasant to run across people one knew in the City, it made it less anonymous. She had started plucking her eyebrows, he thought, and not doing it very well. It was rather touching.

'So. And what did you say to each other at this bus stop?' Frieda picked up the embroidery at which she spent her days; the flat was littered with bright cushions.

'She likes the place she's living at. Nice people she's staying with, she says.'

'Tell me something new. One year she's been there. Three men and one girl till last month, now two men only. I don't know. Things change.'

'These days . . . it's all very innocent.' But this Mark did not believe. He envied the young of his daughter's generation; he imagined the flats of London as constantly curtained, darkened, like the over-luxurious hotel in which long ago he had spent the first night of his first honeymoon. A complex dance of love took place in them. No young man lay quivering alone in a room in which his fantasies were broken only by the sound of his father calling the cat in.

'If it is all innocent, then it is a great pity. But Phyllida is happy. What else did she say?'

'You seem to know it all.'

'Her mother told me. Bridget, your wife, her mother, poor thing, in her tiny flat on her own tonight while you and this girl you have brought into her house dress yourself up for a party.'

Mark got up. 'Now mother, not again. Not tonight.' She was a wicked old woman, he thought. He was amazed at his own goodness at putting up with her. 'I cannot . . . no.'

'Not tonight? Why not tonight? Is Rebecca the only person to have your company tonight? Not your old mother at home all day alone?'

He could foresee the battle before him: his dignified restraint gradually overwhelmed; his resort to threats of an old people's home (once he had gone as far as to inspect some. He thought it was only the impossible cost which prevented him from booking a room); her ready tears and moral death-bed speeches; his descent to childhood with screams that she was ruining his life . . . the whole degrading scene lay before him like a rotting urban landscape through which he travelled regularly. And then the reconciliation, the tears, the embrace and childhood endearments. Oh, mother, mother . . .

He was rescued by Rebecca's foot on the stairs. His mother was a little frightened of this bright and uninvolved young woman. She recognised perhaps that Rebecca would take steps to protect Mark and that she might indeed find herself in the Miller Eventide Home which was so well-spoken of by the relieved children of those incarcerated within. Rebecca was too young to have doubts about the morality of self-protection. Old lives were self-evidently of less value than young lives to her; she wrote campaigningly about the need to care for vanishing species, but it did not occur to her that the argument might be applied to an old person's few and threatened years.

Deprived of her chance to pour her fury and love and reproach like scented oils over the head of her son, Frieda picked up her embroidery again. Rebecca sat down uninvited, her red hair brilliant against a sea-green pillow.

'A pretty pattern,' she said kindly, gesturing at the needle-work in Frieda's hands, not really looking.

'Oh, yes. From the Baltic.'

'Really?'

'Traditional . . . a village on the Baltic. A great-aunt taught it me, she was from those parts.'

'One can see, one can see the folklore origin.'

'It was a fishing village.'

'One can see the motifs, the boats . . .'

Fool, thought Mrs Mayor. She had got the pattern from a Penelope Embroidery Shop, ready marked on the canvas. The book of instructions lay by her side. Such an ignorant girl.

'You should take up embroidery,' she told Rebecca, and behaved quite politely for the rest of the short visit. She then waited eagerly through the next hour for the front door to shut, for them to be safely out of the house. Once they were gone, she felt her way carefully down to the phone.

But Bridget was out, Bridget was leafing through her neighbour's Bible, hunting for Ephesians. It was not till half past nine that Frieda got through.

'Bridget? Bridget, this is me, Oma here, your Frieda here. . . that's right. Now tell me all about your day. And did you know that Mark saw Phyllida today? And that he's gone to that publisher's party I told you about with Rebecca.

She's had her hair done: it looks awful, just like Shirley Temple, all ringlets. I could tell Mark didn't like it . . .'

Bridget held the phone from her ear, tried not to listen. After a bit she said, 'I wish you wouldn't phone me like this . . . I don't want to know, I truly don't want to know.'

'But of course you do . . . he's the father of your daughter, isn't he? You haven't found another man, have you?'

'No.'

'No, how should you, and you all of forty-five when he went, after all? So, still, how to get rid of this Rebecca?'

Bridget hung up. The phone rang again but she did not answer it. The wicked old woman, she thought, admiringly. Such savagery, such shamelessness. Frieda would have thrown that turbot at Samuel's head had he ever, in Vienna or Salzburg or Golders Green, told her of a rather pretty young woman, a journalist. And the Hollandaise sauce after it. Regardless of the cost in eggs and butter.

'MY FATHER'S GONE to a party,' said Phyllida with careful nonchalance, as the evening wore on. 'I saw him today, he told me. He's got fat.'

'Fat?'

'Well, he's over fifty.'

Fat and over fifty . . . Serafina looked disgusted. 'But you said he'd got a new wife!'

'I know. Quite young, granny says. She was his mistress for years, then they got married. Granny hates her. So do I.'

'You don't know her.'

'She's a tinpot journalist, ever so trendy.'

'She must be kinky, I'd have thought, getting into bed with a fat man. Is he really enormously fat?'

'Enormously fat,' lied Phyllida. 'Rolls and rolls of fat lying under, over his collar, absolutely waterfalls of fat cataracting over his belt.'

Giles lit a cigarette. 'How revolting,' he said. 'Actually he sounds just like Martin's new man thirty years on.'

'Yes. Martin's new man's a bit odd, isn't he?'

'Martin's men always are.'

'True.'

In other flats about them other patterns of life evolved and died. Two floors down a merchant banker's daughter told a young lorry driver that her pregnancy test was positive. He was pleased about this which surprised her. Next door Martin's latest pick-up, overweight and unbeautiful, took an overdose of sleeping pills and would be discovered dead the next morning. On the ground floor, at No. 8, Rhadakrishna monks, pale and pimply after a day in London offices, having cast off their everyday disguise of bank cashiers and book-keepers, bowed and chanted through endless incantations. A young man with whom Phyllida had twice slept paused on his way home to Battersea and leant over the Albert Bridge, his arm round a friend of Phyllida's, and discussed the size of log one would need to play Pooh-sticks there. But of course, she pointed out, one would be dead before one saw it emerge – one would be crushed under the wheels of the passing traffic as one dashed across the road.

'Dear Pooh and Christopher Robin. To die for them,' she giggled.

All these people were part of Phyllida's life and Serafina's life. They accepted them without surprise or expectation. London was no longer a city, but a dark continent of ferment.

THEY KNOW ALL of London, thought Bridget once, outraged by their coolness, their detachment, for they spoke openly of these events and adventures to their families, unaware it seemed of traditions of reticence which had for years sheltered older generations from knowledge they did not wish to have. They had asked her to dine one evening. It was one of their unexpected attributes – their old-fashioned ostentatious formal hospitality extended to friends and relatives in such a way as to confuse and bewilder them.

The young man who passed the port, who was wearing a dinner jacket (how could he afford it? How could these young men afford it? Had they wealthy parents or over-drafts?) and who had chosen the claret with such care was – or was not – sleeping with the redhaired girl who had just had a second abortion because her steady boyfriend . . . no stable interpretation of her daughter's world could be found.

The young meanwhile would be considering the sad mess their guests and other relations had made of their lives, aware of how little the gesture of the dinner party could have meant and yet hoping that the evening, to which they had given so much thought and on which they had spent more than they could properly afford, had at least given some pleasure, or if not that, eased some pain. There was no magic wand for them to wave, no way for them to put things right. When it came to it, everyone had to survive by getting on with his or her own life. There was Phyllida's lonely and exhausted mother, Giles's father, as well as the grandfather too old ever to be asked. And as for Serafina's parents . . . let alone the recent scandal of her uncle who was sixty-eight and had just left his wife for the woman next door, and she with only one leg . . . and then there was Jonathan's expensive and un-speaking family in Switzerland. No, it was all too much to bear.

They looked bleakly and directly at their parents' muddled and pitiful lives. They had no responsibility for the muddle, yet it gave them pain, from which they escaped as best they could. They were not able to bear the burden of their parents' disappointments, they felt, but nevertheless their parents seemed to expect their children to do something about it, to provide them with a little vicarious happiness, to assure them the sacrifices had been worthwhile, to comfort them when loneliness could no longer be ignored. Their parents phoned them on obvious pretexts, begged them to visit, bribed them with theatre tickets to listen to hurried tearful confidences in the bar, sailed off saying guiltily that of course everything was all right *really*.

In the flat, the telephone rang once more. Unwarily, assuming that Phyllida's mother was trying again, Serafina answered it, pulled a face at the others, and talked for some time before hanging up.

'I think mummy was a bit drunk,' she said.

'It'll cheer her up, poor darling. Nothing like a bit of booze.'

'Yes, but she can't afford it. You know she can't, Jonathan, I told you. Daddy isn't sending the cheques regularly.'

'Oh, not again.' He took a sip from his glass, and grimaced. 'This sherry is awful, Giles. Why do you always get Amontillado, when you know I only like a really dry one?'

'You fetch it then. Them as buys, chooses.'

'Selfish bugger.'

'Quite. Comfortable one too just now. Why do we go to theatres and discos and the Poly? Why do I frequent Heaven and the Queen's Head? Let's be middle-aged and slip into torpor every night.'

'Giles, I think mummy was drunk again.'

'You said. Forget it. She's a grown-up lady now. So she needs a little alcohol these long lonely evenings. So do I.'

'But she was *drunk*!'

'Look, love, I said forget it. You can't help. And I've got

37

an evening at home for once and I'm going to spend it watching telly. Lovely. Not thinking about all our parents. My father's got hold of my office number now, you know that?'

They looked at him horrified.

'Do you think everyone has such trouble with their parents as we do?' asked Phyllida. And then because she was a nice girl and fond of her mother she added, quickly, 'Not that I don't think mother is . . . '

'Perfectly splendid,' said Giles. 'Quite. You keep saying.'

'She manages,' said Phyllida in reproof. 'But do you think everyone does? Really?'

'It seems to be in the nature of the parent-child relationship,' said Jonathan, since Giles was buried in the *Radio Times*. 'None of the books mention it: it's a conspiracy of silence on the part of the older generation, I expect. We should have been warned while we were still at school, not allowed to stumble into the task unprepared. It's such a shock as we grow up to find how much time they spend in tears.'

'Mummy doesn't cry,' said Phyllida. 'She's terribly bright and jolly. She makes jokes about jumble-clothes.'

'Quite.'

Giles then switched on the telly rather loud and said, 'I've been waiting for this programme actually.' He did not want to think about his father's phone call. His father had been made redundant four months ago. He had written one hundred and eighty-three letters of application without getting an interview. 'One hundred and eighty-four if you count the one I posted yesterday, but they've not had time to refuse that yet,' he had said. He had been an uncaring and irresponsible father. Even now, he was caring for his own father only in order to get a roof over his head, to share his father's council house, his own house having gone down in the wreck of his last business but one. Giles's childhood was littered with moments of panic and marked by alternate periods of splendour and poverty: twice he would have been removed from his schools, at which he had been placed at moments of financial optimism and ostentation, had not his mother's family grimly rescued him. Yet his father's loneliness moved him; it seemed like a warning of his own probable future. It distracted him from his work, it threatened to crack the carefully-built image within which he sheltered his real feelings during the intolerable and conventional boredom of his office life. He knew he should try (but how?) to get his father a job, he should talk to his acquaintances in the City, use his network of friends, who in the past year or two had, a few of them, found themselves moving up in the financial hierarchy. The trouble was that he knew his father to be unreliable, to be a man who assumed that corners were made to be cut and that everyone made a little bit on the side. He was a man who believed reality could be evaded if one were fly enough. Giles could not solve the problem. He could think of it no more today.

'It's a good programme, actually,' he said. 'About David Hockney in California. Just right for a wet evening in March.'

THE RAIN BEGAN during the evening, creeping slowly across from the north-west, pausing a moment over Hampstead, taking a little while to leap the Thames. It splashed upon car bonnets, streamed across roads. People heard it upon their roofs and against their windows. The happy ones thought of those without homes; their firelit rooms grew cosier and warmer, the rain outside emphasising their own good fortune. Others remembered the damp patch on the ceiling, the blocked gutter, the crumbling inadequacy of all defences. In Waddon Bridget started to get ready for bed. The rain marooned her, walled her in, cut her off from all possibility of human contact. The weekend lay before her and she did not want to think about that. She would get up early and walk round the park. Or get up late and go back to bed with the newspaper and a cup of coffee. She would give herself something specific to enjoy. And rejoice, she said, having to construct something wherewith to rejoice. Her mother had written in her autograph book when she was eight, written in a bold firm copybook hand on a sugar-pink page: 'Laugh and the world laughs with you, Weep, and you weep alone.'

'Wherefore rejoice in the Lord,' said Bridget, filling her hotwater bottle and unsure whether she were being serious or satirical. 'Oh, you rainstorms and March winds, rejoice in the Lord.' She hoped her daughter was not walking home through the wet black night. She imagined her daughter's life as one of perpetual parties; she would have been relieved to know that on this night at least she was home, warm and dry and, by now, drinking whisky as she listened to David Hockney's serious and unpretentious voice. Nobody moved to switch the set off at the end of the programme; they watched the third episode of a detective serial, of which no one had seen the previous instalments, with sleepy solemnity. Occasionally Jonathan would say, 'Damn this rain' and Phyllida would say, 'It might stop by morning.' Everyone was slightly and happily drunk. The whisky was Jonathan's: he was depressed by rain and seemed to think it produced a dampness even in centrally-heated air. 'We must keep the damp out,' he would say, gazing into the wild night and pouring himself some more to drink.

'English weather is so uncivilised,' he had said once. 'The trees move about so, and the rain and mist hide things . . . it is all so irrational.'

'Irrational?'

'So unpredictable. So irrational. In Switzerland it snows in the winter and then it looks pretty and one can ski. It's hot in the summer, and then it looks pretty and one can swim. I feel as if the weather were a background for *me*. But here . . . ' So they were drinking whisky.

ONLY THE PEOPLE at the publisher's party in Bedford Square were unmoved by the rain, almost unaware of it. The many floors of the tall narrow graceful house muffled it, the terrace construction excluded it. And then the brilliant competitive conversation going on in every bright room, on the narrow stairs, in the doorways, created such a hum . . . The party was taking place throughout the house. The best food was in the attic as a kind of lure, to counteract the considerable attraction of the senior partner holding court on the first floor. The stars of the evening (people often the last to arrive and the first to go) usually remained on the first floor and were perhaps unaware of the goodies in the attic. Bernard Levin usually dropped in, Kingsley Amis was constantly expected, Lord Goodman always materialised. It was rumoured that the floors might give way if more than sixty people congregated on any one level, and as a result unimportant writers found themselves perpetually on the stairs, rushed hither and thither by charming young copy-editors urging them on and on to meet someone who had so much enjoyed their last book and who always appeared to be either just one floor up or one floor down.

Mark was an old habitué of these parties. He kept his ground near a table on the second floor where there was room to breathe and plenty of wine. He had gone straight to the attic on arrival, eaten well (though he was hardly even plump as yet, Phyllida had been entirely malicious) and was now drinking freely. He could never indulge himself thus without hearing Frieda's voice, disapproving, as she watched a neighbour's husband lurch home after his usual Sunday morning visit to the pub. 'Every gentleman is drunk *once*,' she had said to Mark. He felt when he drank that he was failing her as an English gentleman, failing to live that myth which his parents had so carefully developed to soften their exile; and yet there had always been wine at their table and good brandy for their friends. It was only their son who must exercise restraint. He swallowed the wine in his glass defiantly.

A Germanic voice behind him said, 'I hesitate to comment, Mark, but are you not, perhaps, needing that drink a little too much?'

Outraged, he swung round. Dr Fischenbaum retreated a step and said, reassuringly, 'I would not have ventured, it is only concern . . . your mother phoned me just before I left. She guessed I would be here. Such a loving, such a concerned mother you have, my boy. And after all I was your poor father's closest friend. Frieda wept a little; you need a father's help she said. Who can refuse such a woman? And she asks always after my translations, you know, with so interested a spirit. So I come today a little early and I hunt through the rooms for you, and I find you and now you will tell me what is on your mind.'

'Nothing is on my mind.'

Only pity for the decrepit figure before him kept him from more outright anger, that and the knowledge that the proper target of his anger was the absent Frieda. The ever-present Frieda, he amended.

'But your mother feels . . . '

'What does my mother feel?' Mark controlled his temper with difficulty.

'To speak frankly, she knows of your unfortunate entanglement with a woman unworthy of you; she understands your wish to free yourself; she has asked me (such a delicate spirit she has) to help. As I am a cosmopolitan, one might say, well, she did say, she was good enough to say . . . ' In the face of Mark's rigid expression even the short-sighted Dr Fischenbaum was losing confidence. 'I was after all your father's closest friend,' he pointed out again. 'I might advise, mediate . . . perhaps the young woman, spoken to with the right enticements, might respond, might withdraw?' He sounded unsure. Frieda would have been disappointed in him. 'I know a little of this young woman,' added Dr Fischenbaum, confidentially.

'You do?' asked Mark, incredulous.

'From your dear mother. Her name is Rebecca, a good Jewish name I admit, but I believe her father married out? It never works . . . '

'Rebecca,' said Mark, pouring himself another large glass of wine and drinking it straight off as an alternative to throwing it at the old man before him, who was beginning to look to him vaguely like Frieda, 'Rebecca is a charming and intelligent woman who has done me the honour of becoming my wife.'

He then turned and walked away into the next room, though less pointedly than he would have wished because of the need to thread his way through the crowd, which was thickening, especially so round the figure of a middle-aged poet in motor-cycling gear. Rebecca, he was relieved to see, was not among the nubile young women clustered about this person.

Nor was she in the back room to which he made his way. Disappointed, he helped himself to another drink. Rebecca would drive him home, he told himself.

He knew he was drinking too much because he had started to make lists. He was leaning against the wall making up lists.

Mark made lists to comfort himself, had never managed to break himself of the habit. Now he bent over a plain girl sitting by him, a girl whom someone had brought along to

43

the party and deserted, a girl who he felt pretty sure would never cross his path again, and said that there were fifteen living writers of repute who had published nothing until they were fifty. The girl said 'Oh?' in an uninterested voice and stretched across the table for some olives. He felt irritated; he thought of himself as free of old-fashioned sexist foibles, especially since Rebecca had a sharp eye for them, but he still expected plain girls to compensate for their looks by a generalised and warm concern for the male sex.

'Here,' he said, 'have an ashtray for the stone.'

'There aren't any. Not in stuffed olives.'

He would have abandoned her but he needed an audience. 'And there are sixty full professors in the U.S.A. who were over thirty-five before they learnt English.'

'I suppose if they are professors of foreign languages . . . '

'*Apart* from professors of modern language,' he roared. But he did not know; it was an obvious possibility which had hitherto escaped him. He moved to another field. 'I have followed up all the children of the five analysts and psycho-therapists of my acquaintance and every single one of them is delinquent in a major degree, despite great fatherly concern. Or, of course, because of it?'

'Can you see any salted peanuts?'

'And I am compiling a list of men whom I know and like and respect who walked out on their wives and it has reached the extraordinary total of twenty-two.'

'Do you really know twenty-two men whom you both like and respect?'

'I know far more . . . for God's sake, that's clear, isn't it? It must be. I mean not every single worthwhile friend I have got has walked out, only a minority. Well, not a large majority, I'm sure.'

'I should hope not,' she said primly. 'Though it does seem to be like measles in men of your age. Panic about impotence, I suppose.'

He chose to ignore the last comment. Plain girls had no right to talk about impotence. 'I only mean it's not an absolutely unknown event for men to walk out on their wives,' he said. 'Twenty-two known to me . . . It's quite common. It's so common that it's become perfectly acceptable behaviour.'

'To desert your wife?'

He looked at her in despair. He was really very drunk. 'She's all right you know. And it was five years ago. Anyway one can't live in the past, one has to be free to live one's own life. One owes something to oneself. One cannot allow oneself to be bound by history.'

'I like Gauguin myself,' she stated, as if suddenly finding his point of view acceptable, but it was a leap he was too drunk to follow.

'Gauguin?'

The plain girl caught the eye of the rather beautiful redhead who had suddenly joined them. She hoped she might be eager to widen the discussion. Rebecca ignored her, put her arm round Mark and nuzzled into him. 'Drunk again, love?' she said.

'As a lord,' he agreed. But her presence was sobering him; he loved her too much to need to collapse into alcohol when she was with him. His hand spread across her hip. 'Oh, Becky,' he said. 'I'm bloody tired you know. Let's go home.'

She smiled. The plain girl could see that they were in love. They walked out together, stopping to say a word to Michael, to Jeremy, to Vanessa; they were glad to be leaving, to have the peace of their home before them, to have a weekend before them. 'I was rude to that poor girl,' he said, as they left the house.

'She'll be all right, someone'll look after her.'

'Oh, she didn't mind. She'd written me off as an elderly drunk anyway. Can't blame her. My fault. I'm just tired.'

He turned, before she started the car, and kissed her.

'Dearest Becky,' he said. 'I wish I were nicer.'

'Couldn't be,' she said, letting in the clutch. And indeed she thought so; and he was in her presence, and at other times too, a far more intelligent and sensitive man than the girl at the party could have known.

'You need a break,' added Rebecca, after a few minutes. She began to plan.

T HE SUN SHONE fitfully next morning and Phyllida managed to bring herself to telephone Bridget. Bridget was delighted but apprehensive. She was afraid Phyllida might want to borrow money.

'Is anything wrong, dear?'

'No, of course not. It's only that Giles said you phoned last night. I wondered if there was anything special . . . '

Since Mark's defection Bridget and Phyllida spent a lot of their time refusing to be a burden to each other, yet aware that should disaster strike either of them the other would perforce have to pick up the pieces. The tenderness of their mutual love was no longer heard in their defensive voices; it was overlaid by bright artifice, at which both of them grieved.

'Nothing special, dear.'

'I thought perhaps you were at a loose end a bit, a bit at a loose end.'

'Who, me?' Bridget laughed. 'Not me. Actually, I went to a most fascinating place in Croydon last night. An evangelical church, a black church really. Some odd American offshoot. Such fun.'

'What an odd thing to do.'

'It's for an article,' lied Bridget. As she spoke it became the temporary truth.

'Oh, for an article. You're going to write again, then? Jolly good.' Bridget's writing had consisted of five articles for the local paper on playgroups; they had been written when Phyllida was three.

'I thought I'd pick it up again, yes. Try the local paper.'

'Good-oh. Don't overdo it though, not with all that teaching.'

'I don't think actually there'll be all that much teaching after Easter. They're cutting the evening classes early. There isn't going to be much part-time teaching about soon. Leave me much more time for my hobbies of course, and writing, like I said.'

'Mother's so absolutely splendid that it makes me sick,' said Phyllida putting down the phone. 'She's just lost her job, or most of it, and she's being ever so jolly, you know?'

'Giles's father's lost all his jobs. And his mother went and died so she's no good,' said Serafina. The two men were still asleep.

'What an odd way of putting it. About his mother. As if she did it on purpose.'

'Well, I meant she can't go out to work herself. Splendidly, as a char, as your mother would. Being dead, she can't. My mother could but won't. She just gets drunk. She's selling all the family furniture. I'm saving up to buy my favourite bits before she sells them all.'

'Hasn't Giles's father got any family furniture to sell?'

'No, it appears not. And he's got his own father to look after too, and *he's* almost ninety. Isn't it awful?'

'Perhaps we could introduce Giles's father to my mother and they could be splendid together,' said Phyllida, 'and look after Giles's grandfather and get Family Income Supplement and not bother us. And have your drunken mother as a lodger to redeem her. Is it one of one's duties these days to match-make for one's parents? Would Giles's father do for my mother do you think?'

'He's impotent. Giles says he told him so over lunch. Imagine how embarrassing.'

'My mother would never do anything embarrassing,' said Phyllida, unsure whether this was a pleasing trait or not, but admitting it to be convenient. Then she added suspiciously, 'You and Giles seem to have been getting together rather.'

'Not really,' said Serafina, looking self-conscious.

'Oh.'

Oh, my lovely Giles, thought Serafina inside herself. For he did talk to her more than he used, she thought. Oh, my lovely Giles.

'OH MY SON, Errol,' crooned Bridget, taking over another woman's grief and huddling into the corner of her chair and weeping for it, since tears came and had to be given a focus, grief had at last to be given words, and Bridget had no longer any of her own. 'Oh, my Phyllida, my distant daughter, Phyllida, polite and discreet and kind, living her own life as daughters should, oh, my boring self, oh, Angel Gabriel. Oh, horse.'

'George Eliot had a face like a horse and if you will imagine a very sad horse you will have a clear idea of George Eliot's appearance.'

It sprang into her mind. She wiped her eyes, giggling uncertainly. 'Analyse into clauses,' it had said, the dark red textbook of her schooldays, 'analyse into clauses, George Eliot had a face like a horse, and if you will imagine a very sad horse you will have a clear idea of George Eliot's appearance.'

George Eliot had genius, a lover, a whole life.

Bridget had just a face like a horse.

The telephone went.

It occurred to her that she had become part of the telephone system rather than remaining a part of human society. She lifted the receiver and said in a high-pitched hum, 'Brrr, brrr . . . Brrr, brrr . . . Brrr, brrr . . .'

A puzzled strange feminine voice (she never was to discover whose it was) said, 'Mrs Mayor? I'm sorry is that 641 – '

Appalled, Bridget slammed down the telephone. That was what happened to people living alone, she thought. First they talked to themselves inside their heads, and then aloud as they walked down the streets, and then they started making odd noises. She foresaw the day when she would clump down a rain-soaked street to the shops quacking like a duck to the grey skies; or would suddenly shout at the hairdressers, as she had done the other night in her bath, pointlessly and unexpectedly, to the empty world, 'I hate you. I hate you.'

'I am a horse and a telephone,' she thought, 'and an old woman and a teacher of literature and a householder and a member of the congregation of St John's Church' . . . what, would the list stretch on till crack of doom? 'Rescue me,' she prayed. 'Speak to me.' She felt in her handbag for a handkerchief and found the passport photographs again and also the pamphlet given to her by the minister, the pastor, she did not know how to describe him, by the Rev. D. O. Johnson she saw now it was stamped, only the night before. It was dramatically printed, with italics and capitals and subheadings and indentations and footnotes. She did not feel she could wade through it, it gave her a headache even to look at it.

She felt hurt that the pamphlet had been handed to her without apparent choice, as if she needed some kind of hand-out before she would go, but as if she were not in any way selective or demanding.

'I suppose I'm not demanding,' she admitted. And humiliatingly he had recognised this and handed her some pamphlet about, she supposed, the captivity of Israel or the sufferings of Job. She glanced again at the amateurish production on her way to the kitchen to throw it away.

'Thy bruise is incurable,' she read, 'and thy wound is grievous . . . All thy lovers have forgotten thee; they seek thee not.'

Jeremiah, it appeared, chapter 30. She thrust it angrily into the waste bin. It was not apt, she thought. 'I haven't even had any lovers,' she told the absent pastor. 'Only one legal and unsatisfactory husband.' She was glad now of her earlier certainty that the pamphlet had been picked at random.

'My bruise is incurable,' she repeated. 'Bloody nonsense,' she added, and felt better, though swearing even so mildly was rare for Bridget.

Nevertheless, it comforted her to remember him. It was him she wanted, not sermons or pamphlets, his quiet, tense, masculine concern, and it was so long since she had admitted any such thought or feeling to her consciousness that she side-stepped the implications and thought of his safely disembodied voice talking of obedience to the word of the Lord and then felt a great rush of rebellion, for after all was that not exactly how she had spent five years, obeying, submitting, behaving as caused least trouble to others. She wanted more from him and from the world than this. She could find no words of her own for the confusion within her. 'I shall do such things,' she said. 'What they shall be, I know not. But I shall do such things.'

It was at this moment that Frieda telephoned her, to tell her of the very late return the previous night of Mark and Rebecca, and of their even more shocking frivolity that morning. 'And Rebecca,' said Frieda, 'had a bite mark on her neck and not even the modesty to cover it. The slut. The whore.'

Mark and Rebecca were not late risers, even after a party. They sat over breakfast in the sunny kitchen before Bridget was out of her bath, before Phyllida had stirred. Rebecca sat gazing at Mark, sipping coffee, her pretty cup held in both hands. They had brought the pottery back from Italy six months earlier. Rebecca had an eye for pretty things; the whole house seemed lighter and more elegant than when Bridget had owned part of it. Mark had wanted to move when they married, but Rebecca had dissuaded him. Such a pleasant house it was, she had said. And moving cost the earth these days. Besides, wouldn't it be a little cruel to uproot his mother from her flat upstairs in a district where she had so many friends? Rebecca meant this; she did not intend to sacrifice her own happiness or Mark's to Frieda but she hoped to be able to behave with civilised kindliness to her mother-in-law. It did not seriously occur to her that there might be any difficulty in this. Old people don't like moves, she pointed out to Mark.

He had been a little shocked at the ease with which she had dismissed his tentative suggestion that she might not want to settle among the debris of his first marriage.

'But that was ages ago,' she said. 'Bridget's been gone ages. And one cannot keep remembering the past.'

'That is why I thought you might want to move.'

She looked at him confidently. 'If you keep on I shall think you are still anchored in the past,' she said, happy in her certainty of his love for her and hers for him. 'But we agreed, didn't we, life goes on, one grows, one changes. No need to run away from what no longer matters. And it's a lovely house. And after all,' she added, generously, 'it's not as if you weren't happy here for a very long time. You and Bridget had a good marriage, for years and years. And it ended peacefully enough at the right time . . . you don't need to run away.'

He did not want to visit estate agents, to spend unnecessary money, to instruct solicitors.

He felt too old to go again through the terrible uncertainties of buying and selling houses, of failures to exchange contracts, of calculations about bridging loans.

'Of course, if you like the house,' he said.

'And,' she pointed out, 'we could afford a splendid honeymoon on what it would cost us to move.'

'We shall have a splendid honeymoon anyway,' he had said, pulling her to him. 'If our present form is anything to go by.'

And she had been right, he thought now, pushing his cup

towards her for more coffee. He was proud of his pretty house, his sunny ever-changing house. Rebecca had opened his mind to a whole new way of furnishing. She bought old furniture from frighteningly expensive antique shops. It got moved about, tried against different walls, was placed in different groupings. Sometimes it was returned months later to the shop from which it had been bought and some new table or cupboard would take its place. Rebecca never lost on these transactions. 'But one wouldn't buy from a man who wouldn't repurchase,' she said, astounded by his surprise. Much of her considerable earnings went on curtains or re-papering. He did not grudge this.

'What today?' he asked. She was the one who took the lead. He depended on her for excitement, for stimulus, for ideas.

'Dieppe.' She looked at him with the upward glance he had once thought pleading, learned to see as determined.

Dieppe? She was mad.

'I told you, I said last week . . . you drive down to New-haven and go across on the ferry and stay the night and come back full of French food and wine.'

'But not just on the spur of the moment. It needs planning.'

'For God's sake, it's not Pakistan or Chile. Don't be so provincial. It's next door, really.'

He longed to go. His world sparkled when she was there. He loved her more than when they had married, more even than when he had started the affair and betrayed Bridget, Bridget who was so splendid a wife, so good a woman, who had given him a settled background and predictable love and made him feel his years, who had bored him so, and about whom he still felt guilty, though less and less often so.

'Dieppe,' he said. If to her it was just next door, to him it was an escape, a party.

'But we must hurry,' she said. 'Throw some things together, rush away, Quick.'

'We can't. We've not made arrangements about mother.'

She showed no impatience, though she was already clearing the table, thinking about passports and Eurocheque cards.

'I don't think she'd mind being left alone for twenty-four hours. She's not senile or helpless. She gets herself to the West End occasionally, after all.'

'Not for months.'

'I'll see she's got all she needs in the flat. And I told the Warners we might be away, Susie'll drop in.'

'We usually get someone in, you know we do, if we're going to be away overnight.'

'And she hates it.'

This was true. The agency nurses were talkative and patronising; all old people were the same to them. They spoke to Frieda, she once complained, as if she were a retarded four-year-old.

'She'll be all right,' said Rebecca. 'You'll see.'

'Yes, you go,' said Frieda, surprisingly, when he put the plan to her.

He waited, suspicious. There was a gleam in her eye.

'So you want a little French weekend,' she said. 'You go. I am not senile, you know, not yet. We have that pleasure to come. And however exhausting it is, you know, men who marry women young enough to be their daughters almost, have to keep them happy. All this rushing about. It is the sign of an immature mind of course, but you go. Most certainly. I ask only that you bring me back some of Armand's Tisane,' she added. 'The Tilleul Tisane. You can't get Armand's in England, only in France.'

His heart sank; he foresaw his whole weekend given over to hunting in back street pharmacists' shops for this obscure and old-fashioned drink.

'We shan't have much time.'

'If it is too much trouble, of course,' she said. 'And I will pay for it. But it is my only request. And I am myself too old to hope for weekends in France ever again.'

He wrote it down. Then guilty, excited, hating the rush and tear of this unprepared expedition, yet enjoying the sense of daring, of behaving out of character, he drove Rebecca, rather too fast, across London to the A23. Nevertheless, he did not expect good to come of it all. He expected almost to be forbidden to go on board. He was brought up when foreign travel was a serious undertaking. It surprised him that all went smoothly; he even found his mother's tisane quite easily, at a large grocer. He suspected correctly that she would have chosen some less easily traced purchase had she had more time. In spite of this he was not entirely happy as they returned. The weekend had cost a great deal more than he could think it right to spend on so casual a break, and the car had been scratched in the car park where they had left it, and he had not slept very well. He always found French pillows too hard and these days they gave him a stiff neck. He was not in a good mood as they returned, and Rebecca knew this. It saddened but did not perturb her.

'Here we are,' she said, turning into their street.

'There are lights on downstairs. God, what's wrong? There shouldn't be lights. Not downstairs.'

'Perhaps someone's called. Susie, perhaps. Or your mother's decided to watch our telly, instead of hers. I've often thought she preferred ours but she won't say. Or she's having a whale of a time going through my desk. Don't panic,' she called, but he was already halfway up the path.

The door opened before he could get his key out.

A rather sturdy woman stood there, outlined in the lighted doorway.

Oh God, thought Rebecca, perhaps the old woman has had a stroke or something. Mark'll never forgive himself if anything has happened to her.

She got out of the car as fast as she could, pausing even so to lock the door after her because of the cognac visible on the back seat, and then hurried towards the house.

Mark had not gone in. He was standing on the top step in an oddly uncertain position, as if about to rush back to the car.

'Rebecca,' he said, as she reached him. 'Rebecca, this is Bridget. Bridget, my . . . Bridget, this is Rebecca.'

'How do you do,' said Rebecca politely. Mark's first wife looked quite pleasant she thought, a little stodgy but not without humour. A bit old for Mark, she'd have thought.

'Is mother . . . ?' asked Mark.

'Oh, she's fine. Absolutely fine.'

'I don't quite . . . ' Mark wondered if Bridget perhaps often visited Frieda without his knowledge. He was appalled at the possibility that she had watched the gradual transformation of the house and he had not known.

'Perhaps we could come in,' said Rebecca.

Bridget moved politely out of the way. 'I like the changes you've made,' she said. 'I had no idea.'

So she was not a regular visitor. Mark was surprised in a way that he had recognised her so swiftly. Five years apart, after all.

'You have a new dress,' he said stupidly.

Bridget said, 'You will need to know. I have moved in. My things are in the spare room, the one next to the stairs. And my car's in the garage. You hadn't clicked the padlock firmly. You always were wickedly careless about locking up.'

'I think I left the padlock loose, actually,' said Rebecca.

Mark shouted, 'What the hell do you mean, your things are in the spare room?'

'I told you, I've moved in. I've moved back.'

He regained control. He said very slowly and clearly, 'Would you mind telling me what this is all about? What made you come here after all this time?'

'Your mother invited me.'

'She's always inviting you. You wrote and asked me to try

and stop her a year or two ago.'

'Well, you didn't stop her. And this time I came.'

'Is mother ill? Is she . . . '

'Frieda is perfectly well. She was lonely. She is in the drawing-room and I am making us both some coffee. I will make enough for you as well. And of course for Rebecca. She telephoned me and asked me back and I thought why not?'

Mark was aware of an urgent need to go to the lavatory. It had been on his mind for the last five miles of the journey home, and now it destroyed any possibility of dealing with the situation in the immediate calm and masterly manner demanded. He was forced to abandon the field. Zipping up his trousers a little later he wondered bitterly what unrecorded political defeats and military routs had been due to exactly such physical demands. When he emerged, he found the three women sitting in the drawing-room. Bridget was pouring out coffee. 'It was ready,' she said cheerfully, 'and I found I'd made enough for us all if we only have small cups.' Frieda was looking smug and triumphant; Bridget appeared to be enjoying herself. Rebecca was perched on the edge of an upright chair smoking but chatting quite politely. A conversation about the value of bargain breaks seemed to be developing. It did not make sense.

After a bit he retreated to his study.

'Phyllida,' he said very quietly, despite the shut door, fearful that the sound of his lifting the telephone receiver would somehow precipitate some even worse event. 'Phyllida, don't hang up, please don't hang up. Phyllida, you must come round and help. Your mother's here. Bridget's here. She says she's come back.'

'Back? She can't.' Phyllida sounded suitably horrified.

'No, of course she can't. It's outrageous. Come and tell her so.'

'Now look, I really think this is for you and Rebecca to sort out, don't you?'

'But she won't go.'

'Too bad. Is she all right?'

Phyllida rang off. Mark went back to the drawing-room. It was getting late and he had an important meeting first thing in the morning.

Incredibly, conversation was going on.

'I don't like the curtains, but otherwise I must say the room is greatly improved,' Bridget was saying approvingly. 'I always wanted flowered chintz on the chairs too, but Mark wouldn't have it. He always used to go for Regency stripes, as if he had been frightened by Beau Nash in his cradle.'

'Very good taste, those stripes were, I thought,' said Frieda.

'Oh, ghastly good taste,' agreed Bridget.

'We chose those stripes together,' said Mark with indignation.

'We bought them together, certainly,' said Bridget, 'and actually I paid for them, from my Shakespeare class money, but you chose them. I just said yes. You always got so bad-tempered when I disagreed with you. Does he get bad-tempered when you disagree with him, Rebecca?'

'No,' said Mark.

'Dreadfully,' said Rebecca, 'but of course only if you let him give an opinion first. He can't bear being contradicted, and that's what it is. I don't worry. He gets over it. And usually I'm quicker anyway.'

'What do you *want*?' asked Mark. 'Surely you didn't come back just to tell Rebecca you didn't choose the curtains?'

'She came back because I phoned her and told her I was alone and felt ill,' said Frieda.

'Did you feel ill?' asked Rebecca. 'Ought we to get a doctor?'

Frieda looked at her contemptuously. 'I am always feeling ill. Old women expect it. One day you will find me dead in my bed. But not yet. You will have to put up with me a lot longer, please God. If you are still here. Yesterday I did not

57

feel well but I did not feel more ill than usual.'

'She phoned me,' said Bridget. 'And it seemed like the voice of Gabriel in the hymn. Or Jehovah. "Come," she said. So I came.'

'I do not understand you at all, either of you,' said Mark.

'It was something to do,' said Bridget. 'At the very least, it was something to do. At the most it was the voice of Gabriel.'

'If you thought mother was ill, it was of course kind of you to come. But now we are here, I think you should go. I am sure Rebecca will not mind if I drive you home if you do not feel up to driving yourself.'

'You really were hell to go shopping with,' said Bridget reflectively.

'For God's sake,' said Mark, 'you haven't come all this way to reminisce over my shopping habits, have you? What the hell do they matter?'

'It makes me angry,' said Bridget. 'It makes me angry to think I put up with it.'

'Where's your coat?'

'I'm not going.' She leant back with the air of a headmistress waiting for silence and the silence duly fell.

After a bit Rebecca said, 'Mark is in love with me, you know. You can't put the clock back.'

'I don't want Mark back. Or at least, I know I can't have him. And I really don't think I want him.'

'Well then?'

'This is where I want to be,' said Bridget. 'It's the first thing I've wanted for years. To be here. With people to talk to and something that matters to talk about. With company I haven't had to organise. Just to be here.'

'But you squabbled so all those last years.'

'Squabbling,' said Frieda. 'What couples don't squabble?'

'We don't,' said Rebecca.

'What married couples of standing, I mean. You are only a new . . . a new plaything.'

'We did not squabble,' said Bridget.

'If you like,' said Rebecca. Her shining hair danced on either side of her beautiful oval face. She was quite unperturbed. Mark would get rid of this pathetic creature. Frieda she had never taken seriously.

'Listen,' said Mark, sitting down. 'Perhaps you'll feel better tomorrow. Perhaps you've been overdoing it. You do look a little tired. Now, I'll drive you home and I'll send you a little cheque next week and you can go to Venice or Amalfi or somewhere and have a little rest.' He was uneasily aware that the word little was recurring too often, but could not stop himself. 'You need a little change,' he added.

Bridget considered whether to be indignant at the offer of the cheque. She had made a dignified point in the past of not asking Mark for money even when she had had to . . . she could not, however, be bothered.

'I'd rather be here,' she said, 'squabbling.'

Rebecca said tartly, 'We should certainly be doing that if you were here.'

'Oh, I don't suppose I'd enjoy it exactly,' admitted Bridget. 'But it would seem real. I wouldn't have to wonder how to fill up my evenings.'

She's mad, thought Mark. Or evil. He wondered that he had stayed married to her for so long. A great weight of guilt was lifted from his shoulders. Paradoxically he felt affectionate towards her for the first time for ages.

'And now let's take you home,' he said coaxingly.

'No,' she said. She put her hands on the arms of her chair and stiffened. She was behaving outrageously, she knew. It was indefensible. She had not been so happy for years.

'Make her go, Mark,' said Rebecca. 'It's been a long day.'

'How?' he asked furiously.

She shrugged her shoulders.

Mark went up to Bridget, stood in front of her and, bending down, gripped her forearms. He managed to lift her a little out of her chair. As he stood her up she let her weight sag. It caught him off balance and they fell sideways to the floor. He was used to Rebecca's slight form, he had not expected Bridget's weight. Rebecca curled her legs away from the heaped tweed of Mark's jacket, of Bridget's sensible skirt. Mark removed his hand hastily from Bridget's thigh.

'Now what?' Rebecca lit another cigarette.

'For heaven's sake, Becky. I mean she was my wife for about twenty-five years.' Mark stood up and looked down at Bridget who was huddled up crying. 'I can't just kick her down the stairs forcibly.'

'No,' said Rebecca. 'So I see. Well, if she is going to stay here, we had better go ourselves. She'll get bored.'

'Go?'

'This is London. There are hotels.'

'Do you know what London hotels cost?' asked Mark.

'He always was mean at moments of crisis,' Bridget said through her tears.

'Or we could go to Josie and Max,' said Rebecca coldly.

'And have the whole story round London in twenty-four hours? Nigel Dempster'd have a field day.'

'We're not that important, Mark.'

'Well, Max'd dine out on it for years. And it wouldn't solve anything. She'd stay. She's stubborn.'

'Persistent, you used to say,' Bridget pointed out. 'Courageously determined.'

'I'll go on my own, then,' said Rebecca. 'This is all quite ridiculous.' She walked towards the door, pausing for a moment at a little desk to open it and extract an address book.

'Was it that easy?' thought Bridget. But Mark was saying sulkily, 'If you feel like that, then, of course, I'm coming, Becky.' He really does love her, thought Bridget, and she had known it all the time, but she would still rather be here behaving badly, crying, hurt and living, than watching a serial on BBC 2 because it gave her a fixed point in the week.

I have grown wicked, she thought.

'Don't go,' she said. 'Don't go. I need you.'

Mark was talking in an undertone to Rebecca as they looked through the address book together.

'Don't just go, Mark,' Frieda called sharply. 'She needs you. She is your daughter's mother after all.' She got up, gesturing with her stick. 'Your poor homeless daughter's mother.'

Rebecca, flicking through the pages of the address book, said, 'I would advise you to telephone her daughter tomorrow if she's still here, Frieda. I will leave solicitor's consultations until Bridget has had a chance to consult a doctor. She is plainly ill. Or mad.'

'Such insults from a mere Belgian.' Mark had never understood his mother's insistence that Rebecca was hiding a Belgian descent.

Rebecca smiled kindly, took a step towards the door, and crashed to the ground. Her fall dislodged a glass vase from the desk top; it tinkled about her.

Frieda extracted her stick from between Rebecca's legs and sat down.

'Go, if you must,' she muttered, 'but not taking my son.'

'You did that on purpose,' said Mark.

'What a thing to say to your old mother,' said Frieda, weeping. 'To think you could have ideas like that. What has come over you to believe that I could hurt even your little Belgian girlfriend on purpose? What has she done to your imagination? Your poor crippled dying mother.'

'She has broken my ankle,' said Rebecca. 'No, don't try and move me, don't. And I have a terrible pain in my back.'

'Oh God.'

'I would come and help,' said Bridget who was still on the floor, 'but since you all ask so earnestly, or at least I assume you intended to, no, I don't suppose I'm badly hurt from where Mark dropped me so brutally on the hearthrug but I am bleeding rather profusely from some damage somewhere, my head I think, and I feel extremely giddy.'

She lay back and closed her eyes.

'She is unconscious,' said Frieda. 'She is dying. You have killed her.' She fumbled in her handbag. 'I cannot find my heart pills,' she announced, 'and I have taken none today.'

MARK STOOD ON the doorstep as the doctor got out of his car. A brisk man, an Indian, not the familiar grey-haired Londoner Mark had expected. Of course, on a Sunday one must accept whoever was on duty.

'An accident, Mr Major?'

'Mayor, actually, Mark Mayor.'

'An accident, Mr Mayor?'

'Two actually.'

'Two?' The Indian drew away a little, gave a glance at the quiet room, the affluent house. 'There has been a fight?' He looked reprovingly at Mark. 'Your friends had been drinking?' He had been brought up in England; when the middle-aged English called you to their houses on a Sunday evening it was so often through drink.

'No, no, I assure you . . .'

They reached the drawing-room.

'You were long enough, I must say,' said Rebecca. Her leg was hurting. The doctor ignored her and moved across to Bridget, who was lying motionless, her head in a puddle of blood.

'She fell,' said Mark. It might be drink after all, thought the doctor, but he could neither smell alcohol nor see any glasses. Although of course there was broken glass on the carpet as he came in, they might have cleared away . . . He reserved judgment.

'She is dead,' said Frieda. 'I have seen plenty of dead people in my time.' Her tone implied that the doctor might not have had her advantages.

Mark had seen Bridget open her eyes two or three times since her apparent collapse, but he knew little about the effects of concussion. Perhaps his suspicions were unworthy.

'Not dead,' said the doctor, who was kneeling by Bridget examining her. 'A minor contusion on the temple I think. These head wounds bleed alarmingly.' He produced scissors, dressings, and eventually a notebook.

'Her name?'

'Mayor, Mrs Bridget Mayor.'

'How long has she been unconscious?'

'Oh, seven or eight minutes. Ten perhaps.'

'As long as that? Strange.' He looked suspiciously at Bridget. 'Her pulse is normal, perhaps a little fast.'

'She has opened her eyes once or twice.'

'Just shock and possible concussion I think. Of course if it were not Sunday I should consider a fractured skull.'

'Does one not fracture skulls on a Sunday?' asked Mark.

'Oh, one does of course, but we try not to consider it as a possibility. The X-ray problems are so great on Sundays it is more dangerous to the patient to send for an ambulance than to leave him where he is. I do not however think it is likely that Mrs Mayor has fractured her skull. She may have slight concussion. I should think she probably has.'

'I think so too,' said Bridget faintly. She had come to the conclusion that she was overdoing her unconsciousness.

'So there is really no treatment except of course immobility. I think she might be moved carefully to that sofa, or even to bed if she really wants it, but then at least twenty-four hours bedrest. She must have rest. Now, what of the angry young lady on the floor? Ah, we shall have to . . . ' and he was cutting off Rebecca's boot before she had time to protest.

'This is nasty,' he said. 'Yes. You were right, madam, I should have looked at you first. Now you will need an X-ray:

63

it will take hours.' He looked lugubrious. 'I think, considering the time, I had better strap it up and Mr Mayor can take you into the hospital first thing in the morning. I do not think it is a real break, just a crack, perhaps a ligament. They can be very nasty. Your name?'

'Mrs Mayor.'

The Indian stopped writing just for a second and then went on. Ah, a sister-in-law, one could see him thinking.

'I am Mr Mayor's wife,' said Rebecca coldly. 'This is my house and that', she pointed at Mark, 'is my husband.'

'It is Mr Mayor's first wife who has concussion,' said Frieda. 'I regret to say my son assaulted her. It is very sad, doctor, for you and me, who have both come from cultures where the family is sacrosanct, to see the disappearance of these values among those reared in this once-great country. However. By the way, my name is also Mrs Mayor – I am the first Mrs Mayor of course, not the third – and when you have finished strapping up that young woman's leg you had better make sure that these little white pills are the ones I am supposed to be taking. I found them down the side of this armchair while we were waiting for you, and the bottle looks a bit like the one I lost, but not exactly.'

There was a small sound from the hearthrug. Bridget was laughing.

'YOU CANNOT BEHAVE like this,' said Margery earnestly. She was one of Bridget's oldest friends. Mark had brought her round to the house to talk sense into Bridget. Rebecca was sitting in Out-patients waiting for him to come back and fetch her. Phyllida was at her desk, having refused to take the day off work in order to nurse both her loved mother and her hated and unknown stepmother.

'Skip your own work,' she'd told Mark.

'How did Mark know where to find you?' asked Bridget. She had had a good night on the drawing-room sofa and Frieda had managed to bring her a splendid breakfast using Rebecca's elegant kitchen with a fine disregard of the chaos she was leaving behind her.

'Oh, Mark. Well, of course . . . ' Margery was a very old friend indeed. Bridget had been asked to dinner parties regularly over the last five years, had been seated next to Margery's husband, had been cosseted and spoilt. Now for the first time it occurred to Bridget that there had been other dinner parties to which she had not been invited, at which Rebecca and Mark had been guests.

'Oh, I see.'

'Now Bridget, don't be silly. You know quite well that we thought Mark behaved very badly, and we told him so, but after all he is one of our oldest friends and one doesn't want to take sides. Now, Rebecca is behaving very well, I think, from what Mark says, but it can't be pleasant for her having you here. And of course it's so unlike you, dear, to behave like this and cause all this trouble.'

'It's a relationship,' said Bridget. 'I'd rather be here and be a nuisance than neatly tucked away in Waddon.'

Margery said brightly, 'Now, your lovely little flat.'

'I'd rather *haunt* people when I'm dead than stay neatly in my coffin, wouldn't you?' asked Bridget.

'YOU ARE PERFECTLY *well*,' said Mark. It was now Wednesday morning. 'Surely you see that you must go?'

'I don't see why. Rebecca and I don't actually quarrel and your mother likes having me.' Bridget was scraping carrots for a casserole. For the next day, she explained. Casseroles were the better for long preparation.

It was true, thought Mark, horrified, that Rebecca and Bridget were settling down rather easily. Rebecca's leg was strapped from thigh to toe. She was immobilised.

'Bridget's quite useful actually,' she told Mark. 'At the moment.'

'It's indecent,' he said. 'Don't you care about me? Aren't you jealous?'

'Of her? Mark, she's just a kindly old schoolmarm. I can't imagine there was ever much between you. She's got a good bone structure of course, and she dresses well in a way. But that just makes her pleasanter to have about. Oh, she does no harm. She's been through a bad time, that's all.'

What am I to say to people, he thought. He tried to start a list of people who had lived openly with two wives but could think only of Brigham Young and one of the Dukes of Devonshire. He could not remember whether Stanley Spencer had managed it or not.

'I do wish you would go,' he said to Bridget, over dinner.

'I like it here.'

'Or at least eat upstairs with Frieda. She'd welcome you.'

'I have too much I want to say to you,' she said.

'What?'

'Oh things. When they occur to me. Things rise up occasionally, one can't plan these feelings, they come. I don't want to miss a chance.'

'There's an article in that,' said Rebecca. They were eating in her bedroom; Bridget had cleverly brought up the folding garden table.

'You will have to go out one day,' Mark said bitterly. 'I shall change all the locks.'

'Frieda will let me in. We have discussed it.'

'You never used to be like this.'

'I was always too busy trying to convince you that I loved you. What got me about that . . . ' She saw Mark put down his knife and fork, push his plate away.

'Don't you like it?' she asked. 'It's turbot. I slipped out early, when you went to work, and bought it. It's turbot.'

'Turbot?'

'You must like it,' she said fiercely. 'You must.'

Mark said very soothingly, 'Bridget dear, you are having some form of nervous breakdown, aren't you? We must see a doctor.'

'I saw a doctor on Sunday, remember?'

'I mean we must see a doctor who . . . We must help you feel better.'

'I feel fine. Better than for years. I feel me for the first time for years.'

'Then why are you crying?'

'Because you won't eat your turbot. Please do. I made a Hollandaise sauce. EAT YOUR TURBOT.'

Meekly he ate his turbot.

PHYLLIDA CAME, RESENTFULLY. She did no good.

'Mother has stopped being splendid,' she told Giles and Jonathan when she got home.

'Good-oh.'

'No, it's dreadful. She's weeping and shouting and she looks dreadful. And daddy's young woman is sitting up in bed looking cool and superior and behaving beautifully.'

'Being splendid, is she? Someone in your family always seems to be behaving splendidly. I begin, Phyllida, to look at you with doubt. You may one day blossom into a bosomy County Councillor or something.'

'Rebecca is not my family.'

'She's your stepmother.'

'Oh God, ordinary mothers are enough to cope with. Mother says she's happy.'

67

'You had better keep away if it upsets you so. We have our own careers to get on with,' said Jonathan. 'There is some hope I may be sent to our Paris branch. A flat in Paris at company expense, imagine.'

'When?'

'Oh, not till the autumn, don't worry. You won't have to look for a replacement for ages. I'll be quite difficult to re-place, won't I?' He was so like Giles, thought Phyllida. But he had more money and his parents' problems did not impinge.

'Not at all difficult,' she said.

'My father asked me if we'd replaced Simon yet,' said Giles.

'Whyever?'

'I don't know. I thought perhaps he needed a loan and wanted to know if I was paying a quarter of the rent or only a fifth. I said we hadn't of course. But I could find someone quite easily for Simon or Jonathan's room.'

'One of Giles's little friends,' said Jonathan. 'Oh, how sweet.'

'Well,' said Giles, 'you're talking about going to Paris, so I don't see what it is to you. Phyllida doesn't mind.'

'Serafina might,' said Jonathan.

'Serafina might need replacing too, I suppose,' said Phyllida who had missed any point in much of this inter-change. Jonathan and Giles occasionally showed a certain edginess together; Jonathan would tease, Giles would resent it. Giles was the older, the more beautiful, the more sophis-ticated, the poorer. It was jealousy she assumed, male rivalry. Irritations such as this always arose among flatmates. She herself had snapped at Serafina for leaving her tights soaking wet on the draining board. 'Serafina really isn't going to cope with that job of hers much longer. She'll have a breakdown,' she went on. She worried about Serafina. She hoped she was not becoming a protective person. She fore-saw a life of looking after lame dogs.

'Like your mother? A breakdown like your mother?'

'I don't know. I think now that mummy must have been doing odd things for some time and I never noticed. She gave me this Bible.'

'She gave you a Bible?' Giles put his cup down in astonishment.

'Look.'

They examined the Bible. It was bound in soft pink, a vinyl masquerading as suede and imprinted in gold.

'Pink and gold,' said Jonathan, delighted. 'My mother wouldn't have thought of anything but plain black. I realise now I am a deprived child. I shall write and tell her so.' He began to sing. 'Mummy never gave me a Bible, a Bible . . . '

'Don't be a fool, she didn't *give* it me. I mean it is not a present. She borrowed it in church and forgot to return it so I've got to. She wants me to take it to the vicar, the pastor, she said, because she had borrowed it from someone in the congregation whose name she doesn't know.'

'I'd post it if you've got the address.'

'Well, of course. But you know it is odd because mummy doesn't go to church as far as I know. And then I asked Margery Deacon, you know how Margery keeps phoning me about mummy, and she was surprised I didn't know mummy went ever so regularly, but to St John's or St Anne's or something. Spiky, with confession. But this address is ever so odd. Somewhere in West Croydon. So she borrowed it at that church, the one she just went to last week, to write an article, she said. You remember.'

'No'.

'Oh well, I suppose I didn't tell you. But she didn't like to post it, she said it belonged to a woman who needed it and had lost a son. She got quite weepy about it and awfully guilty. She seemed to think it might make up for carrying it off if she sent me back with it.'

'Why you?'

'Well, I'm her daughter.'

'Sounds mad to me.'

'She is mad, I suppose. I mean sane people don't simply move in with other people. Anyway, I said I'd take it back. It's somewhere in West Croydon. Not even on the tube. I'll go tonight. She made the pastor sound awfully dishy. He's black.'

Giles said, 'He'll be out visiting or rioting or something.'

'That's cheap,' said Phyllida.

'All the way to West Croydon on the offchance,' said Giles.

'I shall phone first, of course,' she said with great dignity. She rather liked the idea of being the welcome guest of a black community group. It would give her status in the office. And at university she had worked quite hard to help organise a neighbourhood law centre. Perhaps, now she was established in her job, she should get involved again. 'Is West Croydon a Deprived Urban Area?' she asked, but none of them knew.

FRIEDA WAS NOT wholly satisfied by Bridget's return. It was an achievement on her own part certainly. Nevertheless the Golden Age she had imagined had not returned. The happy years in which Frieda had felt so well, the pleasurable continuing presence of her small grand-daughter, the delight of her own rich contralto voice ringing freely throughout the large house, these had not returned as somehow, confusedly, Frieda had expected. Bridget had returned without the past. And Bridget herself was older, crosser, moody, strange. Frieda retreated to her attic flat. Trudy would call soon to find out what was happening. Few of Frieda's other friends could now climb the stairs. Frieda would have to discuss with Trudy how Rebecca could best be driven out or otherwise disposed of.

Clearly things would not be normal while she remained.

'We shall have to move,' said Bridget, appearing at Rebecca's bedroom door. The bandaging and plaster were to come off in another fortnight.

'We have no intention of moving,' said Rebecca. 'This house suits Mark and me very well.' She had been dictating, there was a completed spool at her bedside. She intended to ask Bridget, who was very willing to run such errands, to take it to the post.

'Oh, it would be all right if it were just us three,' agreed Bridget. 'But there is Frieda to think of. She will not be able to climb those stairs much longer. We need a place with a self-contained ground floor granny flat. She must be on the ground floor. I'm really a bit surprised you haven't seen that for yourselves.'

'She likes her present place, I believe,' said Rebecca. She looked up consideringly. 'Of course if you feel so strongly, what we could do is, couldn't you get a larger flat and have her to live with you? She'd like that.' She added delicately, 'We'd make it financially possible of course. And it would be company for you.'

Bridget had wandered to the window. She said as if continuing a conversation, 'I've not told Mark yet how outrageously selfish he was after I'd had glandular fever.' Rebecca was growing used to these sudden changes of subject. 'Well, you know glandular fever, it wasn't really after I'd had it, I'd still got it really, it takes ages. I felt awful.'

'My brother had it.'

'Then you remember.'

'I thought young people got it.'

'I *was* young.' Bridget was offended. 'I was younger than you are now. And slimmer too. It was before Phyllida was born. We were only just married, only a year or two. And the doctor said I needed a holiday. So do you know where we went? When I was longing for sun and sea and wine?

Scotland so he could fish. Soggy, boggy Scotland. When I think, when I think of the hours I've spent sitting on damp river banks or in boring hotels so that Mark could fish . . . '

'Why didn't you fish too?'

'Oh, I did later. I was brainwashed into it. If you can't beat them, join them. But not then, not yet. And indeed too late. He lost interest. I expect you go to Italy for your holidays.'

'And Greece.'

'When I think of myself, still exhausted from glandular fever, traipsing over those bogs and rocks. When I think of it . . . '

'Don't waste your energies on me. Save it for Mark. Pity to waste your fury.'

'Yes, it is. Thanks. I'm saving it all right. When'll he be back?'

'You'll have to stop some time you know,' said Rebecca. 'You can't go on pouring out past fury.'

'I don't see why,' said Bridget. 'I can have the same rows again and again, can't I? Now I've started. When I was younger I thought a good row cleared the air. I was angry with my friend, I told my friend, my wrath did end, and all that you know. But it doesn't seem to work like that. It's still there.'

'Then why go on?' Rebecca was quite glad to have Bridget about to go shopping and answer the phone, and then the poor woman . . . as far as she was concerned it was an act of charity. Rebecca was almost the same generation as Phyllida and had been brought up to tolerance and sympathy. But there was Mark for Rebecca to consider and Mark was beginning to look very tired. The evenings were full of loud voices, of Bridget waylaying him on the landing, shouting up the stairs. Mark would dash into Rebecca's bedroom and lock the door. It could not go on.

'You can't be getting much out of it,' she said to Bridget.

'Have you ever thought', said Bridget after a while, 'what it is like to spend five years without meeting anyone, anyone at all, who matters enough to you to make you angry?'

'I'd have thought it was something to make you happy you'd have missed.'

'Yes . . . I'd have thought that too once. But that's beyond expectation really. All I hope for now is feelings of some kind. Even the fact that I resent your wanting to be rid of me is some kind of reassurance that I *can* still feel.'

'It's not a very dignified role for you, is it?'

'I've never thought my position particularly dignified. I've never felt dignified certainly. Of course, I've behaved well, I can see that.'

'Then why let yourself down now?'

'It's not me you're worrying about, is it? Why should you? You wouldn't care how undignified I was as long as I wasn't undignified here. It's awkward for you.'

'It's awkward for Mark. And he's worried about you.'

'He's worried about himself.'

Bridget walked out of the room before Rebecca could ask her to go to the post and did not come back even though Rebecca called for some time.

'I'M WORRIED ABOUT her you see,' Mark said to a Mrs Jean Debbin. He was driving her across London from Waddon to Hampstead. He knew nothing about her except that her name was in Bridget's address book, which he had removed from her handbag without her knowledge. Each day he would spend on the telephone, working through the address book, trying to find someone who would come and talk to Bridget, coax her out of his house, restore her to some sense of proper behaviour. At first, he had moved circumspectly, choosing a name from the old days, asking about the other names. But there were few familiar names, and those were away or ill or had lost touch with Bridget or (on one shaking occasion) had put the phone down on hearing Mark's name before he could explain he was speaking on Bridget's behalf. As it were.

The address book was crammed with unfamiliar names, a lifetime's collection he would have thought rather than that of a mere five years. In his university days Mark had made friends at almost this pace, but never since. The bulk of the names before him gave him hope that somewhere would be someone who would help Bridget solve her problem (this was how he phrased it to himself) and return meekly to her proper place.

Jean Debbin struck him as an unlikely person for Bridget to know. He felt he had probably made yet another mistake in asking her. She was a sprightly woman in her sixties, with flyaway grey hair; her cheeks were criss-crossed with red threads, her eyes round and dark. She was like a survival from the twenties. He was surprised that she was not called Pixie.

'Oh, Biddy and I are great friends,' she said. 'We pot.'

'Pot?' For a minute he thought she was talking of marijuana and wondered if he had the key to Bridget's strange behaviour at last.

'Oh yes. We met at pottery classes. I'm an absolute devotee of potting you know. I have a gift, though I say it myself as shouldn't.'

'And Bridget . . . pots?'

'Not very well, to be honest.'

'But often? You see a lot of her?'

'Not a lot, no, I must admit it, not a lot now. But we're very close, very close. Sharing this great interest, you see. Potters are very warm-hearted people, you know, very loving people. It's the earth contact, I always say, the earth contact.'

He looked ahead at the damp road. Bridget had been with them a fortnight by now. He was growing used to these strange women claiming to be Bridget's friends, eager to observe someone else's tragedy, holding on to Bridget's unwilling hand as they sat next to her on the sofa in the drawing-room. If they had been driven by Mark, rather than arriving in their own Fiesta or Mini, he would soon hear Bridget calling him. With a brutal directness new to her she would say, 'I don't really think we have anything to say to each other. Would you kindly run Paula – or May – or Irene – to the station, Mark?'

They reached Hampstead. As they got out, and Jean Debbin looked inquisitively up and down the road, and then stood obviously working out the market value of the Edwardian house before her, he said, 'A Miss Robertson, a Margaret Robertson came to see Bridget yesterday. I expect you know her.'

'Oh, probably.'

He persisted. '*Do* you know her? Miss Margaret Robertson. A rather thin lady with a Scottish accent.'

'Does she pot?'

'She acts. They met through that, I think. Amateur acting.'

'But Bridget doesn't act. She pots. She's never, never mentioned acting to me.'

Mark had heard this before too. Bridget's life was full of people who did not know each other. Each one of them seemed to know a different Bridget. He was beginning to discern that many of them had been met at evening classes or clubs which Bridget had joined in a moment of hope or determination, only to drift away on finding them full of people also in search of the unattainable.

'Bridget,' he said, pushing open the drawing-room door without much hope, indeed a little shamefacedly, 'Mrs Debbin has come to visit you.'

'My poor Biddy,' said Mrs Debbin, taking a sidestep, almost a jigstep, into the room. She stretched out her hands: her nails suggested she might have spent the day potting.

Bridget, who had got up when the door opened, retreated a step.

'And your poor little flat left so lonesome,' said Mrs Debbin, who had visited the flat only once a good two years ago.

'I've put it on the market,' said Bridget. This was a lie. 'Someone will be caring for it soon,' she said.

Mark, on his way out (it was his habit to murmur tactfully that he would get coffee and then vanish), caught these words, stiffened and returned.

'You can't sell your flat,' he said. 'You can't. Where will you go? Where will you live?'

'This failure to face facts,' said Bridget. 'You kept pretending I wasn't pregnant.'

Mrs Debbin said, 'Come, come, dear, you're upset.'

'I shall live here, as I am already doing.'

'Now dear,' said Mrs Debbin. 'That's not very nice of you really is it? We have to put past mistakes behind us, not', she added hastily, bobbing her head at Mark, 'that I mean Mr Mayor was a mistake, exactly, of course, but we must face our future with a high spirit and a song on our lips. Like in pottery,' she said, warming to her theme, 'we must learn to throw our broken pots into the waste bin with a free spirit – she swept her arm round, gesturing as one flinging a pot through the drawing-room window might do – 'and turning back to the clay, start again with a brave hope. Why not let me go up with you and pack your things and Mr Mayor can run us both back to your little flat, or we can go in your own dear little car if you're quite well enough to drive, and we'll have a cosy supper together and I'll stay the night and help you settle in.'

'That would be very kind of you,' said Mark.

'Perhaps your wife would let us take some eggs and things,' said Mrs Debbin. 'Eggs and things would make us a lovely little supper.'

Bridget could not remember why she had hoped, even transiently, that Mrs Debbin might enrich her life. Perhaps she had met her during that black period when as a matter of discipline, as a rule of life, she had responded to every overture, rejected no invitation whatsoever, telling herself that even the dullest person might have a more interesting side, reminding herself that twenty, or even perhaps thirty, years, lay before her to be filled. Whatever it was, here was an acquaintance, a forgotten woman, met presumably at some social gathering, a coffee party or a poetry reading perhaps, proposing to reorganise her life.

'Please go away,' said Bridget. 'It was kind of you to come, but please go away.'

'Now dear, I can see you're not yourself.'

'I am more myself than I have ever been,' said Bridget, discovering this to be true. 'I am quite hopeful of myself at the moment. So please go away.' A memory of Mrs Debbin's gesture came to her and she picked up a large cushion and flung it at the window. 'Throw your broken pot into the waste bin', she said, 'with a free spirit. I should warn you that the next thing I throw may be heavier and do more damage.'

'I think', said Mrs Debbin in the hall, as Mark opened the door (and he had not been up to see Becky yet he realised, but she must put up with it, he had to get rid of this dreadful woman), 'that your wife – oh, I do beg your pardon, your ex-wife I mean – well, I do think, Mr Mayor, that dear Biddy needs a doctor. I am, I admit, a little surprised that you should expect dear Biddy's friends to help when what she obviously needs is a . . . well, a psychological doctor, if I may speak frankly.'

'Please do,' said Mark glumly. He opened the car door for her. He thoroughly agreed with her: Bridget needed a doctor. But no doctor would come. Bridget did not think she needed a doctor and that was it.

'You must settle your own domestic conflicts,' his G.P. had said brusquely. It had never occurred to Mark that the man might dislike him.

He had telephoned Bridget's doctor, and persuaded a receptionist to give him an appointment for which he had to wait two days.

'Positively the earliest we have,' she had said.

'It's an emergency.'

'So you said. I have given you an emergency appointment. Otherwise you would be seeing Dr Clarke next week.'

'If I were to tell you that Mrs Mayor has a very high temperature, a purple rash, a bad headache and is unable to eat at all, would you . . .'

'Two aspirins every four hours, plenty of liquid, and call doctor back in twenty-four hours. Doctor likes to see what that does in every case of fever before considering other problems. Shall I cancel the appointment?'

'For God's sake, no.'

'Doctor doesn't like patients with high temperatures in the surgery.'

'I only said if – '

'Mr Mayor, there are other patients waiting to be dealt with.'

D R CLARKE TURNED out to be an elegant young woman with carefully made-up eyes and a haircut rather like Rebecca's latest style. She looked at him across the desk as he explained his mission and said nothing as he presented his views of Bridget's emotional state. He explained his concern over her extraordinary decision; he pointed out how wholly unlike Bridget's usual behaviour her present attitude was. Dr Clarke sat back tapping her chin with a biro. She made no attempt to take any notes. Mark continued, he reached a peroration, he said to this quiet and attentive young woman, 'And so, doctor, I should be very glad to have your opinion on my ex-wife's present mental state and to hear whether you have seen some such aberrant behaviour developing over the last months?'

Her voice had an odd Lancashire twinge. It did not go with her haircut.

'Mrs Mayor does not know you are here, I believe you said?'

'Exactly. She does not recognise her need for help.'

'Is she, in your opinion, suicidal?'

'No, no, that's just it, you see. She seems to be positively elated. Unhappy *and* elated. She grows more elated daily. Exultant, even. Would you not say such a lack of insight into her situation is highly significant?'

She looked at him coldly. 'Unless suicide is part of the picture, I cannot possibly discuss the health of a patient with anyone other than a close relative, Mr Mayor, and then only if the care of the patient is involved. Good afternoon.'

'But I am a close relative. We were married for over twenty years.'

'That is probably significant, I agree. However, you used the past tense. You have no legal standing in your ex-wife's life at all. That is what divorce means, Mr Mayor.'

'Damn it all,' he said, leaning forward to thump the desk, catching her lifted eyebrow and sitting back, 'damn it all, she's living with me. I told you.'

'Living with you? You are reconciled?'

'Not living *with* me. Living in my house. I told you. She's moved in. I want to get her out.'

'Then I can only suggest you consult a solicitor. It does not seem to be a medical problem at all. Good afternoon, Mr Mayor. Give my regards to Mrs Mayor.'

'I SHALL SPEAK to my solicitor about you,' he said to Bridget, returning ages later from depositing Mrs Debbin at the small house the other side of London where she presumably engaged in pottery. She had lectured him the whole way about mental illness and his duty to Bridget.

'Yes,' Bridget said. 'It'll reach the papers, of course, I'll see to that.'

She was standing at the foot of the stairs with a tray in her hand. 'Rebecca's coffee,' she said. 'Your dinner's in the oven. It hasn't dried up. I'll get it in a moment.'

He did not love her. He would never love her again. But he remembered her standing there in just such a position with a tray for Phyllida when their daughter had had measles. Or tonsillitis perhaps. And it was not just sentiment but real affection that swept over him. She had once been a nice woman.

'Bridget, please, I don't want you to be unhappy.'

'I know. But you see I am. It's not your fault any more, if that's any comfort. At least, you can't make it better. I must find my own solution.'

He sighed with relief. 'I knew you'd see it . . . '

'And my solution seems to be to live here.' There was a note of triumph in her voice.

He kept a grip on himself. 'Why?' he asked. He noted with some admiration that his voice still sounded quiet and reasonable, even caring.

'This coffee's getting cold.' She shifted the tray in her hands, took a step upwards.

'Why?'

'So that there's someone to hear me when I scream, I suppose.' She went on up the stairs.

TO PHYLLIDA'S DISAPPOINTMENT she was not invited to bring the Bible back herself. She was a little lost at the moment; her boyfriend had gone to Hong Kong and she found herself missing him more than she expected: he had gone to put in a computer system for one of the large Eastern banking houses and it would take years. He appeared to be too busy even to write. She wondered sometimes if he would have married her if she had somehow put it into his mind, or even asked him. She was a liberated woman. He could not have objected, just refused. But she did not want to get married, nobody she knew was married yet, she could not understand how people decided on such an odd step, a purely ritual step it seemed to her, for look at her parents to whom it had clearly meant nothing, and she would turn her mind from marriage to Bridget, whom she could no longer understand. She felt ready for a new occupation. Black London was the thing, she thought, recalling student rallies, and trying to feel ashamed of her recent self-centred enjoyment of elitist frivolities. And besides, bringing the Bible back herself, making a pilgrimage to the southern suburbs, was something specific to do for Bridget, whom she loved and could not help.

'But mother so much wanted me to bring it back in person,' she said on the phone.

'I am sure she would understand. Or you need not tell her.'

'She feels so guilty carrying it off. She would worry like anything if she thought I had risked it getting lost.'

'Even today, post usually arrives, you know.'

'It takes longer. I could bring it tonight.'

'Mrs Brooker has waited for it for some time. She will not mind an extra day now that she knows it is safe. Tonight will not be convenient.'

81

She was not used to being refused, and besides, she had told the others she was going. And he had the most beautiful voice, she thought, deeper than the high pitched middle-class voices around her.

And perhaps, unconsciously, she felt, with a childish patriotism left over from reading *Biggles* at the age of eight that she was an Englishwoman in her own country and he but a visiting foreigner and that it was not for him to tell her what to do. 'One is not responsible for one's unconscious,' she would have said if she had been aware of it. Moreover, she had a more conscious motivation. No man was going to dictate to her, she thought, what to do for her mother. And in this muddle of filial, sexual and political motivation she began to enjoy herself and her voice changed ('Stop putting on that coaxing whine,' Bridget used to say when she was six, but it got Mark every time) and she said hopefully, 'And I'd like to meet you. Mother told me about your sermon.' That should get him, she thought.

'I have to spend tonight preparing my next. Your mother would understand that has priority.'

'Mother isn't at all well, you see. She worries about things.'

'Yes, well, people do.'

He made no attempt to hide his impatience from her. His time was precious. He had nothing to give this young woman and he feared that if he encouraged her to come, her mother (whom he recalled clearly) might come to the church again. Her unhappiness would make demands on his time and pastoral energy, when he already found it difficult to care for his flock. Or, if she recovered, then in time . . . She would join in wholeheartedly, he could foresee it, he knew of these discontented middle-class Englishwomen; she would talk about healing breaches in the community and bring others with her who still believed in integration and pretence. And soon every committee would be dominated by some confident Englishwoman whose eager certainty would wash away the shoots of self-assertion and responsibility he had been so carefully cultivating in his largely middle-aged and defeated congregation. Or she would observe and patronise, and visit occasionally from the secure base of her own established church or secular discussion group, and both her presence and her absence would be noted by a suddenly self-conscious church. He wanted no part of it. He wanted only to be let alone. He was an intelligent man and understood the distances between people.

'Nevertheless,' said Phyllida, 'I will bring it down.' Opposition excited her.

'I RETURNED YOUR Bible,' she told Bridget on the telephone next morning, eager to comfort her mother and wanting to talk about her visit. But Bridget was disappointingly uninterested. Other events were now occupying her. Further demands were to be made.

'You must come and see me,' said Bridget. 'You must come soon. Come tomorrow.'

Phyllida, astounded, went. There was a family dinner party. Bridget sat in her old corner (though in a new and chintzy chair) and said cheerfully that they should do this more often; it was really no trouble to Rebecca, she pointed out, as she herself had done all the cooking. There was a moment when Bridget considered reminding Mark of a distant dinner party at which, bored by a story she was telling, and not realising that the main guest was enjoying it, he had told her in front of the guests to be quiet. He had had too much to drink, of course, she remembered, he often got assertive when he had had too much to drink. But she was too happy at the moment to resurrect this particular quarrel, even though she had regretted for years not telling him what the main guest had said to her later that evening about Mark's behaviour, and how he had asked her out to lunch and how in mistaken loyalty to Mark, she had not gone, even though she discovered later that Mark had been taking the guest's wife out to lunch on the quiet for some weeks. . . the whole ancient turmoil slipped away from her, she buried it peacefully, though with a clear marker stone in case she should want it again, in case this pain was not yet fully over – for she intended to weep alone no more – but she buried it and poured herself another drink, since neither Rebecca nor Mark offered it and she no longer cared whether she behaved according to the etiquette books. She looked happily round Rebecca's pretty room, her pretty room.

Mark, unaware of the escape from yet another of the attacks to which he was daily subjected, was also happy in Phyllida's presence. He made a great fuss of her, and she in her turn was gracious to him, happy perhaps to have been able to return without openly abandoning her long hostility. She could not but recognise moreover that Rebecca, now up and about, back at work indeed, was a young woman of poise, intelligence and wit. She and Phyllida picked up each other's allusions and Rebecca took greater care than Phyllida that these did not exclude Bridget and Phyllida noticed her care, and liked her for it, and dutifully adapted her own conversation. She began to feel that her father must have special qualities to have attracted a young woman like this, though looking sideways at him she could not discern any. Perhaps Rebecca had needed a father figure. She herself would have chosen a younger father, she thought, a man who held authority, a man with a cause. And he had let himself go so much. A kind man, she supposed, but in her eyes a silly one, gentle, middle class and out of touch. But at least he, like Rebecca, like Phyllida herself, was behaving in a civilised and acceptable way. As the evening wore on this did not prove to be the case with Bridget and Frieda.

For Bridget said, as they sat down at the table, 'I must tell you, Phyllida, I find I'm not getting quite the relief I was at first from just being here. I think I've said all I have to say to Mark, really. It seems such a limited vision on my part, now. I am growing more ambitious for myself.'

Everyone was silent. They had learned not to respond too hopefully to such statements.

'I'm beginning to want more,' said Bridget ominously. 'It is not done to say so, I know, but I cannot see why. Wanting is not wicked.'

'Of course you want more,' said Frieda. 'You are not an unnatural woman. You want your family back and intruders out.'

Rebecca said, 'Oh, I think, Frieda, that Bridget and I understand my position.'

'At the moment,' said Bridget, 'what I seem to want more of is your company, Phyllida. You wouldn't I suppose consider moving back here?'

'There isn't room, is there, Rebecca?' asked Phyllida hastily.

'There is room,' said Frieda. 'You could have the study back again. Or there is the little back room, no cupboards, but a good bed. What more does a girl want?'

'I don't think that would be a good idea, mother, really not,' said Phyllida.

The subject appeared to drop, but only for a little. After coffee, Bridget said, 'Then if you will not come here, I will come and visit you at your flat. I like watching you. I like talking to you. I like listening to you. It is not in fact immoral to want one's children's company. Why do we all pretend so hard that we don't? I have decided that I want to have more of your time.'

'We'll have another dinner party, at the flat,' said Phyllida. 'It's time we had another dinner party. Giles and Jonathan will help.'

'What good is a dinner party,' said Bridget, 'two or three hours of seeing you in a group? I should have had more children, I told Mark and the doctor, I said . . . but I have you and I want to enjoy you. I have not stopped feeling like a mother and wanting children.' She felt daring, like an exhibitionist stripping off for the first time in public. 'What good is a dinner party? I will come and stay for a month or two. I would enjoy that.'

'You can't! Daddy, explain to her that she can't!'

'Why can't I? Simon's room is empty.'

'The others wouldn't like it. They wouldn't understand. It isn't done. People in flats don't have parents living with them.'

'The others wouldn't like it, but I would.'

'It's not your flat.'

'True. Do you know I've seen you for a total of exactly three hours on your own this year, Phyllida?' She was breaking all her own rules. It felt wicked, like group sex or standing on the left on escalators.

Phyllida said sulkily, 'I'm always phoning you.'

'Quite,' said Bridget.

'I think you might approach the others, in the circumstances,' said Mark. 'Your mother deserves a little more attention than you appear to have given her.'

'You mean,' said Phyllida, 'that it's a convenient way of getting her out of your house without scandal, of edging her back to Waddon.'

Since this was just what Mark did mean, he denied it with indignation and force.

'I would rather come back here', said Phyllida desperately, 'than face the embarrassment of asking the others to put my mother up in Simon's room even for a week. I will abandon the flat – Serafina will probably have a breakdown without my support but that cannot be helped – and move back here. I suppose Rebecca will hardly refuse your daughter a roof over her head. I will be the daughter of the house again.'

Frieda said, 'Now if Rebecca will only go away with one of those odd men she works with, so much more suitable, or she could go back to Brussels, all will be well. What a Christmas we shall have.'

Everyone ignored this.

'It is blackmail, of course, mummy, social blackmail, but if that is the alternative I must give up my whole way of life . . .'

'In fact,' Mark pointed out, 'it is for Rebecca to invite you back, not Bridget. And while we would not refuse you a roof over your head, as you put it, if you were really in need, the situation is not so dire.'

'You cannot come back here, Phyllida, so there is no need to worry,' said Rebecca. 'I shall be having the builders in. I shall need the little back room for a nursery and the study for an au pair. I am pregnant. The laboratory tests came through this morning.'

'You must have an abortion,' said Frieda immediately. 'Old fathers like Mark have mongol babies. If it *is* Mark's baby.'

There was a moment's awed silence. Mark could not decide which part of this swift attack to repel first. Frieda followed up the advantage fast.

'I'm against abortions on principle of course, but Rebecca has no such principles I believe. So that will not stop her. Mark would be seventy after all by the time this baby was off his hands and earning. Look at him, so worn down, his lined face, his sad shoulders. The poor boy should be thinking of his retirement, not of high chairs and playpens.'

'Of course I am delighted,' said Mark.

'I don't believe you knew,' said Phyllida shrewdly.

'I am still delighted.'

'Don't count your chickens,' said Frieda. 'In any case she will miscarry. Redheaded Belgian women do not often reach full-term.'

Rebecca gave an uncertain laugh. 'You sound as if you were ill-wishing me.'

'Wishes are no good,' said Frieda darkly. 'It will need deeds.'

'Don't you want another grandchild?'

'I want Phyllida, as her mother does. She is enough for me.'

'You must all go.' Mark was desperate. 'And leave Rebecca and me alone.'

'I shall be only too pleased,' said Phyllida, breaking into furious tears. 'It's the first time I've been in the house for years and you can't wait to throw me out. I suppose you want a son this time.'

'I didn't mean you,' said Mark, distraught. 'I didn't mean – ' But she had gone, banging the door behind her.

'You never did think before you spoke,' said Bridget. 'When I told you my father was dying, you said . . . ' but her heart was no longer in it.

Nothing happened for a few days. Even Frieda was silent, wandering about but saying little. Rebecca stayed at the office, where she worked only part-time, for longer than usual. Bridget too was quieter than she had been. Indeed Rebecca and she began to get on quite well, for Bridget took over a good deal of the housekeeping and also distracted Frieda at times when she and Mark might otherwise have embarked on one of their traditional rows.

Mrs Brooker wrote to Bridget to thank her for returning the Bible.

'Dear Mrs Mayor,' she wrote in a fluent and elegant hand, 'Your daughter has told me your name which of course I did not know before (she is a credit to you). My Bible has reached me safely. Our pastor gave it to me and now I have met your daughter who has explained things. I can understand that you did not mean to take it away but I am glad to have it back. Thank you. Your daughter also tells me you are ill. Since we have been linked in this way by my Bible, I would like to pray for you. If you will send me your baptismal name we could pray for you at our healing group on Wednesdays at 8.30. Wonderful things have come to pass (Mark V 34). Yours in Christ, Maria Brooker.'

Bridget was touched by this epistle. She showed it to Rebecca and to Frieda the evening it arrived. 'Not that I am ill,' she said.

'We all want praying for,' said Frieda darkly. 'Some of us more than others,' she added. Later on she searched Bridget's room for the letter and removed it.

THAT WAS ABOUT the time Phyllida came home from the office and found Serafina in tears. She had walked out of school, she told Phyllida, still shocked at her own behaviour, as if she were a child who had run away from boarding school. 'And I've been crying ever since.'

'You look like it,' said Phyllida unkindly. There were times when she heard herself sounding horribly like her grandmother; she changed emotional gear and tried to imitate the proper concern Bridget would once have shown to any weeping girl (one could not be sure of Bridget's present behaviour).

'You need some tea,' she said. 'You'll feel better.' And then instead of making the tea she sat on the sofa next to Serafina and said, 'Now wipe your eyes, here, have a tissue and tell me all about it. High time you did walk out anyway I'd say, from what you've always said.'

'It's so . . . so . . . irresponsible,' said Serafina.

'So who's responsible every moment of the day?'

'Teachers ought to be. And I can't afford to lose my job. You know that. I'll get an awful reference.'

'Serafina, do you want to tell me what happened or not?'

'There was this boy in 4D,' said Serafina, bursting into louder sobs, so that Phyllida could not easily hear her. 'On good days he wasn't there and everyone was pleased. He wasn't much worse than the others really, just . . . and his language. Anyway the class was quiet actually.' Serafina's face lightened. 'They were all writing,' she said, 'or perhaps drawing, one or two. But actually the room had been quiet for at least two minutes – I was thinking perhaps I'd discovered some magic,' she said.

'Magic?' Phyllida hoped Giles and Jonathan wouldn't come in for a bit. Serafina didn't often talk as freely as this, and Phyllida did not want to stop her, but she usually dived into a bath as soon as she got home and if she delayed it much longer Giles or Jonathan would grab the bathroom. And she was going to the theatre later on. Ashamed of such selfishness (but then Serafina did seem to be making rather a meal of the story) she wondered whether Serafina would find hot water and some of Phyllida's new Penhaligon bath essence comforting. 'Magic?' she repeated, as her interruption had apparently bewildered Serafina.

'So that I could start being a teacher. Teaching them something, not just keeping them quiet, trying to entertain them. It was quiet. I remember thinking even the kids might be enjoying it. It was all peaceful.'

And then the triangular-faced boy had said, and everyone had been waiting for it, everyone looked up, it was planned, he had said, 'Miss, Miss, do you smoke after making love?' And she felt herself grow scarlet and knew herself weaponless and felt . . . 'like the cheap novels say, you know, Phyllida? Naked?' And then they had all chorused, 'She doesn't know, she hasn't looked.' Over and over again: 'She doesn't know, she hasn't looked.' 'And I ran out of the room and out of the school and I feel an awful fool, Phyllida, because I didn't work out what they meant till I was on the bus home. And I can't go back, not ever. And I can't stop crying.'

'You must give up your job. They'll destroy you.'

'How can I?'

'People do.'

Giles arrived home. Serafina went off obediently to weep in her bath. Phyllida and Giles agreed Serafina must give in her notice.

'Only she can't of course.'

'There's Social Security.'

'She won't be eligible if she resigns.'

'She will have to get a medical certificate.'

Therefore Serafina did not go to school next morning, though it was the following day before she was able to see the doctor and emerge satisfactorily certificated as suffering from nervous debility. It was therefore Serafina who heard the knock on the door about midday, and Serafina who opened the door.

'Why did you let them in?' asked Giles, later, standing in the window and running his fingers through his hair.

'I didn't think not to. Well, you couldn't expect me to. It was your father after all.'

'How did you know?'

'He said.'

'Oh God.'

'But he was, wasn't he? I mean that is your grandfather tucked up in Simon's bed, isn't it?'

Serafina, Phyllida and Jonathan stared reproachfully at Giles. Before he could say anything, there was a thumping sound.

'He's fallen out of bed again,' said Serafina. She did not

join in the rush down the corridor. She was not a callous girl but her day's experiences had exhausted her. Giles's father had been very odd.

Very odd indeed.

He had supported his ancient father across the threshold, set him in a chair, told Serafina curtly to keep an eye on him, and gone away, to reappear with three suitcases.

'Giles isn't here. He's at work,' explained Serafina.

'I know, I know. At the office. Lucky you being in.'

'Coming when Giles is out.'

'I know. Thought we'd have to wait. Didn't like to disturb him at the office, he gets ratty. Well, I know. Embarrassing. Still, we'd have had to wait. Thought we could sit on the top stair. Silly really. Seemed best at the time to get on with it though.'

'Is Giles expecting you?'

'Good God, no. Wasn't expecting it myself really. It came to me in the morning.'

'What morning?'

'In the morning. This morning, I suppose. What time is it?'

'About twelve.'

'Still the same morning.'

'Shall I phone Giles?' asked Serafina. She could not cope. Giles's father was moving about in a brisk but uncertain manner, unpacking suitcases all over the passage floor.

'No,' he said angrily. 'Can't have people disturbed at work.'

'I think I'd better . . . '

'No.'

She was frightened then.

'Want to . . . want to . . . ' the old man said. 'I want to have a cuppa tea.'

'That's it,' said Giles's father. 'Give him a cup of tea. He's settling in. You think you'll like it, father, then?'

92

'Only seen the passageway so far, boy. Let's explore.'

Giles's father nodded cheerfully to Serafina. 'He's taking to it. I thought he would. He'll be all right now.'

The old man was beginning to walk about. He was after all quite spry. Serafina was surprised at this; he had been hauled into the flat and plumped down in the passageway chair almost as if he were a dummy. Later she was to get used to Herbert Redditch's alternation between liveliness and apparent coma.

She followed them into the sitting-room.

'Oh, yes,' he said. 'I shall like this.'

'Good,' said his son, Giles's father.

Herbert Redditch stood, his hand resting on a table to give him balance while he coughed horribly and noisily for several moments. Then he said, 'Oh, yes, I shall like this. I think if we got that chair over here.'

Giles's father, a tall thin man dressed carefully in a good grey suit, pulled the armchair over into the bay.

'It doesn't go there,' said Serafina. 'We like it where it was. We sit in it to watch TV.'

'Ah, well,' said Giles's father apologetically. 'He's an old man, you see. He has his ways. Giles'll sort it out. You could move the telly.'

'Are you waiting here all day for Giles then?'

'Ah, well . . .'

'I'd like a cuppa tea.' Giles's grandfather's voice had a London roughness, yet his father spoke standard English, and Giles himself spoke in a manner which suggested public school. Serafina could not recall ever having heard Giles mention his school, and she considered this and puzzled over the visitors until the kettle boiled and she could carry a tea-tray back into the sitting-room.

'If you are both going to wait all day,' she said, 'I suppose you'd better have lunch. I wish you'd phone Giles and explain what it's all about.'

'Show me where the things are, dearie, and I'll rustle something up,' said the old man. Of his son, the man in the grey suit, there was no sign.

'Where's Giles's father?'

'Slipped out.'

'For cigarettes or something?'

'You might say so, yes. "Or something" covers it O.K. In a right mess he's got himself, hasn't he? I don't want no part of it, though, I made that quite clear. I said you do what you like. Young Giles will see me right. What's a grandson for? Course if my prissy daughter-in-law'd done her duty young Giles'd have half a dozen brothers and sisters to help him, wouldn't he? Then perhaps his father'd see things different too. Not that I can talk, you're thinking, only having had the one myself, but that wasn't for want of trying, that was just the way things was. We never used nothing, you know.'

All this time he was swilling tea, choking down great gobs of the biscuits Serafina had put out, sniffing into a grubby handkerchief. Nevertheless he remained horribly audible. She did not know what to say.

'Still,' Mr Redditch went on, catching his breath after a particularly violent burst of coughing, 'he's found me a berth and he's welcome to do things his way. Nothing but a pissing misery he's been ever since he lost his job anyway. Got any cheese?'

He looked contemptuously at the Brie Serafina found for him, but ate a hunk of bread, and then fell into a heavy snorting sleep. Once or twice the snoring died away and he was so still that Serafina wondered if he had died. She tried to telephone Giles but he had gone out on an audit and his secretary was unwilling to give the client's number to private callers, for Giles, fearing further calls from his father, had left strict instructions about this.

All this Serafina, in tears, imparted to Giles when he eventually returned.

'Hullo, Giles, lad. That girl you've got here isn't much cop. She's not given me my medicines. At your dad's, he had an au pair special to give me my medicines until he lost his job. Then he did it. It gave him a kind of purpose in life.'

'Grandfather, how good to see you. Even if so unexpectedly.' Giles did not often allow himself to appear socially at a loss. 'And she hasn't got you a drink either. These medicos haven't made you go teetotal yet have they? No. Now I think there's a little whisky, or else it's sherry. Sherry, Serafina? Ah, and here's Phyllida. Sherry, Phyllida? A bit late tonight, aren't you? Or no, I'm early, the client's quite near here. Phyllida, my grandfather; grandfather, my flat-mate, Phyllida. Splendid view from this window, isn't there, grandfather? Is . . . er . . . did father say when he'd be collecting you?' He poured himself out all the whisky left in the bottle.

'Won't be. Won't be.'

'I'm sorry?'

'Dead, isn't he? Unless he mucked that up like everything else. Dead.'

Tears began to trickle down the old man's face. Giles went white.

'He isn't, he isn't,' said Serafina, 'he was here this morning, he brought those great suitcases!'

Herbert Redditch turned a look of infinite dislike upon her. 'He hadn't done it then, had he?'

'Done it?'

'Killed himself. That's what he was going to do. Pills. I got plenty, he took a whole bottle. Doesn't worry about me, oh no. What if I need them, I says? Get some more off the National Health, he says. No wonder the taxes are so high, I says, people killing themselves on the National Health. You ought to get the stuff private, I says. Well, you can tell he was the type to fiddle his income tax, can't you? Never did that proper, either.'

Giles said urgently, 'What pills, grandfather? Was he going home? When did he leave?'

But his grandfather waved the questions aside. He was sunk in the self-centredness of the old. 'Take me to young Giles, I said, he'll see me all right. Course, he may have chickened out. May be sitting at home crying his eyes out. I dunno. I reckon he meant to do it. Someone'll tell us some time. No need to fuss. The coppers always find you if there's a stiff to be accounted for. I ought to have had some of the pink bottle and some of my white pills after my lunch but I never. *She* never give them to me. *She* don't care.'

'I had better phone,' said Giles. He had not been fond of his father who had been an unfaithful husband, and an uncaring parent. Nevertheless, Giles had been moved by his father's distress over the last months and tried intermittently, in ways he knew were futile, to offer encouragement and hope. 'I had better phone,' he said, 'I must get someone to him. A cab . . . no. It's the rush hour, and it's right across London.' He was dialling his father's telephone number, hanging on, hoping.

'I got a list of medicines,' said the old man. Phyllida took the paper from the rather pathetic, repulsive old man and went to look for the medicines. There was a small box on the floor labelled 'Medicaments for Mr Herbert Redditch'. The handwriting was neat. Inside was a list of drugs and times, lying on top of an assortment of pill boxes, bottles, jars, and foil strips containing coloured capsules. She busied herself with spoons and glasses, all the while horribly aware of Giles telephoning first one address, then another, then the police.

'Don't hurry yourself,' said his grandfather, 'I've just remembered. He was going to do it in Rome. Slept with his first girl in Rome, he said. Wasn't true, there was that fat Rita next door when he was fifteen, but he always reckoned I didn't know about that. Still, there was a girl in Rome. He always was a sentimental bugger. Said he'd die happy if he could die in the Borghese Park.'

'The Borghese Gardens?'

'Might have been. No hurry. He wasn't flying.'

'I'M MOVING OUT,' said Jonathan, next evening, returning from the lavatory where he had found a slight puddle on the linoleum. 'The weaknesses of age will hit me eventually, I know, but I should prefer them to come as a surprise, rather than a long-awaited guest. I shall leave.'

'We could all go,' said Giles. He had been in touch with the police, the Foreign Office, the Rome Embassy, the Samaritans, and the Red Cross. He knew he ought to be concerned about his father, but by now all he could feel was anger at the weight of decision and guilt placed on him. 'Let's all run.'

'Let's all go together,' said Serafina. 'London's hell anyway. Let's all go to Rome.'

'San Francisco,' said Giles.

'If we were Chinese we'd think it an honour to look after him,' Phyllida pointed out. 'We would call him venerable.'

'Well, go and give your Chinese grandfather his next dose of medicine and see if you find it easier if you worship him. Joss sticks are the thing.'

'What does one do?' asked Giles desperately. 'I mean, people can't just arrive and plant themselves on you for ever. There must be something one can do.'

'He ought to be in an Old People's Home,' said Serafina.

'Social workers, that's who we want.' Phyllida was suddenly quite certain.

They looked at each other a little shocked. Social workers were for the inadequate, not for the charming middle-class young. But, of course, Mr Redditch was old.

'First thing tomorrow, Giles . . . Social workers. Or I go,' said Jonathan.

PHYLLIDA CONSENTED TO return to Hampstead. Rebecca telephoned to ask her to dinner and in any case she had news to impart to them. Her life had been extremely busy lately, torn between caring for Herbert Redditch and falling in love.

'Giles stayed in all day,' Phyllida said indignantly, 'and we'd had to wait over a week for an appointment anyway, and then she didn't come, this social worker. She said she would, but she didn't. I mean Giles has work to do. Can I have some more pudding, Rebecca? It's so good to eat without that awful old man coughing and spitting over me. And after all that, Giles's father didn't kill himself. Imagine all those phone calls wasted.'

'Phyllida!' said Mark reprovingly.

'Better he were dead,' said Frieda. 'Some people should never have been born. Some people should never be born. Like those with very old and decrepit parents.'

'You *have* deprived us of drama,' said Bridget. 'I was beginning to feel so sorry for Giles, orphaned so tragically, and now it appears he is still the proud possessor of a parent.'

'Oh, no, it's all right,' said Phyllida. 'His father's dead all right.' She blushed and hesitated. 'Not that we're pleased anybody's dead, of course not. What I meant was that it was awful not knowing and thinking he was taking all those pills and so sad and everything. But Giles hasn't got to feel guilty, he didn't *kill* himself and he wasn't going to, I don't think. He'd got himself fixed up with his old girlfriend on the quiet, it sounds like, he was just ditching the old man and running, only of course we'll never be sure because she isn't saying much now he's dead. No, he got out of the train in Rome and a bomb went off and he got killed. Better even than if he'd got run over because then Giles would always have thought he'd walked under the car deliberately. But even Freud wouldn't say you could get a bomb thrown at you through unconscious wishes. Would he?' she asked doubtfully, for she knew Freud could have everything both ways at once.

'How sad all the same, what a shock for the old man,' said Bridget.

'Oh, the old Chinese grandfather. Not a bit of it. He's just upset that it was an accident. He was quite enjoying feeling morally superior to his son, and now it seems that his son had pulled a fast one on him, and he admires that, but he was enjoying his moral superiority so much more. It seems there's no end to what people will do to feel better than other people. Even enjoy their son's suicide.'

'People will even *kill* their sons for a little moral superiority, I think,' said Mark, looking fixedly at Frieda.

'Or for their own convenience of course,' said Rebecca. 'A stronger and more usual motive generally.'

'Abortions are for convenience,' said Frieda. 'Just so that mothers can go on their gallivants. To Dieppe and places.'

'You make Dieppe sound like Sodom,' said Phyllida. 'Who could want to go to Dieppe?'

'Women who have abortions.'

'Once and for all,' said Rebecca patiently, 'I have not had an abortion, not ever, and I do not intend to have one. So will you please stop attacking me? No abortions, understand? No abortions.'

'More's the pity,' said Frieda, changing sides shamelessly. 'Mark has a child already, he does not want all that 2 a.m. jumping about all over again. It will kill him and then you will be sorry. You do not earn enough to bring up Mark's child.'

'Mother,' said Mark, 'I cannot think why you have taken to eating with us every night. You have your own kitchen. It has always been agreed that we keep separate households. How has it happened that Rebecca and I are never alone together any more?'

'This is the second time that I have screwed myself up to come to dinner with you', said Phyllida, 'and the second time you have made it clear you don't want me.'

'Of course I want you,' said Mark, 'I want you. You're my daughter, aren't you? I don't want my ex-wife. I don't want my mother if she bullies Rebecca. Does that make me unnatural? Seventeen Roman Catholic saints left their families to become monks in the first three letters of the Book of Catholic Saints alone, does the Church say they are unnatural? God, no. I can list them: there was Achilles of Cyprus, there was Antony of Capua. There was Antony of Malta, there was Barnardus the Greater . . . '

Bridget said, 'Don't worry, Rebecca, he always quotes saintly lives when things get too much for him. It's his nearest approach to asceticism. When we were just married and he started wallpapering for the first time, he kept saying that if he'd entered a monastery he'd be meditating peacefully. He's not even a Catholic. I remember he got awfully tied up in the wallpapering. It was Regency stripes as usual. He always was unhandy. I notice he didn't do your new paper in the loo very well, but I'm surprised you persuaded him to do it at all.'

Rebecca said firmly, 'This is a very good mousse, isn't it? Do have some more, Mark. Bridget made it.' She was wondering whether to tell Mark yet that she'd been offered a full-time post on *Harpers*. Perhaps not yet in view of the fact that Bridget, who had quietened down so much, had just had that unfortunate lapse about Mark's decorating. Still such attacks were seldom nowadays, and Bridget's presence was essential to Rebecca's plans.

For if Bridget could be persuaded to stay, she could look after Frieda, the new baby, and the housekeeping for far less than it would take to get competent professional help. Tonight did not seem likely to be propitious to open the subject, however. Phyllida was still looking upset. 'Do have some more mousse,' Rebecca urged. 'It must be very trying for you to have that old man under your feet.'

'I think it is quite outrageous,' said Mark. 'There seems to be a madness in the air, first your mother, then Giles's grandfather, settling in wherever they choose, I can't understand it.'

'I cannot but point out, however,' said Bridget, 'that if you had asked me to stay when I suggested it, Phyllida, I would be occupying Simon's room and the old Chinese grandfather might not have been deposited on you at all.'

'Does he speak any English?' asked Rebecca.

'Of course. He's not really Chinese, he's almost Cockney really.' Phyllida was looking quite cheerful again, she had forgotten her last outburst. Indeed she was looking a little excited, a little . . . 'I want to tell you something,' she said. 'I have got engaged. I came to tell you I have got engaged.'

Bridget began to fumble for a phrase to express delight and enquiry at the same time. Mark said jealously, 'To one of those young men, I suppose?'

'Which young men?' said Phyllida, momentarily (and too easily, thought Bridget with a flash of doubt) distracted from her news.

'In your flat. The young men in your flat.'

'Jonathan and Giles? Good God, no.'

'They're too young,' said Bridget. 'And anyway, Giles. . . no, Mark, of course not Jonathan or Giles.'

'May I know', said Mark, who grew pompous when anxious, 'the name of the man to whom my only daughter has got herself engaged?'

'It's a lovely name,' she said, glowing with happiness, and

looking about fifteen. 'It's Daniel Orlando Johnson.'

'*As you Like It*,' said Frieda informatively.

'You don't know Daniel Johnson,' said Bridget, 'you don't know him.'

She was seized with the jealousy she had expected to feel on seeing Rebecca with Mark. She too had wanted Johnson, suppressed her longing as pointless infatuation, forgotten it and him. Now – 'But you don't know him,' she said, and then realised this might be true. Her heart calmed down. 'Silly of me,' she said, 'it can't be . . . Who is it, dear?'

Phyllida looked straight across the table. She was taller than Bridget and she drew herself up, looking like a gawky young eagle. 'It was love at first sight,' she said. 'And I never believed in it, you know that? I had to coax him out to a theatre, I told him I'd got left with a spare ticket and it was Shakespeare and cultural, so he came, and he was done for, poor man. But he wouldn't come again and I'm spending the earth on train fares. I hardly see him, I suppose, but I'm totally head-over-heels in love.'

Mark relaxed. 'Oh well,' he said, 'if it's still in that dewy-eyed stage I see why he hasn't been along to ask my permission.'

Phyllida giggled. 'It must have been funny when people did that,' she said, but she realised that she would quite like her father, who had in a sense deserted her for another woman, to realise that she too was wanted. She would enjoy his jealousy.

'People still *do* do that,' said Mark, thumping the table. 'I tell you, my girl, I shan't think much of that young man of yours if he hasn't the decency to come and ask me for my permission to marry my daughter, if it really gets that far.'

'Balls,' said Phyllida. She got up. 'Actually,' she said, 'he's not exactly a young man, he's fortyish, and we're not exactly engaged, because he won't be. But give me time.' She swirled round the room, she was triumphant, she was trying not to dance. She sang, 'Give me time, give me time, give me time.'

'You are engaged, you are not engaged, what a world,' said Frieda.

'You said you were engaged,' said Rebecca.

'Well, I think of myself as engaged. I had to say something, don't you see? I just want to talk about him. It's no good at the flat, Serafina's in tears and there's that old man and it gets buried. And I just want to keep talking about him. And it's difficult because he doesn't . . . but he's brilliant and odd and ever so handsome, and kind of reassuring and stern. You'll love him. Mummy, you liked him, didn't you?'

'Yes,' said Bridget. 'I'm jealous of you actually,' she said, trying to see if voicing the truth to her daughter neutralised it.

Phyllida laughed politely. Bridget saw that it was impossible to those round the table that she was not joking. The humiliation of the denial of her sexuality recalled with precision her feelings when she had peered with shame at her passport photographs. At the same time she was relieved. She could not easily accept that she was jealous of her own daughter. And on such tenuous grounds. Such emotions were for women built in a Sophoclean mode. Her own place was with Mrs Beeton cooking turbot. Yet this time the picture of herself lovingly spooning Hollandaise sauce over slabs of white flesh no longer helped her regain what she had always thought of as a proper sense of proportion. The proportions of the past were no longer true for her. Something had changed. For a shameful moment she had truly been jealous of her much-loved daughter. But the recognition did not shame; the adjective 'shameful' was left over from a previous existence. She sat indulging herself in a concern for her own feelings. Her daughter must look after herself – marry or not marry, as she pleased, cope with her own desires and disasters. It was an extraordinary liberation to divest herself, not of love for her daughter, but of self-abnegation. As for Johnson, she realised what she knew Phyllida was too young to accept, that what she had felt (for already the event was slipping away into the past tense, but it had altered something, it had existed, it was part of her history) was largely a result of her own fantasies projected on to the first striking male figure who had entered her life for some time.

'Who', Mark was roaring, 'is this man of forty-two with the Shakespearean name to whom you consider yourself engaged despite, apparently, his protests? Do I gather you are pursuing some poor middle-aged gentleman who flees your embraces? Are you trying to force him into honourable matrimony by announcing an imaginary engagement?'

Phyllida was too happy to resent Mark's patronage. 'He thinks marrying me would interfere with his work.' This was true but did not distress her; she had no doubt that he would give way, she looked forward to teasing him, to the battle, to the conquest. 'He thinks his people wouldn't like it.' She was not thinking of marriage; an engagement to her was a temporary licence for embracement. That there were still those who didn't sleep with their fiancés would have been incredible to her, though she accepted that many older people felt it wrong to sleep with those to whom one had no such commitment. But after all, to sleep with one's fiancé was not to be promiscuous. She understood the objections to promiscuity. She was prepared to adapt, she did not want to give offence, she just wanted to sleep with Daniel. She would have been quite like a mediaeval peasant had she not excluded children from the desiderata of the relationship. 'But,' she said, 'I'm sure that once we were engaged they'd be quite pleased. No trouble.'

'What possible objection could his family have to you?' Mark was indignant.

'Not his family, daddy, his people. His congregation. They wouldn't like him marrying a white girl, he says. I say they're not racist.'

'Who is this man?' Mark was very quiet. 'Bridget, you seem to know. Who is he? How did Phyllida meet him?'

'I think she is talking of the black pastor of a South London church called the Congregation of the Children of Sinai. I have no idea how she met him.' Bridget had forgotten the Bible, the message. It was hidden in oblivion, she had stopped recalling the past.

P HYLLIDA HAD FOUND him, as he had said, working on his sermon, in his small flat above a tobacconist's shop.

'I've come,' she said, and sat down. 'How do you write a sermon?' she asked in honest curiosity.

He was an intelligent man, an educated man. He had been born in Ohio, had studied first there and then, under better teachers than he might have expected, at a small theological college in Missouri, had eventually come to England in response to a call . . . Phyllida's lively mind attracted him. He had met no other graduate since his arrival three years earlier in England. One can fall quite deeply in love in half a dozen meetings, and how was he to avoid these meetings when Phyllida was determined to engineer them?

She could not imagine that he was serious in his refusal to come out with her after that first theatre visit. She accepted that a clergyman (as she thought of him) might perhaps find it difficult to commit himself to an atheist. 'But then,' she said, perching on his study table, careless or ignorant of the gossip she was causing, 'convert me. It's your job, isn't it? Convert me?' She was unaware of the fact that she was playing a sexual game; her previous lovers had needed no provocation or enticement, had joined her in bed as a matter of course after an evening out. It did not occur to her either that her colour might prove as big a barrier as her lack of religious conviction. All in all, she was more ignorant of the power of both emotion and ideas than many a Victorian Miss. She was now using the evening with her father to boast about a sexual triumph which was not yet hers. She was not as seriously involved as she thought. The same could not be said for Daniel.

'Is she serious?' asked Mark, when his daughter had left. 'Is this a serious plan of hers? Is it a serious relationship?'

'He is very attractive,' said Bridget. 'He is a serious man. But of course it cannot be serious.'

'I will not allow it,' said Mark.

Frieda laughed. 'You cannot stop it,' she pointed out. 'And what will you say? Why is it unthinkable? It is of course your own fault, turning the poor girl out of the house, her own home, by bringing in that other woman, but once you have done that you must see you have lost your influence. And what will you ever say to her?'

Bridget saw with mingled amusement and sympathy the trap in which Mark found himself. He could not protest that Daniel was too old for Phyllida, since the age gap was no greater than that between himself and Rebecca. He could not protest on grounds of colour, since he was a noted, and to be fair to him, a sincere, liberal, a contributor to anti-apartheid funds and to the Brixton Defendants' League. There was a moment's pause while Mark sorted out his feelings and his arguments.

'These fringe cults,' he said. 'How can a girl of Phyllida's basic good sense get herself mixed up with one of these fringe cults?'

'You know how,' said Rebecca, sad for him, yet retaining the honesty which had on the whole led Bridget to respect her, 'you saw her.' They all remembered, as Rebecca

106

gestured to the patch of carpet on which Phyllida had stood, her flushed cheeks, her bright eyes. 'Sexuality really does override good sense. It is a driving force. We know we're on a disaster course but we enjoy the ride. We become mad.'

'You admit it,' said Frieda. 'You were on a disaster course when you married my Mark. He was mad when he married you. Sexuality overrode good sense.'

Rebecca said she was speaking generally. 'The "We" embraced all mankind,' she said. 'Sexuality drives us all mad.'

'I suppose', said Frieda, with the air of one really wanting to know, 'you are quite sure that Rebecca's coming child is yours, Mark? In view of your age and that remark?'

The evening broke up in pleasing chaos.

REBECCA HAD MADE up her mind. 'Your mother must go,' she said to Mark. 'We must put her name down for a bed at the Miller Eventide. We may have to wait to get her a single room, but she wouldn't be happy sharing, and I don't want to be unreasonable. I'm prepared to wait till she can have a single room. But I cannot finish my pregnancy and bring up a child in this hostility.'

'Darling,' said Mark miserably.

'Can I?'

'No. Only how can we possibly afford it? It was £150 a week for a single room last time we asked. Of course, there are cheaper places.'

'No,' said Rebecca kindly, 'she is your mother after all and I would not like her to be unhappier than necessary. In any case,' she added, 'there aren't any cheap places, not really cheap.'

'Where is Bridget?' said Mark. 'Where is mother? How does it happen that we are actually having a private conversation? Why do I feel uneasy?'

'Bridget is getting dinner ready for us. She has a new recipe that she wants to try out. Frieda is entertaining Trudy Goldberg. I am afraid that means that the news about Phyllida's love affair will spread all down the avenue, which is a pity because I had hoped, now she is visiting us more often, to introduce her to that nice boy at Number Five. However. So they are both busy and we have a chance to talk. And I must say, little though I ever imagined saying it when Bridget arrived, it seems to me now that her arrival here may have been absolutely providential. Listen.'

Rebecca had it well worked out. The job at *Harpers*, were she to take it (and she did intend to take it, it was the chance of a lifetime, she had been waiting for a suitable moment to explain it to him, surely he must see . . .), the job at *Harpers* would cover much of the expense of the Miller Eventide Home. Along with Frieda's pension they could manage it. That would leave Frieda's flat unoccupied. Bridget could move up there ('rent free,' said Rebecca magnanimously), run the house and look after the baby. 'Think how convenient it would be. Of course we'd pay her a little, we wouldn't want to be mean. And I could keep the study as a study which would be nice, Frieda would be in a good home, Bridget would have what she seems to want, a niche in the family.' Rebecca was pleased with herself.

'Isn't it perfect?' she said.

'Perfect? Having Bridget about for the rest of my life?'

'Only till little Oliver's old enough to start school. She could let her present flat and live on the proceeds till then, and it'd be there for her when Oliver didn't need her.'

'Oliver?'

'Oh, Mark . . . Jason, then. I thought you preferred Oliver.'

'She bullies me.'

'Not any more, she doesn't. Only occasionally, really. I think I've been rather clever actually. All right then, you solve it. *You* organise your mother and a baby and get Bridget out of the house and free the spare room. Because I'm going to take that job.'

'If we could just persuade Bridget to go back to her flat and stay there, that'd be a start,' said Mark.

'Listen, I wasn't going to tell you. But listen. Your mother phoned my mother yesterday and said I ought to leave you for my own sake because you were so angry about the baby coming that you might become dangerous and beat me up.'

'My mother said that?'

'Yes.'

'And your mother believed her?'

'No, of course not. My mother never believes anything. In any case Frieda's clearly a bit odd, isn't she? I mean, she looks a bit wild-haired these days. She sounded . . . well, my mother had a job to understand her at times.'

'She's aging a bit, I suppose.'

'So my mother didn't believe her. But she phoned me up and told me.'

'My mother said I was dangerous?'

'She said you'd been expelled from school for violence. I must say it doesn't seem like you.' Rebecca examined Mark in a way which made him wonder uneasily if she thought him incapable of forceful physical action.

'I got promoted captain pretty fast, considering,' he pointed out, but she was not following him. The war was not a point of reference in her life.

'She swore on the sacred grave of her grandfather in Lodz that you had been expelled from school for violence.'

'The wicked old bitch,' said Mark.

'It's obvious nonsense. But Trudy's up there now and being told it, so it'll get round the district. It's not very nice to think that the neighbours will be watching me to see if I'm a battered wife. They already think I'm a complaisant one.'

'Complaisant?'

'Having Bridget here. Not that I used to mind what the neighbours say, I know, but with little Oliver on the way, I mean, one doesn't want him to hear rumours from the kids he plays with. So now I do mind. A bit.'

'I'll speak to mother.'

'And I'll speak to Bridget. It would solve all our problems so conveniently.' They set off, Mark to the attic, Rebecca to the kitchen.

Frieda stood her ground.

He had been expelled from school for violence, she said, sadly. 'It was a great shock to us to be asked to remove you. Trudy, I think it would be tactful of you to remove yourself while my son and I have this painful conversation. I am sorry that you did not see this for yourself.'

There was a pause while Trudy reluctantly gathered her things and left. Mark realised too late that he should have asked her to stay and hear the truth, whatever that should turn out to be.

'I was never expelled from any school,' he said. 'What school was I expelled from?'

'Mrs Jones's. Such a nice place. Such a nice class of child.'

'But that was – for God's sake mother, that was a playgroup. I was two. I can't remember it, I only remember the name.'

'Three and a quarter. You were three and a quarter. You kept pulling the little girls' plaits and you started hitting one of the boys, Isadore or Theodore or something, every time you saw him. She wouldn't keep you.'

'And you phoned Rebecca's mother about that?'

'It showed a character trait.'

She folded her hands complacently. She is mad, he thought, mad. He must consult a doctor, she had no one but himself to care for her, and the burden of childhood descended on him. He must speak to a doctor. He recalled, however, that he had recently had two unpleasant interviews with doctors on a rather similar topic. It became less possible, dangerous even, to raise it again. 'And in how many other people do you discern the beginnings of madness?' his G.P. might enquire with alarming professional sympathy. It was after all supposed to be an early sign of mental disturbance, to think the rest of the world mad, and yet truly, as Mark considered, the world was surely most perturbing, less sane than it used to be? It was not just Frieda and Bridget, there was Phyllida pursuing some unfortunate middle-aged clergyman, and Rebecca determined to become a great journalist and a devoted mother simultaneously. Yet something must be done. Rebecca must be protected. He plunged down the stairs to reassure her that something, he knew not what, would be done.

In the kitchen Bridget was drying her hands. 'Oh, no,' she was saying, 'no, I'm not prepared to do that at all. Yes, I can see it would be convenient for you, Rebecca, but it's not what I want at all. No, actually, I'm finding this all a bit unsatisfying now. I think I'll move on.'

'I'm sure you're right,' said Mark eagerly. One mad woman in the house was enough, he thought. 'You're ready for your own flat again, I'm sure, he said. 'We'll come and visit you.'

'Move on, not back,' said Bridget.

'THERE'S NOWHERE FOR you to sleep, Mrs Mayor, honestly there isn't,' said Serafina, almost in tears. 'And Giles and Jonathan'll never forgive me if they come home and find out I've done it again.'

'Done what again?'

'Landed us with an extra person. Oh, I'm sorry, I didn't mean to be rude, but they all seem to think Mr Redditch is my fault. Please do go away. There honestly isn't room.'

'Room will appear,' said Bridget. 'I do find that if one actually embarks on a course, it becomes quite possible. Perhaps the social workers will remove Mr Redditch. I will go and introduce myself to him.'

'I shall phone Phyllida,' Serafina called after her in despair.

Phyllida arrived half an hour later. 'You can't mean it,' she said. 'You can't, you simply can't. We've already got Giles's grandfather. He's just taken over Simon's room and it's awful. He smells. Giles baths him, but he still smells. We can't have you too.'

'I don't smell,' Bridget pointed out.

'We haven't room.'

'That is in a way your own fault. After all, as I have already explained, if you had encouraged me to come to stay when I first expressed the desire to do so, I should have been occupying Simon's room and it is possible, it is just possible, that Giles's father would not have thought of dumping Giles's grandfather here. And then perhaps Giles's father would not have fled to Rome to kill himself or live with his aging girlfriend or whatever, and then the bomb would never have dispersed him. It is a lesson to me', said Bridget, 'to do what I want when I want it.'

'It is not the moral most people would draw from the present situation,' said Phyllida.

'But then people always draw the moral which suits them.'

'You said, you always said, that one must consider other people. Consider other people, it is the story of my childhood.'

'Yes, but I have learnt better. "Consider" is not a rigid term. It spreads like melting jelly.'

'If you try to stay here you will inconvenience us all and embarrass me.'

'Probably. On the other hand I don't expect permanently to damage your chances of happiness. It is no good, Phyllida, trying to appeal to my better nature. Causing other people minor inconvenience or moderate embarrassment does not any more outrage my moral sensibility.'

'I was thinking of your social sensibility.'

'I was thinking of me.'

At that moment the doorbell rang.

'It will be Serafina's mother,' said Phyllida, gesturing to the heavens in a caricature of despair. 'Drunk as usual and announcing that she intends to move in here with all her gin bottles. Or Jonathan's father on his way from Geneva to Washington, to say that he's been stranded at Heathrow for days and given up the forward flight. He can have the kitchen table to sleep on and Serafina's mother can share the bathroom with you.'

The doorbell rang again.

'Or seven total strangers who want to rent the hall cupboard,' she added on her way to open the door. Serafina was weeping in her bedroom but could not be heard, for Mr Redditch, in his bedroom, had turned Radio One on full blast.

'I am from the Council,' said the caller.

'Come in,' said Phyllida. 'They've discovered us as a solution to the housing problem rather faster than I'd expected, but I suppose news spreads. How many of you are coming to stay? Do you expect unfurnished accommodation? Would you rather share with me, my mother, or Giles's Chinese grandfather who smells?'

'I don't quite . . . Oh, it's a joke,' the girl smiled uncertainly. She was Phyllida's age. She looked tired. Her denim skirt drooped and her shirt, though clean, was unironed. 'Were you expecting . . . I called to see a – ' she glanced hastily at the clipboard she had been hugging to her – 'a Mr Giles Redditch.'

'He's at work. Will I do?'

'I don't know . . . it's about a Mr Herbert Redditch. It ought to be confidential.'

'Nothing about Mr Redditch is confidential from me,' said Phyllida bitterly. 'I help him put his trousers on in the morning. And his underpants as a matter of fact. I buy the Steradent for his false teeth. Come in. I suppose you're the social worker.'

'I'm the Junior Community Care Officer for Area Ten.'

'Quite. The social worker. We expected you several days ago. Giles took the afternoon off from work. Your failure to arrive was irritating to say the least.'

'Yes, I'm sorry about that. There was an emergency . . . something came up.'

'What?'

'Actually, I don't exactly remember. There's been so many lately. One after another, really, and we're short of staff . . . ' The girl pulled herself together, said in a new, professional tone, 'And of course our clients' emergencies have to remain confidential in any case.'

'It was extremely annoying for Giles.'

The girl looked round the sitting-room, weighing it up. 'Of course, if we'd realised he had a job . . . perhaps we could make another appointment.'

'It's quite simple. Four of us live here. We share it. Mr Redditch has nothing to do with us. He used to live with his son, who is dead. He's eighty-four and he can't live alone and he's only got the retirement pension and £400 in Indexed Bonds. And there's nowhere for him to live. Over to you.' She sat down.

The girl sat down too.

Bridget wondered whether to go and make coffee but decided she was too interested in what was coming.

'I cannot quite see your problem,' said the girl. Phyllida realised too late that she had made an enemy. She should not have mentioned the broken appointment. She should have been more courteous. It was her mother's fault that she had been so aggressive, she thought. She had been feeling aggressive even before she opened the door. There seemed no possibility of explaining this.

'Our problem is Mr Redditch. He cannot stay here. We do not want him.'

'That is sad for Mr Redditch, of course,' said the girl reproachfully.

'Perhaps you would go and see him. You can find the way quite easily, it is the room Radio One is blaring from. He wouldn't get up today. I don't know why. That's another thing, it's not safe to leave him alone. He's too old. He falls over. He spills things, he couldn't boil himself a kettle.'

'Who looks after him now?'

'Serafina's home from her job. She's having a kind of breakdown.'

'Well,' said the girl briskly, 'you've solved that problem then. If there's someone here, I really don't see why you worry.'

'It's only temporary. What happens when she goes back to work?'

'Breakdowns are nasty things. With luck you won't have to face that eventuality. In any case one mustn't cross one's bridges until one comes to them. Things seem to be quite all right at the moment, don't they? I'll go and see Mr Redditch and we'll put him on our list for visiting. Perhaps his doctor would send the community nurse round to bath him, if he smells. Old men often do, you know; one just mustn't keep one's old bourgeois prejudices. Let me know if things take a turn for the worse of course.'

'But he *can't* stay here. He just dumped himself. He's – a squatter. It's your job to do something.'

'I didn't get your name.'

'Phyllida, Phyllida Mayor. Miss Mayor.'

The girl looked at Phyllida's expensive office dress, at her slim soft leather shoes. She said patronisingly, 'Now, Phyllis dear, there is no cause to get upset. His grandson lives here and it is quite usual, you know, for grandchildren to look after their grandparents. Have you a granny or a grandpa who will need help one day, I wonder?'

For a split second Phyllida envisaged Frieda also arriving at her door. She forced her mind in other directions, said furiously, 'But Giles doesn't want to look after his grandfather.'

'Council policy is to expect relatives to care for their elderly folk. Of course if Mr Redditch were alone somewhere – but luckily that isn't the case, is it? He's already happily established here.'

'He's only staying here. It isn't his home.'

The girl looked up sharply. 'I have this down as Mr Redditch's home address. What is his home address then?'

'17 Marsham Drive, Noel Park.'

'That's North London, isn't it? Beyond Finsbury?'

'Somewhere that way. I've not been there.'

'In any case he's not our problem then. I will take him off our list. We should never have been involved. You should approach his home borough.'

'And start again?' Phyllida gave an incredulous wail. 'Right at the beginning?'

'Well, yes. If you can, of course. They may claim he's given up residence and refuse to accept him.'

'And then you'd take him back on your list?'

'We should fight it of course. But if it were eventually established that he was now a bona fide local resident, we should give his grandson every help in caring for him. There's an incontinency service for when it becomes necessary. And we are rather proud of our mobile library service. We are a Caring Borough. I can find my own way out, thank you. Goodbye. I see no point in my disturbing Mr Redditch now that I have uncovered the true situation.'

Serafina emerged tearfully from her room as soon as the

front door closed. She and Phyllida shared what had once been the big dining-room which was now divided by a hard-board partition; it opened off the sitting-room. 'I heard,' she said.

'I noticed the door was ajar,' said Phyllida.

'Oh, Mrs Mayor, whatever shall I do?' Serafina's voice was choked with hiccuping sobs. Tears did not become her. 'I can't go on spending every day shut up alone with that awful old man. He talks about boobs and bums.'

'Perhaps you could persuade the doctor to let you go back to work.'

'They talk about boobs all the time there, too,' said Serafina.

'The teachers talk about . . . ' Bridget was surprised. At the college where she had for so long and so dismally taught part-time the conversation was almost entirely about contact hours and the Burnham Further Salary Scale.

'Not the teachers,' said Serafina impatiently. 'The children.'

'Oh.'

It seemed to be an impasse.

After a bit Serafina said, 'You won't tell Giles, will you, what she said about it being all my fault?'

'All your fault? I don't remember her saying it was all your fault. She didn't even meet you.' Phyllida was wondering whether she might pour them all some whisky. It did seem a little early though, and it was after all Jonathan's bottle.

'But if I hadn't let them in, we mightn't be lumbered with him. That's what she said really. I heard her.'

Bridget said, 'You could hardly have slammed the door in their faces. And after all, you could argue that if Giles hadn't had a grandfather . . . I really don't see how he can blame you.'

'He doesn't exactly. Only I feel so guilty. And he's so

117

unhappy and I can't bear it when Giles is unhappy.' She was still sobbing.

'Proper little waterfall, that girl,' said a voice from the hall doorway. 'God knows what anyone'll ever see in her. I tell her, I say, my dad had a saying, never go out with a leaking boat or a weeping woman.'

'I hate you,' screamed Serafina.

'I know,' said Mr Redditch. 'And if you marry Giles I'll have you for a grand-daughter and I hate *you*. It's time for my medicine. And you never brought me my sandwiches I asked for for tea.'

'She would go home to her mother,' said Phyllida in an undertone to Bridget, 'but she doesn't want to move away from Giles.'

'If I were here,' said Bridget to the assembled group, 'I wouldn't in fact mind looking after Mr Redditch. While it suits me of course. Just for a week or so while we investigate other plans. I will stay tonight anyway. I feel like some young company. Your father really seems to be growing rather dispiritingly elderly. I shall sleep on the sofa, don't make a fuss. I shall manage perfectly well.'

'I will not be here,' said Phyllida. 'I will not be manipulated. I shall move out.' Tears of anger filled her eyes.

'How these young things do cry these days. No stamina. If they'd had the life my old mum had they'd have had something to cry about, I could tell them. Proper little madam, though, that daughter of yours . . . ' Mr Redditch continued his commentary until Phyllida and her hurriedly packed suitcase were gone. 'Pity it wasn't that Serafina who went, all the same,' he added, loudly so that Serafina could hear.

Then Bridget put his tea in front of him and he stopped talking, though his eating habits were such that he could not be said to have fallen silent.

A FEW EVENINGS later Bridget, sitting at the table with Jonathan and Giles one each side of her, and two or three of their friends and Serafina there as well, realised to her surprise that she did not miss her daughter. The young men were amusing company. They were glad to have her, it was convenient. Bridget managed to settle the old man in his own room in the evenings; she had hired another television set for him, she put him firmly to bed before dinner. The room was small, hardly more than a cupboard, so that she could well understand why Simon had moved out (though her guess was wrong, but she had no information about Simon). Still it was cosy and Mr Redditch was not sorry to be comfortably ensconced among piled pillows.

He would lie there brooding over the brief telephone battles he occasionally had with Frieda, battles of which Bridget was entirely unaware.

'She's not here, she's at the shops.'

'Say "Mrs Mayor" when you talk of my daughter-in-law.'

'That's who you are, is it, her ma-in-law? Can I give her a message, ma?'

'And you may call me Madam.'

'That'll be the day.'

'My daughter-in-law was born for better things than caring for you, I may say. Oh, yes, I've heard about you. Don't think I don't know. Battening on her good nature, you are, my man.'

'Heard about me, have you? What lies has she been putting about then? I'll have something to say about that, I will, gossiping old harridans taking away a man's character . . .' but Frieda had hung up. She had enjoyed the little spat and had chosen, more than once, to phone for brief conversations at times when it was probable Bridget would be out.

Nor did Mr Redditch dislike these moments of life; so he too said nothing to Bridget whom, moreover, he knew that he could not bully. He was too dependent, she was too detached. She controlled him.

'You are splendid, Bridget,' said Jonathan over dinner. 'We haven't had a peep out of the old horror all evening. I can almost forget him.' He glared hastily at Giles and added, 'Not that I see this as going on for many more days, you understand. Something will have to be done.'

'I'm sure the solution will appear,' said Bridget untruly, concerned only to maintain the present position as long as possible. 'Have some Bavaroise with raspberries . . . do you like crêpes, I wondered? Would you like crêpes with Grand Marnier tomorrow night, or would you prefer Drambuie?' She bribed them, she enticed them, she made life easy. They were glad of her presence and it aroused no resentment. Indeed Giles was thankful to have someone older to discuss the problem of his grandfather's future with.

'I wonder where Phyllida is,' said Bridget speculatively over the cheese. 'I suppose she has friends . . .'

Jonathan's raised eyebrow made her feel suddenly naive.

'Well, of course she might be with Daniel Johnson, I see that. But he is in Holy Orders, he has a reputation to think of.'

Giles said drily, 'Even love wouldn't persuade Phyllida to live in West Croydon . . .'

They fell silent. Bridget was carrying on a conversation with herself. She was discovering that she rather admired her daughter. 'Would I have had the courage', she wondered, 'to approach Johnson without an invitation?' She remembered sadly the lost chances of her own youth. Perhaps the young men she had watched across the lecture hall at university or met momentarily at sherry parties would have responded to an invitation to tea, to an openly voiced desire on her part to see them again. Faces long forgotten glowed in her memory, those of men she had longed to know and never did.

The unapproached ones would probably have proved boring, she knew. 'But why did I deprive myself of all those opportunities to find out?' she thought. 'I know my "lovers seek me not". Why didn't I go looking for them, though? What led me to believe that to initiate a relationship is simultaneously to abort it?' She wished Phyllida well in her pursuit of Johnson. This did not mean she wished her success, that was not the point, but she wished her to survive without humiliation, without a loss of the readiness to go hunting another day, in another place, for she thought Johnson would escape Phyllida. She might have turned her thoughts towards herself, have examined her own emotions, her desires and residual jealousies, were she not enjoying the dinner party so much, and recalled to it so delightfully by the laughter which greeted some joke of Giles's and by Jonathan offering her some more of his excellent wine.

As she drank she relaxed. She had always wanted sons, had accepted too readily she now thought the doctors' advice not to have a second child. She delighted in these two young men, in their poise, their looks, their wit. She felt as proud of them as if they *were* her sons. They, on their part, behaved enchantingly, not in the least as if she were their mother . . . They had fallen into the way of paying her outrageous compliments; they offered confidences; they had taken her to the cinema. They ignored Serafina, who doped herself with valium and was now keeping her fixed gaze on every move Giles made. It was altogether a splendid evening and Jonathan produced whisky with the coffee even though it was not raining.

'How angry Phyllida will be to miss her share of my whisky,' he said. 'I expect the Children of Sinai are all teetotal.'

BUT PHYLLIDA HAD fled to Hampstead, not to Croydon. She was a practical young woman and aware of the worth of a centrally-heated bathroom. Moreover she needed allies against her mother who would understand what was happening, who had suffered a similar incursion.

'She never thinks of anyone else,' she said bitterly. 'Not any more. We've got no room for her and she knows it. She's got a perfectly good flat and a job – '

'Yes,' said Mark. 'What happened about her job? Term isn't over.'

'It was only part-time of course,' said Phyllida, a little guiltily.

'Still, it was a job. It had kept her happy for years.'

'She phoned and told them she was ill,' said Rebecca. 'I heard her. And when she put the phone down she looked extremely happy, not ashamed at all.'

'All those deserted students!' Phyllida was shocked.

'Nonsense', said Frieda. 'Do you not read the newspapers any of you? I do not expect people who pretend to be journalists to read, of course, but that my son, that my granddaughter should not be aware of what is happening about them . . . of course the school will be very glad she has solved the problem. Principals and headmasters are human beings. They will not like all this sacking and redundancy-making they are involved in. They are getting rid of the part-time teachers to keep the others in their jobs. She is doing them a favour. And they will think she has let them down and feel superior.'

'That is not why she did it,' said Rebecca.

'It is the result of her action, though. Are people not to be credited with achievements?' Frieda looked reproving.

'She will never get a decent reference.'

'If she has no income . . . ' Phyllida's voice trailed away. There was a moment's silence. Mark was considering the unpleasant possibility that he might have to increase Bridget's allowance at the very time when he would have another child to support and Rebecca would no longer be earning, for he could not see how she could accept the *Harpers* job.

Frieda said, 'It is all the fault of that dreadful divorce. She should be here and none of these fusses would occur.'

'I offered her a job looking after my baby. She could have been here.'

'My mother's going to be like Giles's father was. I can see it coming. Even if we get her back to Waddon she won't have a job. She'll need one, well obviously. And she'll see that when she's back to her normal self. It'll be awful. She'll keep on phoning me up and weeping. She's got my office phone number too. Oh God.'

'You and Giles will just have to console each other,' said Rebecca.

'Oh, Giles is all right. His father's died. That's all over. And I know there's his grandfather but after all once he dies all Giles's problems will be solved. And he's eighty-four you know. I keep reading *The Times* and the average age in the deaths column is a lot less. And our actuaries say that a man of eighty-four has a life expectancy of only – '

'I am eighty-five,' said Frieda furiously. 'Which of us are you wishing dead, Phyllida, me because I'm old or your mother because she's a worry to you?'

'Neither,' said Phyllida desperately. 'I was speaking generally. I was answering Rebecca. I was referring entirely to Giles's grandfather.'

'No one could wish you dead, mother,' lied Mark, furious with his daughter for making him conscious of the reason for his own recent habit of reading the deaths column in *The Times* before he glanced at the headlines, even though it was no longer conveniently on the back or front page. 'We only want Bridget quietly back in Waddon again and not disturbing us all in this extraordinary way. She is charging about the country like a mad bull. We all have Bridget's best interests at heart.'

Still, death was often a solution though one must not recognise it. When people would not stay conveniently in their places and would insist on intruding into other people's lives, thought Frieda and Mark and Phyllida (and Giles) of various people, one did find oneself wishing that the natural conclusion of life might bring the obvious solution at some helpful moment. Only Rebecca, cushioned in pregnancy, felt uninvolved.

'Of course,' said Phyllida, who was a truthful girl in awkward ways, 'if Giles's grandfather had only gone to Rome as well, life for the rest of us would be easier. Can I stay here for the night, please?'

DISTANT COMMUNICATIONS WERE resumed between Hampstead and the flat. It was Frieda who first telephoned; her phone calls became daily events, sometimes recurrent. There were days when she phoned three or four times and her vehement articulateness was often at odds with the content of her conversation.

'The milkman was late this morning,' she phoned to say. 'The country is falling to pieces. That woman' (which was how she now usually referred to Rebecca) 'won't complain. It's my belief she puts him up to it. They conspire against me so that I shan't have enough milk for my morning coffee. The pettiness of a peasant.'

'I'm sure Rebecca would lend you some milk if you're really short; after all, if she's out you can help yourself and replace it later.'

'It is the conspiracy not the milk which troubles me. Really, sometimes you are very dense, Bridget. If it goes on I shall ask you to accompany me to the police station to complain; and Mark bought her a new painting for the drawing-room yesterday. He never bought you any paintings.'

'We hadn't enough money then.'

'No, poor girl, you helped him in his early days and now he brings that woman presents. I tell him, I say, "And what have you brought for Bridget?" '

Bridget, who felt sorry for Frieda as often as not, was no longer distressed or threatened by the stream of news about Rebecca and Mark, only bored. She stood by the phone murmuring agreement without listening closely, and then found herself jerked into attention by some wholly bizarre statement which linked with no apparent situation.

'I need advice, Bridget. Shall I feed the tigers?'

'What tigers?'

'You know perfectly well what tigers. The ones in the garden. They were there when you lived here only there are more of them. They only eat tinned raspberries and that's so expensive.'

'I expect they forage for themselves,' said Bridget helplessly.

'I hope they will eat Rebecca up one day.' She rang off.

Frieda was mostly concerned, however, that Phyllida and Rebecca were getting on so easily. 'She is stealing my grand-daughter,' she said once, in tears of rage and self-pity. 'I shall have no one at my funeral but Trudy. I shall die alone. That woman will leave me to die alone, she will take Phyllida out to a party and pretend I am quite well. She is a witch. She should be burnt alive; oh, they knew what to do to witches in the old days. I would burn her with my own hands. Poor Bridget, poor Phyllida.' She rang off.

Sometimes Phyllida, stiff with resentment, called in to remove some dress she wanted or to collect her post.

'I see you've made yourself at home in my room,' she said bitterly to Bridget. She saw that her decision to stay in Hampstead had spared her mother from sleeping on the sofa, which might, she supposed, have got rid of her fairly fast.

'Yes, thank you, dear. It's made settling in much easier. Jonathan put in an extra plug for my electric blanket.'

It was only too clear that life in the flat was continuing cheerfully.

With Bridget to care for Mr Redditch and listen to Serafina, Giles and Jonathan resumed their usual social life, appearing occasionally in the company of beautiful young men or pretty and intelligent girls. Bridget fed them all, rediscovering cooking skills she had not practised for many years.

Phyllida, furious, stayed in Hampstead. Mark was at first delighted. Frieda retreated to her attic to plan further assaults on Rebecca. Rebecca found herself having to be cook again, and for three instead of two. She would have regretted Bridget's departure and Phyllida's arrival were it not for Mark's regained contentment.

She began to ask her friends about the expenses of full-time nannies. If Frieda continued in her new-found placidity the necessity to pay for the Miller Eventide Home would retreat. It was possible that the salary from *Harpers* would then cover the cost of a nanny, or almost so. The need for action had disappeared; a perilous equilibrium had been established. It was almost an equation, with Serafina, Giles, Jonathan, Bridget and old Mr Redditch in Battersea and Phyllida, Frieda, Mark, Rebecca and a coming baby in Hampstead.

It was of course untenable. The accident of geographical distance was a major disturbing factor in that it exacerbated Phyllida's fury and led to a lessening of Mark's comfort in his sleepy evenings. From Hampstead to Croydon is a long journey. Phyllida would go to West Croydon by train from London Bridge after work.

There was a service or a meeting of some kind most nights.

'Eat at my place,' Mrs Brooker had urged, and Phyllida often did.

'You don't look after yourself,' Mrs Brooker would chide. 'You should eat more . . . If you were one of my daughters . . . ' She was sorry for Phyllida: she had heard all about her pregnant stepmother and her distressingly fat and unreliable father. And there was the sweet aging grandmother . . . and of course Phyllida's mother, whom she had once met. 'How's your mother?' she asked, filling Phyllida's plate with a stew of spicy vegetables, okra and peppers and two kinds of bean, with sweet potato served separately in a rich brown sauce.

'Still very . . . disturbed. Not herself,' said Phyllida. 'I worry.'

'A nice lady. I wish my daughters . . . '

'I would like to meet your daughters. What do they do?'

'One is in a bank, the other is studying to be a nurse.' Mrs Brooker herself worked in an insurance office; she had made the leap to a white-collar job and dragged most of her family with her.

'Will they be at this evening's service?'

'No. They are not members of the church. They have their own lives.' She was a little ashamed of this.

'Perhaps they will join later,' said Phyllida kindly. She would have liked to add, 'We might pray about it together,' because this would clearly have comforted Mrs Brooker, and Phyllida had grown fond of the warmhearted woman who fed her such strange and delightful dishes, but she had enough honesty left to feel that she should not sink to quite such hypocrisy. Moreover she had a certain doubt as to whether she could say the phrase without guying it.

Mrs Brooker looked sadly at Phyllida. She had an un-recognised hope that caring for Phyllida, whom she saw as a slightly pathetic waif, might somehow absorb some of her own grief. She thought about Phyllida's unhappiness rather than her own as a device for getting to sleep at night. It was a secret concern. She never spoke to Phyllida of the vanished Errol, who was referred to only in the ritualised screams which were released in church.

'I wonder if he's still alive?' Phyllida would think on the dull stretch of line between Selhurst and Thornton Heath, while she journeyed home. But she did not ask.

As Mrs Brooker was trying to use Phyllida, so Phyllida too was using Mrs Brooker, though not knowingly. It was the innocent self-centredness of the young perhaps. Mrs Brooker was part of the dramatic machinery which Phyllida intended should make Daniel Johnson admit he loved her. Or at least make him kiss her. Or make him admit that he wanted to kiss her.

Consciously, Mrs Brooker saw Phyllida as a young girl in need of the love of Christ. She observed her growing friendship with the pastor with an approving eye.

DANIEL JOHNSON, HOWEVER, began to dread every service. He lingered talking to the elders till Phyllida had left the church. He delayed his return to his rooms, above a tobacconist's shop not far from Surrey Street Market, as long as he could, knowing that when he got there she might be propped against the door waiting. He was glad that the last train back to London left at 11.02, and dreaded that the time would come when she would deliberately miss it. She was shameless.

'You are causing gossip,' he said. She laughed; she had never been part of a small community.

He was aware that the intensity of a girl's feelings for a man so much older than she was must have in it some degree of father worship, and he knew enough of Phyllida's deep hurt at her parents' divorce to realise that this was part of Phyllida's reaction to him, but of what use was that elementary pastoral knowledge (instilled into him by his remarkably good theological college in his own longed-for country) when it in no way made Phyllida's behaviour less demanding?

'They are watching her, not thinking of the service,' he told himself as he sang the concluding words of a hymn. They were watching with a variety of reactions; this he knew from their expressions but also from many embarrassing conversations. Old women with kindly maternal voices would seize opportunities to say, 'Of course, a pastor should be married, you know,' or look across at where Phyllida sat and murmur, 'Such a sweet child.' Others saw her presence as an infiltration, a betrayal: the words 'Beware, let us beware of the Scarlet Woman, of strange Jezebels' had entered into prayer at Thursday prayer meeting. The next night three middle-aged men called on Daniel and offered to pray with him. More sophisticated members of the congregation saw her as out for a cheap sexual thrill and developed their own sexual fantasies of humiliation, eying her dangerously.

A couple of teachers in the community saw Daniel as merely the victim of a teenage crush, and angered others by their casual dismissal of the situation. Alignments were beginning to take place, the congregation was revealing itself as a collection of groups, each with its own ethic, each as far from the others as Hampstead was from Croydon or one flat in the Duke of Cornwall Mansions from its neighbour. He was experienced enough to recognise that this fragmenting of the congregation was more damaging than a theological split. It undid all he had been working for.

She could not understand why he was so disturbed.

'I have come down here to see you,' she said. 'And it's inconvenient for me too. But you won't come up to London.

Mondays you are free, come Monday. I know a friend's flat we could borrow.'

'Phyllida,' he said hopelessly, 'I am a Minister of Religion.'

'Well, just to talk,' she said. 'Nothing wrong in talking, is there?' She was enjoying the battle. Somehow or other she was going to get this man into bed: she took it for granted. 'After all,' she said, 'it's not as if you were a Roman Catholic priest, is it? You haven't taken a vow of chastity.'

After a bit, she said, 'Have you?' It was an intriguing thought.

'No.'

'Well then.' She could not understand his difficulty. London was safely anonymous.

One evening – they were standing by the news-stand in West Croydon station – it dawned on him that he would have bought her flowers from the flower-seller whose daytime presence was evidenced by damp stone and fallen petals, had the man not long ago gone home. He had walked down with her, he had thought, in order to pack her on to a train, refusing any more to let her into his rooms, and unwilling to leave her standing in the dark street. Now his sudden intense desire to buy her something brilliantly coloured, sweetly scented, not violets or anemones, something more dramatic, he could not even imagine flowers passionate enough for her, frightened him.

'You must not come here any more.'

'If you will come to the flat on Monday, I'll stop coming down.' She wondered if her mother, announcing that she had arrived to live with Mark and Rebecca, had had this same sense of pleasure, of freedom, of saying, as it were, that one would choose one's own place and not be pushed out or away.

'You must know it is impossible.'

'Why is it impossible? You like to be with me.'

'You must stop coming down,' he said. 'You must stop wanting me. We have nothing in common, nothing, nothing.

You have no idea of my world, no idea of it. You have no idea of me.'

'You can tell me.'

'And I cannot afford to get married.'

The phrase escaped him as unexpectedly as the great bunch of scarlet and purple flowers had flashed upon his imagination. It was ludicrous in its context; it diminished him. She grabbed his hands and he let her hold them for a moment but he thought she was laughing and he freed himself.

'My calling comes first . . . '

'As to that, why argue?'

She did not even pretend to listen, he thought, and walked away. She ran down the steps to the platform triumphant.

But back in his room he sat looking at the telephone, clear in his own mind that Phyllida's family must be approached. He was uncertain only whether it should be her mother, whom, after a fashion, she seemed to love, or her unsatisfactory father, with whom she was so oddly living. Someone must control her and rescue him. Or he would sleep with her or marry her or something.

He was a very lonely man.

NEXT MORNING, HOWEVER, it was Frieda to whom Bridget answered the telephone.

'Supposing, Bridget, I were to ask you to buy me a live cockerel, would you do it, do you think?'

'Day-old chicks, surely, you mean?'

'Really, sometimes I think your wits are not what they used to be. Day-old chicks were what I used to buy in the old rationing days, when we lived in Dappleton . . . fancy your remembering that story . . . Now are Mark and Rebecca likely to want a poultry farm in their backyard? A live cockerel is what is traditional, I believe.'

'Whatever for? No.'

'But if you know a Japanese. Do you know any Japanese?'

'I don't think so . . . why suddenly do you want me to know a Japanese?'

'Because I suppose a day-old chick might do if it were the right sex. All Japanese can sex chicks, you know. It's in their blood or something. Perhaps it's the slant eyes.'

'I know no Japanese chicken sexers and I have no source of poultry. No.'

'Oh well, I don't suppose it would have worked anyway.'

'I could bring you round a frozen chicken. Or a fresh one come to that.'

'We are not short of food. The Express Dairy leave me what I want if I find the weather inclement.' She rang off.

That afternoon she rang up again to say, 'Could you join me perhaps at exactly six o'clock every night in a chant?'

'A chant?'

'Thus doubling the rays.'

'A kind of Women's Day of Prayer? But that's a midday effort, surely?'

'You are irredeemably stupid at times. I wonder that Mark wants you back sometimes; Rebecca is after all not entirely a fool.'

'Mark doesn't want me back.'

'He does not always recognise what he really wants. He was like that as a little boy, I could never trust him to make out a sensible Christmas list.'

Frieda rang off.

There had been many such phone calls. But when Bridget lay awake at night it was not of such puzzling coded messages that she thought. It was of Phyllida, playing her games of possession with Daniel Johnson. It was of Serafina, eying Giles with growing dependence. It was also of the pretty girls who came and went with Jonathan, who occasionally and as a matter of course stayed the night in Jonathan's room. Sometimes she looked back at her own quiet youth, but could find within her no feelings of either regret or satisfaction. 'It was all so long ago,' she thought. 'I was a different person. Now is a different time.'

The truth was she enjoyed the comings and goings. She enjoyed preparing little dinners which often turned into parties. She was surprised at herself as she accepted extravagantly insincere compliments from Giles's young men (though occasionally and confusingly there was a girl and Serafina was edgy) or accepted an offer to do the washing-up from Jonathan's young woman of the moment.

'I am behaving irresponsibly,' she told herself. But she did not care; she was simply enjoying the life, the movement, the frivolity. She felt impatient with Serafina's misery; she was as brisk as a hospital nurse with Mr Redditch, dealing with him conscientiously but forgetting him once he was packed off to bed, as she ensured he was before Jonathan or Giles got home. She did not recognise any duty to Serafina or Mr Redditch.

SERAFINA INDEED TRIED to force her into the role she would once have filled.

'Mrs Mayor,' she said, 'don't you think you ought to do something about helping us to get rid of Mr Redditch? I mean, someone's got to do something. He ought to be in a home. He can't just stay here forever, can he? Couldn't you phone the Social Work Department and ask why they haven't even acknowledged Giles's last letter?'

'Why me, Serafina?'

'Well, Giles tried. He doesn't get very far though.'

'True. Why do you think I should take over?'

Serafina looked shocked. 'Well, you're older than us, aren't you? Surely you ought to be kind of sorting things out for us if you're going to live here at all?'

Bridget saw that for Serafina women of her age existed only to serve and protect the young. It was an oddly dehumanising view of middle age. It was one she could dimly recall having held herself.

'You ought to be more responsible,' said Serafina with uncharacteristic daring. 'That's what I think. It's bad enough my mother not helping us, but she has some excuse, I can see that.'

'Oh, what?' asked Bridget, interested.

'Well, she drinks.'

'I may try that yet.'

'And Dr Adams has refused to give me another certificate. He says I'm fit for work. He's signed me off at the end of this week. And I'm not.'

'So?'

'So I don't know what to do. I can't go back. Ought I to find another doctor? Could I?' Serafina put her head down on the sofa arm and wept. 'I can't go back. What can I do? Tell me.'

But Bridget made no move towards her. She felt no guilt over Serafina or Mr Redditch; she had not driven them to their present needs. She would help them only so far as suited her.

'It is no good, Serafina, you are too old to be mothered,' she said. The only guilt Bridget felt these days was at Phyllida's absence from the superb parties, and that guilt was slighter than she liked to admit.

'You wouldn't say Phyllida was too old to be mothered if *she* were crying.'

'No, I do seem to be inconsistent,' agreed Bridget. 'But I do not mind my own inconsistencies any more. The truth is that your crying irritates me and Phyllida's would distress me.'

'It's her sniffing that gets me.' Mr Redditch had been sound asleep in the big armchair, now permanently in the big window. Even Frieda's phone call had not led him to stir. Now however he glared at Serafina and then at Bridget, waving an arm towards the sofa. 'Her sniffing. And her bloody moaning. God help the kids in her class is what I say . . . No wonder they try to cheer life up with a few larks. Drive anyone to it, she would. If you don't get me to the lav damn quick you'll have some pants to wash.'

'How did you make your money, Mr Redditch?' asked Serafina. 'Blackmail?'

'Bookie's runner,' he said, a little breathlessly, as Bridget hauled him to his feet. 'Won it on the pools. Selling things that fell off the back of a lorry.'

At the door he paused, looking over his shoulder. 'Ran a brothel down the Mile End Road. Sold old cars. Black market in the war. You couldn't begin to know,' he said.

DANIEL JOHNSON DECIDED to approach Bridget; he spent long hours drafting letters which he failed to post. He might have done better to speak to Mark, who was finding Phyllida's presence in his home less rewarding than he would once have expected. She filled the house with her exaggerated gestures, her clumsy rushing about. She ran up and down stairs, she called up to Frieda from the bottom of the stairs and down to Rebecca from the top of the stairs. She and Rebecca were becoming friends and Mark sometimes felt excluded. They shared a copy of *Spare Rib* and had a bad influence on each other, so that Rebecca's insistence on her need to work full-time became more insistent. Phyllida's presence and closeness to Rebecca emphasised Rebecca's youth and made Mark feel tired. But then he *was* tired. He left the house half an hour earlier than was his habit so that he could drive Phyllida to work, an offer he had made in the first exhilaration of having his long-lost child once more under his roof and was not now able to retract, and he was frequently woken, just as he had fallen into his first sleep, by the sound of the front door slamming as Phyllida returned, very late, from her visits to her so-called fiancé.

'Couldn't you try to be quieter?' he would ask next morning.

'Sorry.' Moreover there was the irritation of the fact that Phyllida was paying him nothing. He was humiliated by his desire for her to contribute to his income; 'I don't need the money,' he told himself. On the other hand it was an expense having her; she drank vodka and whisky which Rebecca ordered but he paid for. And there was the moral problem. 'Is it good for a daughter to live at her father's expense?' he asked himself. 'On the other hand, does a good and loving father expect a daughter, home for a visit for the first time for years, to pay for her keep? Is it a visit? Or has she moved in for ever?' He was ashamed to find he would not welcome this prospect. On what terms were they, on what terms should they be?

He lay awake pondering these problems. He began to ask people at work if their grown-up children lived at home. He never found one who answered affirmatively so he had no chance to move tactfully on to his prepared questions about their contribution to family finances. He began to feel put upon.

'I'm afraid it's inconvenient for you, out here at Hampstead,' he ventured one evening.

'Yes.' Phyllida's voice was tart. She after all had her problems. One evening, when she did not go to Croydon, for Daniel was away at some conference, she attacked Mark directly.

He learnt, to his indignation, that she considered it to be his duty to dislodge Bridget from the Duke of Cornwall Mansions.

'I'm your daughter, after all. You've done nothing for me since you broke the home up and now you sit smugly by and let your ex-wife dislodge me from my own flat. I expect you encouraged her to do it, really, as a way of getting her out of your own hair.'

He defended himself but she did not listen. 'Your ex-wife,' she kept repeating. 'Your ex-wife.' He would have to do something about it, he realised, even as he made debating points about Bridget being Phyllida's mother as well as his own ex-wife. He would have to make an effort, get Bridget to see reason.

'There's nothing wrong with the Waddon flat, is there?' he asked, smitten with new guilt.

'Of course not. She's been perfectly happy there all these years, hasn't she?'

'Of course . . . Well, we must get her back there.'

'Oh, big deal. How?'

'Your mother was always a conscientious woman, you know, really. Always bought Christmas cards from UNICEF, I remember, and things like that. Perhaps you and I are too involved. Someone else is needed to bring her back to a sense of proper behaviour. To her true self. If the medicos had been co-operative of course . . I expect it's her time of life, you see.'

This was intended to calm Phyllida, and Mark, who did not read *Spare Rib*, was therefore astounded to discover that it merely added to her fury. Women, everywhere, had breakdowns and got ill and *died* she said, they just say it's your age, any age between thirty-five and sixty, she said, you try convincing a doctor you're really ill, if you are a woman, she said, unless it's a broken leg absolutely hanging off by a thread. 'I wonder', she said, 'they didn't tell me it was the menopause when I had chicken pox the year before last, I was quite twenty-one after all.'

'You had chicken pox the year before last?' he said, appalled that his enchanting, furious, newly-returned daughter had been ill and he had not known of it.

'Badly,' she said.

'I didn't know.'

'Quite.'

'Are you quite better? I mean,' he fumbled, 'I wish I'd known. I'd have visited, I'd have brought magazines, grapes . . .'

'Have you had chicken pox?'

'Of course I've had chicken –' He broke off and ran up the stairs, returning swiftly to say that, no, actually Frieda said he hadn't had chicken pox.

'So you wouldn't have come to see me even if you'd known,' she pointed out.

'Yes I would.'

'No, you wouldn't.'

They glared at each other.

Upstairs Frieda closed a detective story. It was useless. She had no access to South American arrow poison.

'PERHAPS,' THOUGHT BRIDGET often on these late spring evenings, as she awaited the return of Jonathan and Giles, or looked round the table at one of the parties which, now that her cooking skills were more widely known, were replacing some of the evenings at discos and cinemas (being as well so much cheaper for everyone, except Bridget, whose savings account at the Building Society was for the first time in her memory below £500), 'perhaps I am a more maternal person than I have hitherto realised. Or perhaps,' she added, recalling her impatience with Serafina and the comparatively unregretted absence of her own daughter, 'I am the kind of woman who should have had some sons.'

She relaxed with her pseudo-sons, not just Giles and Jonathan but Jeremy and Nicholas, Roger and Martin, Ahmed and Kurt. At times their knowledge of the world made her feel naive: they were, for instance, travelled. Their families had money, or they had jobs with multi-national companies or international agencies, or they worked for airlines. Roger brought her back some junk jewellery from California.

'I got it for you in San Francisco, it's the rage out there,' he said, flourishing the dazzling shapes, dropping the present on her lap and kissing her. 'I kept fishing the package out of my flight bag all the way over in order to look at the wrapping paper, it made a kind of link with S.F. But it didn't stop me wanting to cry when we took off.'

'Oh, we all cry when we leave San Francisco,' said Giles.

'You've been there too then?'

'Only once. My father gave me a trip there for my twenty-first birthday. I stayed months. That was before he went broke.' He helped himself to some olives.

'I never knew he went bust,' said Roger. 'How very dramatic of him. Was it for millions and millions, like it always is in the *Sunday Times* stories?'

'It was enough,' said Giles gloomily. 'And he'd even mortgaged the house and that went too . . . all the family money down the drain. Bloody fool.'

'So now you're penniless?'

'Dependent on my friends,' agreed Giles, as they sat down to table. 'And my salary, of course. But that won't take me to America. Oh, Bridget, soufflé. How clever of you.'

'Imagine,' said Jonathan. 'Having to make one visit last a lifetime. Poor Giles.'

'Have you been too?' asked Bridget, recalling with renewed bitterness the damp Scottish hotels to which Mark had taken her.

'Not yet.' He was cheerful. 'I'll go when I'm ready.'

'He doesn't need it like we do,' explained Roger.

'In a way, I've been twice,' said Giles. 'I was born there. Only I don't remember that of course.'

'Born there?' said Serafina. She opened her eyes very wide. 'Do tell.' She leaned towards him in a pantomime of concern.

Was it possible, Bridget wondered, that she was unaware of Giles's sexual leanings? Were any girls these days as ignorant as that?

'Nothing to tell,' said Giles. 'My father was out there on another of his business disasters. Grandad made the money in shady property deals, father lost it. We came back when I was three months old.'

'I was born in Ootacamund,' said Laura or Lorna or Leila or whatever the girl's name was. Jonathan had brought her in for the third time; they would have to find out what she was called.

'Snooty Ooty,' they all chorused with delight.

'And,' she said, 'my aunt married a Sikh and we're not allowed to speak of her in front of granny.' She beamed triumphantly around the table. 'And my granny was born in Poona.'

'Ooh, Laura (or Lorna or Leila),' they variously chorused, 'you are lucky.'

'I went to Jersey last summer,' said Serafina loudly.

'How nice,' said Bridget as nobody else responded. 'How very nice. Giles, go and see if your grandfather wants any of the crown of lamb, will you, or if the soufflé was enough for him? I made sure he had several of the goujons of sole in his portion, he doesn't want much at night . . .'

The meal came lazily to an end and they cleared up together, the young ones tumbling over each other yet neatly efficient. It was a warm evening; Serafina and Laura-Lorna were in bright silky blouses, the young men had changed not into the dinner jackets of their own more formal entertainments of the previous year but into creamy jeans, better fitting than their grandfathers' expensive hand-tailoring, and into white open-necked shirts. Roger had rolled his sleeves up. How tanned they were, how clear, how sweet-smelling, how much more beautiful and fascinating than the young men and women of her own generation had been, thought Bridget. She sat in Mr Redditch's armchair, out of the way, half listening to the Archduke Trio on Jonathan's hi-fi, and recalled summers long ago when Phyllida had played in the sandpit with the little girls next door, and Margery had brought her little boy, and Bridget would sweep up the first small child to stagger within reach in an ecstasy of physical response.

'I'm going, Bridget. Thank you for a super meal. Marvellous soufflé.'

Roger was one of her favourite young men. They had gone to a concert together the previous week. He had told her about his parents. They all told her about their parents.

'Come again soon.'

'Of course. See me out.'

She laughed. It was an old pretence of his that he couldn't open the front door, which did indeed stick. Giles and he had a teasing ritual game dependent on the fiction that Roger did not have a home to go to, and hence would go to any lengths to stay the night with friends.

'You could stay the night. The sofa's available.'

'Bridget, I'm too tall for the sofa. No, seriously, see me out.'

In the hall he said, 'And I did enjoy the concert. We must do it again. Goodnight.' Then he looked at her a moment, smiled delightfully, and kissed her goodnight, as everyone did these days. Never such a kissing world as this she now lived in, Bridget thought sometimes, as young men and women kissed each other hallo and goodbye, kissed each other on giving presents or bidding goodnight. Such loving, casual, self-indulgent, meaningless embraces. A world of friendly kisses on cheeks, on foreheads and fleetingly on lips.

But this swift kiss of Roger's at the door was, if swift, deliberate. Roger's open lips felt for, found, her lower lip, paused gently, widened to press a moment on her open mouth. His tongue flicked against hers.

'Bridget, sweet,' he said, and then, with no difficulty at all, opened the door and went.

Bridget was not fool enough to persuade herself that Roger had just made a declaration of love. He had had rather a lot to drink, and was in any case a creature of impulse, of immediacy. Perhaps even of mild mischief. She smiled to herself and went back to the Archduke with a feeling that something remarkably but trivially pleasant had occurred, as if she had been given a wholly unexpected present. The kiss could have no significance to Roger, or indeed to her, so she need have no embarrassment at meeting him again, have no need to indicate the inappropriateness of such open sexuality given – given what? So many objections flooded into her mind that it became impossible to name any one, even the most obvious one of age, without giving the impression that it was the only one or indeed magnifying the incident by suggesting it was worth discussion. She laughed in affection for Roger and dismissed the memory before it formed.

Laura and Jonathan were gossiping in a corner; Giles and Serafina were looking through records with Kurt, but Kurt was not staying either, he said. He could walk Laura (it was Laura, apparently, Kurt had no doubts) to the tube. But Laura was staying the night, Jonathan said.

B RIDGET SETTLED MR Redditch, doling out his pink pills, his white pills, the teaspoonful of medicine, helping him down the corridor to the loo and calling Giles to help her get him back into bed. It took two of them, one each side of the bed, to drag him to the head of the bed so that he sat upright against the carefully-piled pillows, though she could do this by herself earlier in the evening, when he was less tired and confused. 'Bath tomorrow,' she

142

told him. The old man greatly enjoyed bath days. The community nurse came in twice a week to bath him and he liked embarrassing her by making sexual comments.

'No good,' he said, glumly. 'The blonde's on holiday, she told me. It'll be that bitch of a Scotswoman.'

They laughed and left him. Giles settled down with a book. Serafina sat dozing before the telly, and Bridget went off to bed. She preferred to slip away early and discreetly on the nights Jonathan had a girl to stay, an action of hers which, however, she was hardly aware of and never examined. She ignored the situation with ease, did not allow it to impinge on her or to evoke wonder about Serafina or Phyllida's possible guests in past days. Tonight she fell asleep swiftly, but was woken later, after about an hour or two she thought, by hushed voices. Someone flushed the loo, ran a tap. There was a laughing call – immediately stifled – down the corridor. Silence reigned again. She knew with instant certainty that she had heard Jonathan and Laura after lovemaking. She knew the resettling for the night, the second and different, amused, happy, conspiratorial settling into bed that was now going on: the straightening of sheets, the retrieval of pillows. In the morning Jonathan might say to Bridget, 'Did you sleep well?' meaning that he hoped his postcoital conversation in the corridor had remained private and she would say, 'Yes, very soundly,' to reassure him.

She lay astounded by the specific vividness of her memories, building them into imaginings about Laura and Jonathan, and gradually finding herself developing fantasies in which she herself was an actress. They began with Roger at the front door, and developed into strange situations involving Jonathan, Giles, Kurt, Jeremy . . . It was an extraordinary and unforeseen relief to her to discover that she had still within her the sexuality of her youth; it was a part of her which she had long thought dead, and she had thought of herself as a lesser person, less feminine, less human, because of this. It was as if the power and pleasure of her fantasies reassured her that she was still alive. That the loss of sexual satisfaction was one of the misfortunes of war, probably inevitable for many if not indeed for most people, she had long recognised and accepted; only now did she realise that unsatisfied sexual desire could itself make a positive contribution to sexual life.

She fell asleep to lyrical dreams of rivers in a dry country and awoke to comically adolescent uncertainties about Roger. She hoped she had responded as he wished; she wondered whether she should let him know she expected nothing more; she tried and failed to recall how – or whether – she had, or should have, kissed back. And she thought how absurd she was being and discovered that though she knew this it did not spoil her new-found self-assurance to know that she was being ridiculous. She wished she had kissed Roger back passionately, even at the cost of embarrassing him, and making a fool of herself, because it would have been so good to have kissed someone, anyone, like that again. She remembered an old woman once seen in a pub, drunk, grotesquely attempting to sing 'If I were the only girl in the world', her old skin flushed in transparent happiness, and wondered how she could have pitied one so enviable.

Eventually and reluctantly she got up, forcing her relaxed body to activity.

Only Serafina and Mr Redditch were still home. Giles, Jonathan and Laura had gone. There were two letters for Bridget on the kitchen table.

'Fancy that,' she said to Serafina. 'Two clergymen want to call on me. How respectable it makes me sound.'

Father Long, from her Waddon church, had responded to Mark's carefully pitched plea; Dr Johnson made it clear he was in need of her help. Both of them wrote to her, it struck her, in terms which saw her as Phyllida's mother rather than as a separate person. She put the letters aside in mild irritation and went to get Mr Redditch up for the day.

'I see Giles brought your breakfast in,' she said.

'Least he could do.'

'What else do you expect?'

'Bit more concern from my only grandson, I'd have thought. Bit more company. Not that I've ever had much time for him, poncing about London as he does. Still, I'll say one thing for him, doesn't go for the rough trade, never did I reckon. Most of them do, you know. Or guardsmen. When I was a guardsman –'

'Were you ever a guardsman, Mr Redditch?'

'About six months I lasted. Got invalided out. Best thing that ever happened to me. Well. Still, lucky for him you're here to look after me. Not that you've any right here from what that Serafina girl tells me. Squatter like me, aren't you?'

'Yes.'

'Not as much right as me, really, seeing I've got a relative here.'

'No.'

'Married above him, my son, you know. Didn't take her long to find out she'd made a bad choice. They had rows. . . well, you ask Giles.'

'I wouldn't dream of it.'

'No, you got to keep in with him, if you're going to stay here, I can see that. Wonder you've got the nerve really.'

She was not perturbed by this nor ashamed of the realisation that came to her that she had absolutely no intention of using any energy or intelligence finding a home elsewhere for Mr Redditch, since his continued residence at the Duke of Cornwall Mansions might turn out to be a condition of hers.

Occasionally she could not help testing the water, as it were, dipping a finger into the feelings of the young people to test the warmth.

'I could go back to Waddon if I'm in the way,' she would say daringly.

They stared at her in panic. 'Who would look after Mr Redditch?' said Serafina at once, more open about her needs than Jonathan or Giles, who would feel for more flattering phrases to ensure her continued help. They made her certain, with their eventual delightful flattery, that she was welcome, cherished even. She relaxed in their need for her.

At the same time, she knew that on the day Mr Redditch left the flat she would become an intruder, a restraint upon their lives.

If Mr Redditch left, it was possible, she supposed, that Phyllida might return, for there would be room again.

'But not even for Phyllida', she admitted to herself, 'would I move willingly back to Waddon.' Not even for Phyllida would she happily accept a possible break with Giles and Jonathan and their friends, who loved her, whom she loved, but who would not accept the family atmosphere with which she had cushioned Mr Redditch's presence once he had gone.

'I am using you,' she thought, as she cut his toenails. But there was no need for guilt, since he too would rather be here than in some strange and antiseptic institution. Though of course it would not, could not last. Jonathan would go to Paris, or marry his Laura, or some similar girl. That she could contemplate with ease. It was the loss of her witty, enchanting, swaggering Giles, with his self-assured smile, and occasional tenderness that she dreaded. How had he ever sprung from the awful old man she was helping into the sitting-room?

Serafina ostentatiously left the room on Mr Redditch's arrival. She sat at the kitchen table, holding a book up to the inadequate window.

'You'd be happier at work.'

'No, I shouldn't.'

Serafina went on reading. It was Fay Weldon's *Remember Me* but Serafina was missing the humour. No flicker of action crossed her face as Bridget cleared the table, washed up, made a shopping list and answered yet another of Frieda's telephone calls. This time Frieda said, 'She's here you know. She can hear every word I'm saying.'

'Then I hope you'll be polite.'

'Polite? To that one? She was sick last night, all of a sudden, in the dining-room. Poor Mark, I could see he was disgusted. Always such a fastidious little boy he was.'

'Be quiet, Frieda. Rebecca can hear you.'

'Oh, you can't shame that one. No sensitivity. Sick all over the table. Of course, Mark'll get fed up with fat Belgians who vomit all day. *We* know faithfulness isn't one of his virtues, don't we?'

Bridget hung up. 'That was my ex-mother-in-law,' she said to Serafina.

'Again?'

'Again.'

'She's worse than my mother for phoning,' said Serafina, suddenly confidential. 'Do you think I ought to go and look after her? It'd be better than the brats at school, wouldn't it?'

'How can I tell? Could you afford it anyway?'

'If the doctors'd say I'm temperamentally unsuited to teaching, if they'd say I mustn't teach again for my health, I'd get unemployment benefit I suppose, or Social Security. That's why it's so awful for me that Dr Adams says I'm all right. If I leave voluntarily I'll have ages without any cash. Though I could cash in my pension money.'

'Even on Social Security, you'd find it a tight squeeze.'

'Oh, I shouldn't try and live on that. But I reckon father'd be so relieved, he'd subsidise me. Us. I'd get it all tied up legally, it'd have to be mother's income on condition she gives me a home or something, so that it didn't affect my unemployment pay. He could afford enough to make quite a difference. He imports American video tapes. It is a growing market. He's dead selfish and ever so mean, but he's got the money you know.'

'No, I didn't know.'

'Enough for that. He's not rich of course, not really rich, not like Jonathan's parents. He's quite fond of me; I'm the one who can't stand him. And he hates mummy. But he'd like an easy life, she makes scenes in public . . . Oh, I could wangle it out of him. Of course, if he were really rich, it'd be easier.'

'It usually is.'

'If my father were very rich,' confided Serafina, 'really, really, very rich, I think Giles'd marry me.'

Giles would never marry you in a thousand years, thought Bridget. The girl had become quite pasty-coloured during her weeks at home, and her hair straggled lankly about her forlorn face. She said nothing.

'You don't believe me,' said Serafina.

Bridget shut the door to the corridor; she did not want Mr Redditch to hear . . . 'Is Giles really the marrying type, do you think?' she asked.

'He sleeps with girls, you know, at least, I'm pretty sure he does. There was one called Margaret, you've met her, well, she keeps cropping up. And last year he went away with someone called Lisa.'

'Still . . . '

'It's only fashion, you know, all these other young men, that's what I think. If Giles were happy with a wife to look after him, in a different place . . . we could have a country cottage and keep horses.'

For all her apparent knowledge of the world Serafina was, thought Bridget, still as hopeful as the daughters of the Victorian vicarage who married drunkards or rakes with the certainty of their imminent reformation.

'Whoever marries Giles had better make up her mind to take him as he is,' she said drily. 'Boyfriends and all.'

'Oh, you needn't worry. I'll never have enough money. You don't think he'd marry me, I can see that, but you don't

know it all. He hates his job, did you know that? He absolutely hates it. And he likes the good things of life. He'd be
relaxed with me if I could make life easy enough. And it'd be
more natural, wouldn't it, so he'd be happier?'

'Natural?'

'Well, people aren't meant to be gay, are they?'

'Who is doing the meaning in that sentence, Serafina?'

They stared at each other in mutual incomprehension and
dislike.

Bridget was busy about the house for some time. Serafina
read in the kitchen. Mr Redditch sat looking out of the
window. Capital Radio was playing very loud. After a bit he
said, turning the radio down, 'Don't know why you don't get
that lazy bitch in there to give you a hand.'

'She's unhappy.'

'She and who else? Get her off her arse, make her help you.'

'I heard that,' called Serafina. She came in.

'Why don't you do something then? Sitting around like a
sick hen.'

'I would,' said Serafina resentfully. 'Only Bridget's not
doing things that have to be done. She's just making work for
herself. I'll do my share, I always have, well, almost always,
but look at her.'

They both stared at Bridget, who stopped ironing and
stared back. 'What's wrong now?' she asked.

'You're doing Jonathan's and Giles's share. You're ironing
their shirts. I don't think shirts need ironing anyway, but I
know they like them done. Only they can do their own. I
won't iron Jonathan's shirts; he doesn't iron my blouses.'

'Quite right,' said Bridget. 'I wasn't thinking. It's the
maternal conditioning I got in pre-women's lib days.' She ran
a hand down the shirt on the board, a new one of Giles's
spread out before her, and thought how good it had looked on
him, and that in another seven hours he would be coming
through the door; she recalled Roger's kiss and Giles's smile

and said, with great self-control, because she wanted suddenly to pick the shirt up and hug it, smell it, examine it in great detail because her feelings were no longer hidden from her, no longer contained within the safe conventional mould, because she could no longer shelter behind the approved maternal excuses, despite all these urgent and surprising emotions she said quite calmly and slowly, 'But I will stop, Serafina. You are quite right. I shall go for a walk. I will leave you to care for Mr Redditch. You can be invalids together.'

BATTERSEA PARK WAS full of tulips. Mark had taken her there in their courting days. It was a memory now without hurt: compared to Giles's sweetness and flamboyance, Mark was someone dull, crumpled, well-intentioned, unexciting. He had never had the lithe strength Giles exercised so regularly, never even as a young man played squash and gone running, or spent time skiing and swimming. Bridget was herself wholly unathletic; she had never before found Mark's lethargic life a matter for discontent. Now she did. Mark, she thought, had always had his limitations. He could hurt her no longer. He was just someone of whom she was rather fond, a friend.

The park was golden and scarlet with flowers, the sky a mosaic of branches and birds. Two women in white saris moved across a freshly-mown lawn; an elderly man in a red track suit jogged past her. Round the corner in a patch of grass between the back of a park bench and a semicircle of shrubs a solidly-built Chinaman was wholly absorbed in moving a foot slowly forwards, an arm upwards, his eyes fixed on the top-most branches of a budding chestnut tree, but clearly not seeing them, waiting for the exact moment to halt his move-ment and stand poised, perfectly still, perfectly self-aware. Separate lives surprised and delighted her, flowered as brilliantly as the once foreign, now domestic tulips. Swooping assuredly from side to side of the path two rollerskating boys came towards her, parted to pass her on either side, and vanished into her past. 'That,' said a middle-aged woman, stopping in front of her and pointing to a bush, 'is a thrush.'

Bridget smiled uncertainly. The woman was rather dirty and wore a shapeless tweed coat, old boots.

'I thought you'd like to know,' said the woman. 'I tell people things. People don't know. That is certainly a thrush, I think.'

'Oh, yes, thank you.'

The woman said kindly, 'You're welcome. We used to have a robin about here. Keep a look out. Our feathered friends, I always say.' She nodded, as if pleased with Bridget and life and went away.

Bridget rather thought the thrush was in fact a blackbird; she could not see it, only hear its song. But it did not matter. It was a world in which nothing broke any rules. The telephone kiosk at the edge of the Thames was working, was unvandalised; the graffiti were illegible or witty; she had the right change.

'Giles,' she said when she got through, 'will you lunch with me?'

They met at Leicester Square by the kiosk selling theatre tickets, as he had suggested. She had not seen it before and she realised how much of her life had been spent in the sprawling suburbs. She was there early. She saw him coming through the early tourist crowds and walked towards him. He bent to kiss her as always, as everyone under thirty did. This time she kissed him first, as she wanted to, returning to him the kiss Roger had given her, and he did not pretend not to know the difference. He looked down at her (only now did she realise that Mark was too short really, for a man), and raised an amused eyebrow. 'Well,' he said, 'well . . . ' and he was not puzzled or embarrassed as far as she could see, though nor could she pretend to herself that he seemed particularly delighted or responsive. He accepted it, she concluded, as an interesting event. Possibly Giles's main demand of life was that it should be interesting.

'We are going to Manzi's,' she said. 'I am celebrating.'

'May I know what?'

'The emancipation of women, the colour of tulips, and the fact that Serafina is giving your grandfather his morning pills.'

'I thought it might be your birthday.'

'No.'

'Then let's pretend it's mine.'

They met that evening with no mention of lunchtime. No private exchange of glances indicated that any advance of intimacy had been made. Bridget was not sure that Giles considered any new state had been arrived at. Nor, puzzlingly, did she care.

The evening was calm. They left the curtains open and saw the clouds drifting slowly across a sky which never darkened; the moon was full and the street lights could not compete. Even the pinprick of brilliance of the lights on aircraft circling for their approach to Heathrow seemed a natural part of the night.

IN HAMPSTEAD, HOWEVER, life was less harmonious. Frieda's morning telephone call had been too much even for Rebecca's self-assurance. 'I was not sick,' she had said angrily as Frieda put down the phone. 'I spat it out neatly into my napkin.'

'Spitting neatly, is it, now?'

'It was the taste,' said Rebecca. 'I said so at the time. Soap powder mixed with the sugar. You weren't there, anyway. You just heard about it.'

'Of course, you should not eat sugar. Mark has given it up

and Phyllida also is slimming. The Belgians are always too fond of sweet things. You eat far too much. However. But I could buy some saccharine, some Sweetex. I am going to the chemist's. My pot plants have whitefly and I need some insecticide; a walk will do me good. Trudy is coming with me to give me an arm occasionally.' She turned at the door. 'Spit or vomit, it was not nice for Mark, you know.'

'SHE MUST STAY out of my kitchen. I'm sure she put soap powder in the sugar bowl deliberately. I've locked the kitchen door actually, I got a locksmith in this afternoon to put a lock on it. There don't seem to be any keys to any of the inside doors, did you know? I don't want anyone in my kitchen but me from now on.' Rebecca sat, angry and tearful, clutching the glass of sherry which was the only aperitif she allowed herself now that she was pregnant.

Mark wondered if pregnancy was liable to produce mild paranoia. He tried to recall Bridget's behaviour when she was expecting Phyllida, but he had been less conscious of her condition than he was of Rebecca's. He had been busy making a career; the pregnancy had seemed less exciting, less a matter for him to concern himself with. Or perhaps it was the fashion. In any case he could scarcely recall it. But Rebecca was upset and this could not be good for her. His mother had a wicked tongue he knew, but then she was an old woman, a fragile old woman . . . 'You mustn't take what she says so seriously,' he said.

'She put soap powder in the sugar bowl.'

'You can't know that. It is most improbable.'

'And she bought some systemic insecticide this morning, for her pot plants she said. She will empty it into the soup one day when you are eating out.'

153

'You are not seriously suggesting that mother is prepared to murder you, Rebecca? Because if so – '

'She is trying to frighten me. I don't think she is trying to kill me, no, though I'm not sure that she's alert enough to know how dangerous some things are. But obviously she's trying to frighten me. You just won't face unpleasant facts, Bridget said that, didn't she? You won't face facts. Frieda's trying to frighten me. And by God, she's succeeding.'

'A few aggressive jokes,' Mark said weakly.

Rebecca said, 'The ladies at the public library have asked me to let her know that they cannot fulfil her last request.'

Mark held his whisky up to the light, enjoying the moment before he filled his mouth with its golden tang. 'Reading again, is she?' he said. 'Well, that sounds normal enough. She used to be very fond of Trollope, I remember. Trollope and Dickens and Priestley. Couldn't bear Conrad.'

'The ladies at the library were very apologetic,' said Rebecca coldly. 'They could not find her any books in large print on the subjects she required.'

'Odd she reads large print but still embroiders,' said Mark.

'It is just to make more work for us finding her books,' said Rebecca.

'So she's looking for specialist reading, is she? What on, peasant embroidery?'

'Voodoo and Black Magic.'

He threw back his head and laughed. For a moment Rebecca looked desperate, but his laughter was infectious and she was in any case essentially a cool and sensible young woman.

'It is funny, I suppose.'

'Shall we offer her some Plasticine and a supply of pins for her next birthday?' asked Mark.

'They asked me if she'd like some Dennis Wheatley instead.'

'We can always get Phyllida's reluctant bridegroom to

154

exorcise the house if she really does raise the devil,' said Mark, cheerfully. 'First use I've thought of for a son-in-law in Holy Orders. I'd always rather fancied one in the wine-importing business myself. I suppose Phyllida hasn't had the courtesy to say whether she'd be in for dinner?'

'I think she did say,' lied Rebecca, 'but I've forgotten.'

'Back after midnight again and waking us all up, I know. Costing her the earth, too, all this travelling, and she looks like death warmed up. It must be interfering with her work. She really ought to get home at a reasonable time. Well, I'm resigned. Midnight, she'll wake me up.'

B UT IT WAS much earlier than that when the door slammed and Phyllida, tearful and indignant, plunged into the room.

'Had a squabble with lover-boy?' asked her father.

Rebecca remembered one of Bridget's assertions, in her first week as uninvited guest, about Mark's use of facetiousness to cover his failures of tenderness, and realised sadly that she would never see Mark as innocently as before Bridget's incursion.

'It's granny. She's ruined my life. She's ruined my chances with Daniel.'

'Granny? She doesn't even know him.'

'And', said Phyllida dramatically, 'we shall all probably be reported to the Race Relations Board, I should think, and serve her right. I hope she gets sent to jail. And there'll be photographs of the house all over the *Sun* and the *Mirror*.'

'What has Frieda done?' asked Rebecca. Images of Frieda rising halfway through a service in some great cathedral (Rebecca had never seen the Croydon church) to denounce Daniel as a seducer of youth arose in her mind and mingled with others of her marching upon Daniel's house at the head of a column of teenage skinheads. Common sense reasserted itself.

'She can't have done anything,' she pointed out. 'She's hardly left the house, only to go to the chemist to get something to poison me with. Oh, and the pet shop the other day, I suppose she was thinking of a kitten, thank goodness that came to nothing. She certainly hasn't been all the way to Croydon. She couldn't get there, she's not fit enough. She can't get on and off buses any more.'

'She has written an insulting letter,' said Phyllida.

'Felt like it myself, sometimes,' said Mark. 'That man ought to send you packing or accept one of your repeated proposals.'

'Not a letter to Daniel, that wouldn't matter. To my darling Mrs Brooker, and she won't believe I didn't know what granny was thinking, she won't believe I knew nothing at all.'

'Who is Mrs Brooker?'

'She's like a mother to me,' said Phyllida, feeling that to have been true in that Mrs Brooker had petted her, admired her, and never hinted criticism. 'She trusted me. She looked after me. She used to feed me before service if I went straight to Croydon from the office, and I usually did. You can buy yams in Surrey Street.'

Mark felt that he was going mad. 'What have yams to do with all this?'

'Nothing. Just they came to mind. To show you how she cooked for me. She led the group that didn't mind about me and Daniel. And now she won't have me in the house and Daniel says this'll show me once and for all how far apart our worlds are and he's furious. No, I could understand if he were furious. In an awful way he's glad. As if he'd been proved right.'

'What can Frieda have said?'

'Oh, I can tell you what she said. I can show you. Mrs Brooker had photostats made on the office machine and showed them to everyone, the elders and the choir leader and the table-tennis organiser and everyone. I got one too, you bet. The humiliation. And I explained about granny being old and gaga but they didn't care. Well, Mrs Brooker was so hurt, I can see that. And I'll never see Daniel again – or have supper in Mrs Brooker's kitchen again.'

'I could learn to cook yams.'

'That is not the point.'

'No, I'm sorry. It was a silly thing to say.'

'Anyway they're not very nice.'

She was fishing in her brief-case and produced the letter. Rebecca and Mark, trying to disguise a rather pleasurable curiosity, bent over it. Frieda's continental copybook handwriting was remorselessly legible, despite places where her hand had clearly jerked involuntarily, or lost power, so that an occasional word finished in a meaningless scrawl across and off the page.

> Dear Mrs Brooker,
> You kindly wrote to my ex-daughter-in-law, Phyllida's mother, offering to pray for her recovery in your Healing Sessions. I must tell you she will get better when she is in her RIGHTFUL PLACE again. My son is BEWITCHED by a young woman who is no better than she should be. I use the word BEWITCHED advisedly as I believe her to be casting an evil spell on him and on the house. What is needed is some counter spell. It would be a good act to RID the world forever of this woman who is keeping husband and wife apart but if she could just be removed from this house (I have tried in vain) the cause of good will be served. I do not, I must confess, believe in magic or religion, which to me have always seemed the same, but I pride myself on my open mind and it is certain that the witch doctors of Africa have much secret knowledge. In any case when reason fails as it does in my

son's case one must turn to the unorthodox. So I ask you to use your Healing Sessions to heal my daughter-in-law Bridget by getting rid of the USURPER by methods known to the tribal elders of Africa and doubtless handed on by your slave ancestors. I will pay for any special ingredients you need though I believe ritual to be largely a matter of words (Chanting and Rays).

Yours sincerely,
Frieda Mayor

'You don't mean to say that anyone took this farrago seriously?'

'It hurt them.'

'It hurt them? This old woman's nonsense?'

'Look, Mrs Brooker's an educated woman – well, she's got her typing and shorthand speeds I mean, and a couple of O levels, you know – she's sensible. Her mother taught in Barbados. This is denying all that. It's like saying over here all we notice is the colour of your skin and we don't think much of that. It's saying we all know you're just out of the jungle really, like we get a bit cross, even if we don't admit it, when the Russians tell people we live just like Dickens says. And of course she thinks I'm part of it. She thinks I've talked about her to granny, she doesn't know how granny heard of her otherwise. So she feels betrayed. She doesn't know I hardly see granny, really. Oh, I can understand her reaction all right, can't you?'

'Yes,' said Mark. 'Of course.' He was surprised that Phyllida, whom he tended to think of as a lovesick teenager, could achieve such detachment. He looked at her with a new respect. It occurred to him for the first time that she was holding down quite a responsible job. People were so fragmented. Nothing should surprise him, he felt, and yet he heard himself saying, 'I can understand your Mrs Brooker. . .

but I must say I'm surprised at your pastor. You've always told me what a serious intelligent chap he was.'

'Oh, he needed this,' said Phyllida, realising it for the first time. 'It was a godsend to him, I suppose. It's convinced me. He couldn't. Perhaps he wasn't as forceful as I've always imagined . . .'

Rebecca and Mark kept quiet.

After a bit, Phyllida said, 'Do please try and get mummy out of my room, please do. Hampstead's awfully inconvenient for work and we've got some pretty interesting cases coming up at the office. She's not doing anything to get rid of Mr Redditch, you know. I might as well take that campaign over. I bet I could do it.'

'Do you want us to speak to Frieda?'

'Oh, let it die. Do you know, I think I've gone off Daniel after this? He looked so sheepish and pleased and yet he made an awful little sentimental speech about permanent friendship and seeing each other just now and then. Well, I can't see the use of that. I'm going to have better things to do than traipse down to Croydon twice a year to hear him preaching, no future in that. I told him to hell with that.'

'What are we going to do about Frieda, though?' persisted Rebecca.

'I suppose,' said Mark sadly, 'we may be forced into reconsidering the idea of the Home. Only not tonight. Let's, just for once, have an early night.'

He had recently been given a *Book of Lists*, one of Rebecca's rare misjudgments, and had put it away resentfully. Ready-made lists removed his comforting and defensive preoccupation. It was a sign of perturbation over his mother, his wife, his daughter and his ex-wife that on going to bed he found himself unable to settle, got up, went downstairs, and retrieved the book from the drawer where he had thrust it. He sat up in bed reading it long after Rebecca was asleep.

BRIDGET TOO FOUND herself restless next day, but more happily so. She wandered about the flat without tidying up, recalling her lunch with Giles and aware only of a longing to pick up the telephone. This she refused to do. She would not so soon consider a second lunch with Giles. It was not just some shaming remnants of adolescent calculation which led her to this restraint; it was, far more, though not exclusively, a concern for Giles, a desire not to discommode him by making real or apparent demands. In a sense too she was more absorbed with her own feelings than with the relationship between herself and Giles. She felt introspective. She indulged herself in fantasy.

'Been staring at that phone a good five minutes, you have,' said Mr Redditch. 'Expecting to hear the cops is on their way?'

At this moment the telephone rang and he jumped as if some misdemeanour of his own past might have come to light and he was to be warned to take cover.

Bridget was ridiculously hopeful that she would hear Giles's voice, but it was of course Frieda, Frieda who now called at least twice daily, Frieda unexpectedly and uniquely in tears.

'I miss you, Bridget. I am so alone.'

'Dear Frieda, but you have Phyllida, you have Mark.'

'That woman has Mark.'

'He loves you too.'

'If I could pray I would feel better, Bridget.'

It saddened Bridget that this deeply cynical woman should reach so conventional a conclusion, even if it were one which Bridget as a good churchwoman (though only since her divorce, only since there was no other way to mark an empty

Sunday) should so wholeheartedly have welcomed.

'But Frieda, you have always been so passionately anti-clerical. So unbelieving, so . . . I cannot . . . ' She felt deeply hypocritical, but over what she was not sure.

'And who says I am not still? You must learn to listen more precisely, you really must. It must be a great trial to your friends, this fuzziness of mind. I said *if* I could pray I would feel better.' To Bridget's relief the aggression was overcoming the tearfulness. '*If* I could believe in God, obviously it would be comforting. I could pray for her to die then. But I do not believe in God – she will not go away, I begin to see that, and the help I have been seeking from others does not seem to come. I expect she intercepts my letters. Do you think she could intercept my letters, bribe the post office perhaps?'

'No, no . . . ' Bridget could make little of this.

'I get no answer you see. Ah, well, I am on my own. But she stays here, in spite of all my efforts, she stays here to spite me. She is evil, she wants me to be unhappy. Tell me, I wonder, truly, do you believe in God?'

'I go to church. Well, I did in Waddon.'

'These evasive English. Do you believe in God, I asked.'

'Sometimes.'

'Do you think one of those times you could pray for me?'

Bridget was touched. 'But Frieda, I always do. You and Phyllida, and my friends. And Mark, recently. And my god-children. One does.'

'Listen! Think! Not one of those prayers *for* people, so patronising, so insulting, you must leave me off your list at once. Will you pray on my behalf, I meant? To God? Just in case it works? Pray for Rebecca to – '

'No,' said Bridget and put the phone down.

Serafina said in shocked tones, 'You hung up on her.'

'She was very trying.'

'Is she very old?'

'I suppose so.'

'You should be more patient then. My granny went senile you know. She lost her time sense. Mummy would go into her room and bring her tea and come back two minutes later with some more cake and granny would be in tears because she'd say nobody had been near her all day. She'd been so frightened, she said, she thought perhaps everyone was dead. Mummy and I got frightened too. That was when daddy left actually.'

'Very sad,' said Bridget, knowing it was indeed so, and recalling the deaths with which her own life had been littered, and yet feeling nothing because of the happiness within her.

'What does the doctor say about Phyllida's granny? All the doctors would say to mummy was that granny was fraying round the edges. "Well, she's fraying round the edges," that's what our G.P. said. It didn't help much.'

'I don't think she's seen a doctor lately. She's not ill, you know.'

'Isn't she? I thought all old people were. I wouldn't let my mother not see a doctor if she were very old. But Phyllida's father is a bit odd I gather.'

'Odd?'

'Letting himself get so enormously fat for one thing. It's a sign of emotional inadequacy, isn't it?'

Bridget could make little of this nor did she try. She was growing almost fond of Serafina who seemed to have a stimulating effect on her in some way.

'By the way, I am going out to lunch, Serafina.'

'Again?'

'Again. I am taking your advice. I shall speak to Phyllida's father about Frieda's well-being. And about one or two other matters as well, perhaps.'

'Don't leave me alone with Mr Redditch,' wailed Serafina, but Bridget was already dialling Mark's number.

HE AGREED UNEASILY to meet her for lunch, suggesting a wine bar which he knew to be reasonably cheap. 'Quite good food,' he assured her, 'it's in the *Good Food Guide*.' It was just off Leicester Square in Cranbourn Street, so for the second day running Bridget passed near the kiosk selling theatre tickets and eyed its small hopeful queue. It was a pity Mark had not suggested Manzi's. She said so when they met: 'I'd rather have gone to a proper restaurant, where we could sit down and be waited on and have lots of room,' she announced, entranced to discover she no longer needed to pretend politely to non-existent satisfaction. She was going to add 'Like Manzi's,' but she decided to aim higher: 'Like the Savoy,' she said.

This was a mistake, as Mark did not take so extravagant an idea seriously. 'Let's make it the Connaught if we're fantasising,' he said cheerfully, which made her cross. Muttering in indignation, she followed him down the stairs to the cellars where the food was served. 'This is exactly the kind of place you would choose,' she said, but he did not hear. It was in any case an unfair charge, for Mark hadn't been consistently mean; he had been at times a good and generous host: it was only that responsibilities of his future fatherhood were weighing heavily upon him.

However, Bridget did not feel inclined to consider this, knowing as she did that Mark's income was enormously more than hers. He had bought her her flat as a large part of the divorce settlement. She wondered, without much hope, whether the courts would increase his small payments to her, even though her drop in income was she supposed largely her own fault, since she had abandoned her teaching so irresponsibly. And that was not a point she wanted to raise, actually. 'It is just,' she thought, 'that this is a dispiriting place to be taken for the first meal with an ex-husband since one's divorce.' She looked round the dark and crowded cellar after she had struggled back from the self-service counter, carrying a glass of wine, a plate of exotic salads, some French bread, her handbag, a large carrier bag labelled Fenwicks, and a knife and fork wrapped in a paper napkin, and wished she had asked for a bottle of something expensive.

Luckily the table was in a corner.

They talked about Frieda in a desultory manner. Both of them had other, more insistent matters to discuss. Mark was feeling for an opening to point out how greatly Phyllida needed to return to her flat. He told her of the Croydon disaster. He was about to offer to forage for a second glass of wine when Bridget spoke.

'I'm in love with Giles,' she said.

It made her extremely happy to announce this and she considered repeating it.

'You can't be.'

'One wouldn't think so,' she agreed. 'You know, this is a nice place, you were right. The salad was awfully good. And it's clean.'

He looked at her uneasily, wondering if he could pretend she had not made the earlier remark.

'Good value, these little wine bars, I always think.'

'But all the same, I am in love with Giles.'

'You can't be. He's over twenty years younger than you are.'

'May I remind you of Rebecca's age? And you seem extremely happy.'

'It's entirely different. Women often prefer older men, never the other way round.'

'We have been brought up to believe so, certainly.'

'Oh, in other societies . . . but you are a product of this society. So is Giles. You must be an old woman in his eyes.'

'There was Mistinguett,' pointed out Bridget. But this was

too much for her seriousness and she dissolved into giggles. 'I've tended to think of George Eliot as my standard where looks are concerned though, not Mistinguett. I don't feel that fishnet tights are my thing. Did she wear fishnet tights or have I got her wrong?'

'Why George Eliot?'

'She had a face like a horse.'

'Did she? I must say I think you're a bit hard on yourself. You're prettier than that. You've got quite an interesting face.'

'Have I?' said Bridget, brightening. 'You never said. Actually, did you know, well of course you do, George Eliot set up house with a man young enough to be her son and it worked very well.'

'Giles would be horrified,' said Mark, trying to remember what if anything he knew about this young man. 'Horrified. You can't embarrass him like that, you mustn't tell him. You mustn't let yourself down like that. Though you're joking of course.'

'What happens to older women,' said Bridget passionately, 'that makes you think all we want is peace and quiet and grandchildren?'

'It's all Frieda wants.'

'Is it? Look at her. And I'm not Frieda's age. I want people and achievements and money and men and pretty clothes.'

She dived into the paper carrier and produced a large and flowery hat. It attracted eyes as she whirled it round before plumping it on her head.

'Take it off,' he said. 'You look grotesque.'

'I don't mind,' she said, 'don't you see? I don't mind being laughed at. Laugh at me if you like. I want the hat more than I want approval.' She pushed the hat more firmly on, tilting it a little forwards. 'Go on,' she challenged. 'Say it. It's a hat for a young woman, say it. Only I like it too.'

She took it off, the great hat, enormous on her, a hat turning her into quite a different person. Its removal diminished her. He was relieved when she became quite an ordinary person again, but he had a sudden vision of Renoir's 'Chapeau de Paille'.

'It is a pity in a way', he said, 'that women don't wear hats any more.'

'Royalty does. And *Vogue* says they're coming back.' She had not read *Vogue* for months but *Vogue* was always saying hats were coming back.

'Just hopefulness, I expect.'

'Anyway I don't care. I shall wear it to walk in the park when the sun shines. I shall parade among the joggers.'

'You could give it to Phyllida,' said Mark. 'It would suit her.'

'It suits me too.'

'Well, in a way. But it seems a waste.'

'I am not giving it away. It was very expensive. And it will amuse Giles.'

'I wish you wouldn't say that.'

'What?'

'I wish you wouldn't drag that young man's name into the conversation like that. It's grotesque.'

'It embarrasses you?'

'No, of course not.'

'You've gone extremely red.'

'Oh, all right then. It embarrasses me. It ought to embarrass you.'

'Ought it? It doesn't. I'm just extremely happy. I don't expect anything to come of it, you understand. I just enjoy the feeling. And it does nobody any harm, after all, my loving him.'

'It's harming you.'

'How?'

'Well, listen to you.'

'You think I ought to keep my feelings to myself?'

'If you are unfortunate enough to have them.'

166

'Hug them like a guilty secret? I don't feel guilty and it's no secret.'

'If you've no proper sense . . . and to be more practical, of course, it's harming you. It's making you extravagant. You can't afford hats like that.'

'Can't I?'

'No. He won't like it anyway.'

B UT OF COURSE he did. He had come home happy and he was ready to be amused and to share his happiness. They laughed a lot and he adjusted the angle of the hat carefully and then kissed her. Serafina watched from the window. He followed Bridget into the kitchen and told her about Max who had telephoned from Edinburgh and how he had never expected to hear from Max again and she shared his happiness and they looked at each other with the warmth of those who did, despite Bridget's earlier denials, share a secret. 'I'm out tonight, Bridget,' he said, slipping off the table, 'see you tomorrow night. Tell you what, meet me for drinks. Wear that smashing hat.'

'It's a garden party hat. A fancy dress hat. I'm giving it to Phyllida.'

'Meet me anyway. Jules's at seven.'

'Of course. Where's Jules's?'

'Jermyn Street.' He was clearly surprised she didn't know.

W HEN SHE FOUND it she realised that Giles's taste was probably no better than Mark's but pleased her more. Jules's was plainly outrageously expensive. She said so, happily, when they were sitting at a table in the back room. She had asked for a gin and tonic and Giles was admiring an extraordinary concoction of brilliant colours in a glass decorated with oddly cut and arranged fruit. He said it was called a grasshopper and she realised that the decoration did indeed attempt to evoke a Walt Disney view of grasshoppers. She almost expected some music to strike up as he lifted the glass, some sentimental version of an old fable sung in a little girl voice, an old Judy Garland tape perhaps. He was too absorbed in looking round for acquaintances to have heard her quiet comment so she repeated it.

'I said it's dreadfully expensive here, isn't it?'

'I know,' he said. 'It comforts me after work.'

'Do you really hate your work?'

'It gets me down. All those establishment figures, and the hideous offices. I don't suppose you liked teaching much though, did you?'

'Oh, yes. Yes, I enjoyed it.'

'Really?'

'No,' she said, surprised at the discovery. 'Not really. Not the last years. I did once, I can remember. The job changed, I don't know how. Or perhaps it was I who changed. The bits I thought mattered suddenly didn't matter any more, I suppose. Or I just got bored.'

'Well, then. So I come here to spend money and pretend it's all worth it.'

'What do you want to do?'

'It isn't so much what as where, I suppose. I don't mind the work. I'm quite good at it in a way. Well, I would be, wouldn't I? It's about money, and money interests me. I like it. It's meant to be a demeaning thing to say.'

'It's honest.'

'I enjoy things so much, you see. It's hardly an excuse, everyone does. But I don't dislike accounts anyway, however undignified my motivation. It's the place. I hate London, it's dirty and tired and the sun never shines.'

'Giles, you can't have looked. It was a beautiful day.'

'Was it? I didn't notice. That makes my point, I suppose. You don't notice in London. You have to live indoors anyway and wear dark suits . . . it's in my contract of employment, do you know that? That I must wear suits of sober colouring to work. An act all the time I'm in the office. So have another drink. Gin and tonic, isn't it?'

'No,' she said. 'I'll have one of those things you're drinking.'

'You won't like it, you know. You've got better taste. You're stuck with gin and tonic. Or something with campari?'

'I have drunk my last gin and tonic,' she announced, as if ending an era. He went away without asking further and returned with two Manhattans. 'Next time we'll start with one of the champagne cocktails,' he said, 'but not after gin, I thought. It was silly of me not to think of that first.'

Pleased that he had chosen the same drink for them both she returned to their earlier conversation.

'What do you want to do?'

'Oh, go back to California. Lie in the sun. Get a job in an art gallery in Monterey or San Diego. I could, you know. I know about art, and I can sell. Or run an office or get into a bank even. Or just keep books for someone. Anything.'

'A bank? Accounts?'

'I know about money, I told you. I'm quite precise. I understand it. And I've no blots on my record. Nobody'd have difficulty in getting fidelity bonding on me . . . And I imagine my British education might help; they don't give away accountancy qualifications for nothing.'

'But the same kind of work?'

'In California.'

'How would California help?'

'Well, you've been to the States.'

'No.'

His eyes widened. 'Bridget, love, you've never been to the States?'

169

'No.'

He considered. 'Then I can't explain,' he said.

They walked home across St James's Park, over the Thames.

'Why don't you go?' she asked.

'At the end of the month I shall have exactly fifteen quid in my account. It'd get me to Heathrow I suppose.'

She said nothing. He put his arm around her. 'Oh, Bridget, you know me. I could save my fare I suppose, given time. But then what? I've got friends over there, several, people who've been through London, one or two who write, not that Americans write letters really, did you know? But I can't expect casual friends to stake me for more than a couple of weeks, if that. And then, I'm not exactly a student am I? I'm past sleeping on beaches with a bedroll. I like my creature comforts. I want it all ways.'

'I love you,' she said.

'I know. Isn't it fun? Whatever next?'

He opened the flat door for her and they went in. The evening went its accustomed way and the next day it rained.

THERE WAS A short ring at the door a few afternoons later. When she opened it and saw the two clergymen standing there, two clerical collars, two neat old-fashioned dark grey suits, two earnest polite shy faces, one black, one white, she thought of old Bing Crosby films, of dancing, of sentiment, and inevitably of love.

'Come in, come in,' she said, thinking that they should do a soft shoe shuffle through the door and finish with a neat double tap and hands on hips. But of course they walked in politely, out of step, apologetically. Father Long had an umbrella and hung it carefully on a hook.

'How nice that you are both here together,' said Bridget,

not at all sure that this was so. She recalled guiltily the casual postcard she had written to each of them inviting them to tea – 'any Tuesday or Thursday that suits you'. What bad luck they had called together. Though it would get it over faster.

She introduced them. 'Father Long of St John's; Dr Johnson from the Children of Sinai. Perhaps you have already met.'

She was not sure whether as fellow-clergymen but in such very different denominations they would see each other as brothers or rivals. The two were of course not mutually exclusive. It would be a difficult tea-party she felt; and frustrating for each of them presumably, given that neither of them could embark on whatever topic had brought him here, or so she hoped.

She looked round the sitting-room. 'Serafina, may I introduce Father Long? Dr Johnson? And this is Mr Redditch. Mr Redditch, Dr Johnson, Father Long.'

But convention could carry one just so far. Once everyone had sat down, there was silence. Mr Redditch coughed. Silence again. All Bridget could think of was that there were no cakes to offer anybody.

'We have no cakes, I'm afraid.'

'I'm running out of my ginger biscuits,' said Mr Redditch. 'I hope you're not going to fall back on my ginger biscuits.'

Father Long and Dr Johnson proclaimed, simultaneously and awkwardly, a fortunate inability to eat ginger biscuits, a common happiness to drink tea without eating cakes.

'I'll make scones,' said Serafina. Bridget was effusive in her thanks.

'It will take some time. I'll bring tea when they're done.' She escaped thankfully through the door.

'Delightful girl,' said Father Long.

'Yes . . .'

After a bit Bridget added, since some comment had to be found, 'She's a teacher.'

'Oh. Half-term, is it?'

'No. She's been ill.'

'Oh.'

'How is everyone at St John's, Father Long?'

'Very well, very well.' He caught himself up. 'Old Miss Taylor died last week. A sad loss. Such a loyal member of our congregation.'

'Oh yes, yes.' She had no idea who Miss Taylor had been.

'Of course,' Father Long hesitated, looked sideways at Dr Johnson, decided to continue, 'we all miss you. I hope we may see you back among us soon?'

Such a discreet question, thought Bridget, such gentle pressure. It was tempting to give him a meaningless assent, to say, 'Oh I should think so. I should think so.' It would satisfy him. Yet even so vague an agreement would open up the possibility of going back. To embody an idea in words half created it, made it a possibility. She stiffened.

'I'm not coming back to Waddon, Father Long.'

He looked sad. 'Such a charming flat. It suited you.'

'I did not like it.'

'You are moving elsewhere?'

'She is staying here,' said Mr Redditch. 'She has to look after me. I need her. I shall need her for a long long time.'

'I will try to make arrangements for you, Mr Redditch, you know that. But I'm not staying here for long either.'

'Ah.' Father Long looked brighter, leaned back. 'So your daughter will be able to return here?'

'Has Phyllida been – surely Phyllida hasn't been talking to you about this – she doesn't know you.'

'Oh, no, no, I assure you . . . but after all, people do like their own places, don't they? I don't expect you quite realise how upset she is at not being here?' He was not good at deceit.

'Father Long, I gather that someone has been speaking to you about Phyllida.'

'Her father and I did have a few words actually. Yes, a few

words. Just on the phone you know. As it chanced.'

'Her father telephoned you by chance? It was a wrong number?'

'I did not mean to imply that the phone call was not intended.'

'And it is not that you all miss me at St John's, it is not that I will be happier in my own little flat, it is not for this that you are here. It is because it will be comfier for Mark and Phyllida and because you like to smooth things over?'

'Oh dear. You make it sound as if we are all manipulators. We are thinking of you and your future.'

'Father Long, I am going to do what I want to do. Whatever that is. I am not going to do what is least trouble to other people.'

He looked at her seriously. She knew her charges were in a way unjust. He was thinking of her well-being too, but he could envisage it only in terms of security and familiarity. 'I hope you find happiness,' he said. 'What do you plan to do?'

'My immediate plan is to sell the flat. My next step is a little more uncertain. I shall wait to see what happens.'

'That seems a trifle unwise . . . '

'The lilies of the field . . . ' she said.

'Luke XII 27,' Daniel's voice broke in. 'But then one must also recall the parable of the wise virgins.'

'Matthew XXV 1,' said Father Long.

It was like the Masonic handshakes Bridget had often watched being exchanged by visitors to her college under the impression that they were secret.

'Be a bloody prayer meeting in a minute.'

The two clergymen exchanged amused glances. Bridget, momentarily embarrassed by Mr Redditch's interpolation, realised that both men had coped with other Mr Redditches often enough.

'Not but what we could do with a bit of prayer here. Having it off with my grandson, or trying to, isn't she, thinks

I don't notice but I do, I do, I hear her creeping about the place at night. Disgusting I call it, no privacy, no shame. Ought to pray for her, that's what I say, mooning after him with those great eyes.'

Bridget felt herself going scarlet. She fumbled for a dignified way of denying or wiping out or sidetracking the speech. But it was Serafina's furious voice which spoke, and it was at Serafina that Mr Redditch was staring. She had come back into the room without Bridget's knowing.

'Shut up,' she said, 'shut up, you dirty old man. What if I do love Giles? There's nothing wrong in that. You're making the rest up.'

'I heard you. Creeping about in the middle of the night.'

'Well, I can go to the loo if I want to, I suppose.'

She was shaking with anger. It seemed possible she might attack the old man and he ducked his head as if expecting to be struck. Father Long stood up to reach Serafina and put a restraining arm round her, but before he was fully out of his chair Daniel Johnson said, 'Let us pray', and plopped down on his knees in the middle of the carpet, thereby penning Serafina into the space near the doorway just as she was about to take her first step towards the big armchair.

How ingenious of him, how shameful, to use prayer as a diversionary tactic like that, thought Bridget, torn between admiration and indignation.

'Oh Lord,' he began. At this point Father Long, in haste, as if he had hesitated too long, lowered himself carefully to his knees. Rheumatism, remembered Bridget. Mark had a touch of it too. These elderly men. She did not kneel, but the remnants of her good manners led her, unwillingly, to lower her head.

'The prophet Malachi,' said Daniel . . . Serafina sat down next to Bridget. Mr Redditch reverted to his Congregationalist Sunday School days and clasped his hands tightly together. They all listened, in some surprise, to the words of the prophet Malachi. They seemed wholly inappropriate to any minor domestic squabble. (Daniel Johnson would have been pained had he known of this, for he felt that only in the words of the minor prophets could a recognisable description of the city in which he dwelt be found.)

'Behold, I will corrupt your seed and spread dung upon your faces,' announced Daniel, and even Father Long did not realise that the passage was leading to the great and perhaps not irrelevant question, 'Have we not all one father? Hath not one God created us?' So that when Daniel paused after the words, 'for the priest's lips should seek knowledge and they should seek the law at his mouth', Father Long took it upon himself to say 'Amen' hastily and scramble up, before more images highly unsuitable to a tea-party emerged, or before, even worse, he was invited to continue this extempore recitation from the Bible. He was anxious to break in on other grounds too. 'I smell burning,' he said.

'I smell burning, I smell sin,' said Serafina amazingly.

But Father Long completed the couplet. 'I see Satan beckoning me in,' he said. 'Well, well, so the old rhymes are not wholly forgotten.'

'The children skip to them. They don't know who Satan is, though, I asked.'

'But I do smell burning, you know.'

'My scones!'

How like Serafina to burn the scones, thought Bridget, and felt ashamed of her unkindness. They were, when Serafina brought the rescued tin in to brandish it before them, plainly past praying for, as Father Long put it with a cheerful chuckle. He was proud of the joke and smiled benignly. Mr Redditch had fallen asleep.

'Prayer calms,' said Johnson, failing to pick up the idea.

'It does not calm me,' said Bridget. 'I do not intend to seek the law at anyone's mouth. Not a man's anyway, and as for "For they should seek the law at his mouth", indeed.'

'The priest . . . ' said Father Long, 'the priest is of course a kind of metaphor for the Church.'

'And what about Ezekiel?' asked Bridget.

'I do not follow you, I cannot recall . . . '

'In Ezekiel I discovered some weeks ago, also from Dr Johnson, and I came home and checked it afterwards, all the imagery about Jerusalem, whenever Ezekiel was being rude about her, all that imagery is feminine, calling Jerusalem a whore and a harlot and a fruitless wife and a treacherous daughter. Jerusalem was clearly a man's city anyway. How much you all hate us and keep us in our place. Why shouldn't Serafina have shown Mr Redditch how angry she was? Why must the good metaphors be masculine and the evil ones feminine?'

'It is not so,' said Daniel. 'The Church is a bride. And "I have likened the daughter of Zion to a comely and delicate woman", remember. Jeremiah VI2.'

'Exactly,' said Father Long. 'My very point. A most apposite quotation. I really do think, Mrs Mayor, that you are being a little over-sensitive.'

'I am being sensitive, inconveniently so. I'm overstating, I admit, but it feels as if we have to behave meekly and you don't.'

'Historical tradition . . . ' murmured Father Long, looking at Daniel.

'Who can find a virtuous woman? for her price is well above rubies,' he replied.

'Ah, but if we begin upon quotations, of course, we must steer clear of Ecclesiastes. One must not quote Ecclesiastes VII 28.' This appeared to be a covert joke on the part of Father Long.

Long and Johnson were closer to each other than to her. Perhaps it was their cloth rather than their sex. 'Have some tea,' she said crossly, Serafina having brought a pot in.

'Are you perhaps over-influenced by the Women's Movement?' asked Father Long, in a forgiving voice. 'My niece at Cambridge is quite enthusiastic about it, but then she is young. At our time of life . . . '

'I cannot be accounted for entirely by my age,' said Bridget. 'I am me, I am not a typical suburban woman, if such were to exist outside the statistical tables, predictable because you know her birthday.'

'Each individual human soul is of course itself.'

'I know why you came,' said Bridget. 'You came because Mark asked you to do so. To turn me back into an ex-wife. But why did you come, Dr Johnson? You did not say. Has Phyllida been nagging you to come and winkle me out of the flat as well? Are you both on the same errand? Am I to be made to behave?'

'Your daughter has not been talking to me about this or anything. She has stopped coming down to Croydon. She agreed with me in the end that she was quite out of place there. She has no idea I am seeing you.'

'How people do go on about proper places. I had not thought of love as being out of place. Phyllida loves you, I thought, however inconvenient that is for you.'

Father Long, embarrassed, got up.

'I did not realise this was a private matter, a personal family discussion. I am so sorry, I will go, no, really, I must go anyway.'

'It is not private,' said Daniel. 'Well, not from Mrs Mayor's spiritual directors, not from her own pastor. I hope you will add your voice to mine. I have come to beg her, as a mother, to carry out her parental duties and ensure that her daughter stops . . . ' He stopped too.

'Yes?' Bridget's voice was sweetly encouraging.

'Stops pestering me.'

'I understood you to say she had already done so. And pestering is not a word I like to hear used in connection with Phyllida. Is that how you feel about it?'

'Course it isn't.' Mr Redditch was not asleep after all. 'He loved it, who wouldn't, stands to reason, pretty girl like your Phyllida chasing him all round the houses. Nice tight little bum she's got, that girl, hasn't she, my lad? Bet you got your blackie hands on that once or twice. Or if not, bet it made you feel no end of a fellow to know you could and give her the go-by. Pestering you indeed. Do us a favour.'

Father Long said hastily, 'I hope still to see you in church in Waddon, one day, Mrs Mayor,' and was gone.

'I'm not going to protect you from Phyllida,' said Bridget. 'It is not my job to protect you. It is your own. And you have done so, it seems. She has agreed with you. I had heard that. It puzzles me that you have called on me, seeing that the situation which gave rise to your first letter is now at an end.'

'After her grandmother's letter . . . can't we discuss this in a little privacy?'

'I think Mr Redditch has dozed off again. Serafina is in the kitchen. There is only my bedroom.'

'He does seem to be sleeping. Well, after her grandmother's letter she quite saw . . . she hasn't been down again. But the effect will wear off. She will be back. She will not be able to keep away.' He sat back and she saw him smile. It was a smile of self-congratulation; suddenly he looked like Mark, it was the exact smile with which Mark had told her, on the Night of the Turbot, that he had spent the night with another woman. She had forgotten the smile and the pain and never till now felt the anger.

'You are sure she will be back?'

'But of course . . . she is self-willed and energetic, isn't she, and not used to failing? It is part of her charm, of course. One sees it in the way she sits on the corner of tables, like an American college girl. I'd forgotten the pose. And she can be relaxed and intense at the same time, I don't understand it.'

He needed to talk about Phyllida, then. Pity threatened to overwhelm her anger. She remembered Phyllida's need to talk about him on the night of the dinner party when Rebecca had announced her pregnancy. Her own more and more frequent lunches with Mark were opportunities for her to talk about Giles. When her life had been emotionally empty, her days had been filled with activities, and her evenings too, for the evening classes of London were the major state provision for the lonely. Now that her world was crowded with plans and people she did little but talk. She moved from conversation to conversation.

'You have come to talk about Phyllida.'

'I have her interests at heart.'

'Too close at heart perhaps. You will have to forget her, you know.'

'How can I? She will be back. One day I will go into the pulpit and see her back in her usual place. I must work out what to do. Perhaps I was wrong to turn her away. Whom have I to talk to about it?'

She felt no pity for him after all. His conceit was too irritating. 'No,' she said. 'She will not be back. Her father tells me there is another man, at the office, a disillusioned Scot with a broken marriage behind him. Another challenge.'

'She will be so unhappy . . . '

'Oh, I think not. Men are not the most important thing in Phyllida's life. Surely you realise that they are a kind of game, a spare-time consolation, for her. Her work is what she really cares for. And she is getting more responsibility, more demanding work. Her work is absorbing her, she will be successful, important. You should understand the importance of work, you talked about it enough.'

'For a man.'

'For women too, it seems, if they are allowed to discover it. Some people just enjoy their job more than anything else. Your work matters to you. It is why you turned her away.'

'My work . . . ' He sat looking down at the floor, his hands dangling. Serafina looked in, hesitated, and went away.

'When you came to the church that day, do you remember?' he said.

'I said when you left that you would not forget us. I was angry that you called your visit to us just a mistake. It was an insult.'

'I did not mean it as such. It was a fact not a judgment.'

'I said that the visit was not something you could dismiss. The visit was part of your history. The converse was also true of course. You were part of my history. Its consequences have altered me.'

'You will get over Phyllida.'

'There is a Dutch proverb, did you know, that the pain goes but the scar stays?'

'So?'

'Results stay.' He looked at her, wanting to hurt her, for she was not on his side. 'You may not miss your husband any more, you may not weep, but his desertion has permanently altered your life. You will be poorer in your old age, to begin with.'

'To end with.'

'I am not playing word games. So, my work . . . the scar is there too. The church is full of enmity and cliques. I am not so good at leading it as I thought. I came, you know, from a different kind of congregation.'

'From the States, yes.'

'A different country. But a different class as well. A settled middle class. I try but I don't understand my people here; I can't even pick up the class cues. I don't know whether, in English eyes, in their own eyes, they're making it or are underprivileged. They seem pretty poverty-stricken to me, but some of them I offend when I say so. The children drift away, they become Rastas, they read the Bible and it tells them to smoke pot. They drop out of school. Their parents split into groups. They distrust me or they mother me. There is no one to talk to.'

'There was a good deal of warmth I thought the night I was there.'

'Phyllida made me want different things. She reminded me what it was like back home. She made me want different things, and she made the church different too.'

Bridget froze. 'She may have revealed weaknesses, Dr Johnson. She did not create them.'

'And she is so young.' He did not seem to have heard her. 'She is young and I am almost forty. Too old for her, really. You must tell her that.' He raised his hand to cover his eyes and Bridget saw the beginnings of veins standing out on his hands, on the back of his hand, and recalled Giles's strong deft fingers. Only weeks ago Daniel had attracted her, and she had not dared admit it because he seemed too young for her. Now his defeated appearance, the incipient signs of ageing, almost repelled her.

'You have come to tell me, or so you pretend, to tell her to keep away from you, but she has no intention of coming back. She is otherwise engaged. You say you want no more of her, but you come and see me, and you keep talking of her. Now you want me to give her messages. It doesn't make sense. You have come here only to keep in touch with her.'

He looked up. 'If you went back to Waddon, she could live with you as a daughter should do with her mother. It is so near Croydon. I could work better for my own church if I had people – you, her – people of education, people to talk to. I am fond of Phyllida, I just cannot marry her. Tell her I want to develop a freer relationship with her. There is only good in friendship. It could go no further, but with you in the flat there could be no gossip. She has her work, I have mine. There need be no final break. I cannot face a final break. Just to keep in touch.'

'And I?'

'You would be making a home for her, I suppose. It is what women do. It is their calling.'

She said, 'It is not mine. And as for Phyllida, you want her on your own terms, on the edge of your life where it will do no harm. Speak to her yourself. I want no part of it.'

'You must despise me. I despise myself.'

But before she could answer, Giles came in.

'I will not be able to fall in with your plans in any case,' she said, stretching out a hand for Giles, but Giles was already standing behind her, his hands on her shoulders, his face near hers. 'I will not be able to do so because, as I said earlier this evening, I shall be selling my Waddon flat. What I say three times is true,' she said, discovering that by stating the plan she had brought it about. 'I need the money. It has gone up in value quite a lot and I need the money. And now if you will forgive me, Giles and I have things to discuss.' She saw him out.

'WHAT DO YOU need money for, Bridget?' Giles asked. 'One shouldn't enquire I suppose, but other people's money is so fascinating. And of course people with money are always so attractive.'

'It is not the usual opinion.'

'Their characters may be pretty awful I suppose. But they always look so healthy and beautiful. I tell myself it's orthodontists and good infant feeding and skiing holidays, but they just are good to look at.'

'I shan't get money enough to transform me. It's not that kind of wealth.'

'I like you the way you are. Don't change. But what kind of wealth?'

'Oh, thirty thousand, thirty-five. The legal fees and things'll reduce it a bit.'

'Fun for you though.'

'I hope so. Let me take you to Jules's tomorrow night,

where we won't get interrupted and I'll tell you what I'm going to do with it.'

'We won't get interrupted here . . . '

She ignored this. Snatched moments of tenderness in corridors were not enough.

And the next day she put her flat on the market. The agent said that it might be advisable for her to move back in order to sell it. She was not sure how she felt about this, whether she dared move away from Battersea, even in order to acquire money. The link with Giles was very fragile. She put it to him over Campari sodas.

'If you go,' he said, horrified, 'who will look after grandfather?'

She would rather he had expressed his desires for her to stay in more personal terms, but did not really expect it.

'Serafina could.'

'Like hell she could. She'd get out quick.'

'Perhaps I could come up two or three times a week.'

'It wouldn't be much. I'd miss you, actually. Look, I've got tickets for the Olivier. You said you wanted to see it.'

She was overwhelmed. 'Someone at work couldn't use them and I thought of you straight away. You're the only one of my friends who likes straight theatre, did you know? It's Friday. So you can't go till Friday. You can't be in such a hurry.'

'I am rather. I have plans for the money.'

'What plans?'

So she told him.

SHE POSTPONED HER move back to Waddon. This gave her a chance to see Mark for lunch on Friday.

'We are going to San Francisco together,' she told him as soon as they had sat down.

'Exactly who is "we"? *Who* is going to San Francisco?'

'Come, come, Mark, you know better than that. Giles and I are going to San Francisco. Giles has always wanted to go back there, and he does make it sound great fun.'

'So Giles wants to go back to San Francisco. All right, all right, I'm keeping calm. Actually what I've seen of him, he seems a pleasant enough young man, I've nothing against him. It's you I'm concerned about. And people may think things.'

'People will be right.'

He looked uneasily at her and said, 'He can't possibly want to go on holiday with a woman old enough to be his mother.'

'I amuse him. And don't you think it's a little schoolboyish to spend your life working out exactly how old everybody is?'

'No, I don't actually. People are different as they get older. I am, I'm a bit stiffer, a bit slower, and I've got a good deal less sparkle than Giles has. It makes a difference.'

She looked at him with respect. 'You always were capable of honesty, I'd forgotten. It's nice to remember that there were reasons for falling in love with you. You weren't really a bastard, were you?'

'Good God, no. Whatever makes you say that? Not a saint, exactly, bloody difficult at times. Not a bastard.'

'When a woman's husband leaves her, that's how she usually sees him. Of course she does. Until she falls in love with someone else. And of course if she's over fifty she usually doesn't, so she goes on thinking of him as a bastard. However, I'm prepared to admit you can be quite a pleasant man. For example, asking me to your club for lunch today.' She had been touched by this; in the days when they had been married she had never been there, women were not yet admitted even as guests. She had accepted this without resentment. Now she felt that she should have resented it, but was too pleased at satisfying her curiosity to feel very deeply about this. 'I imagined it would be all brown leather and books and smoke, not light and airy.'

184

'Oh, it's a pleasant place. Rebecca suggested I should take you here.'

'Did she? How nice of her, it's much nicer than the wine bar.'

'The food's not so good.'

'No, but to talk.'

'That's what Rebecca said. She was quite cross with me when I told her where we usually went.'

'I do *like* Rebecca.'

'Thank you.'

'And I like you again, now.'

'Thank you. But your judgment, I gather, is based on the fact that you've fallen in love with someone else? That you fancy someone else?'

'I'm sorry?'

'You fancy someone else? You fancy Giles. You've got an itch for him, a letch for him. You fancy him. And you call it love.'

Mark had planned this attack, worked it out for hours and now used it more brutally perhaps than he had intended, unexpectedly and unadmittedly hurt by Bridget's cheerful and patronising assurance that she liked him. Somehow or other, he had felt, thinking over Bridget's confidences about Giles, Bridget had to be brought to her senses. He owed it to her, he had some residual responsibility surely for her happiness. They had after all once been married for twenty-odd years.

'You just fancy him,' he said. 'Mind you, I can see why.' This was true. He thought Giles an attractive young man, nothing special perhaps but someone with the capacity to be happy, to enjoy the moment. He was obviously intelligent, fit, well-groomed. His face lit up with amusement, with delight, with interest, as he talked to one person, listened to another, avoided a third. He was the kind of young man who rowed for his college, got a decent second, spent a year at Harvard on an exchange scholarship, kept his friends, and made no later splash in any more important world. His youth gave no indication of what his future might be.

Bridget watched Mark's fingers, splayed on the table-top, press downwards as he tensed against her expected reaction of fury or tears. No, he would not expect tears or he would not have brought her to his club. It must be a proper and discreet repentance he expected.

She hesitated. The phrase Mark had used gave her difficulty. It was not part of her vocabulary. 'An inability to use some phrases,' she began . . . 'I can't cope with them. It's like four-letter words. An inability to use quite commonly spoken four-letter words is one of the language limitations of my age group.'

'You throw the word "love" round easily enough,' he jeered. It was a just criticism. She nerved herself, not to the admission, which was easy enough, but to the phrase which he had chosen and which to her was cheapening, vulgar, and out of character. And yet, in this situation, necessary. 'Yes, I fancy him,' she said. 'I do fancy him.'

'Well then.'

He sat back as if that were his mission completed.

'It's enough.'

'It's nothing. It's degrading, to let it matter enough to lose your self-control like this.'

'It doesn't feel like nothing, it feels good.' He was horrified at the lazy contentment of her smile.

'Oh, Bridget . . . '

'All right, I know love is better. Or so we're taught. But what you can't understand is how marvellous it is to want something again.'

'That's it, isn't it? Something you said, not someone.'

'I want Giles. But, yes, apart from that, if you want to know, I want something. Do you want me to spell it out?'

'No!' he said, panicking now, remembering for the first time that Bridget's voice had a fatal carrying quality, and noticing that the room was emptying now so that the background hum was lessening. 'No!'

'Because I will.' Yet she could not. She felt for a way round, for an allusive explanation. 'When Geoffrey Smeedon went to Majorca with his typist, do you remember, two years after Marina died, years ago, Phyllida was quite little, you said, good old Geoffrey, getting his oats again, good for him. You said a good many more explicit things about the typist's bottom, I recall. Quite envious, you sounded, and I was supposed to accept it. Well, I did. I do.'

'I was drunk, I expect.'

'Not at all. Or if so, it makes no difference. Anyway, I enjoy Giles. I enjoy his talk and his company and the way he looks. And if it's all a romantic disguise for fancying him, as you put it, for wanting him like Geoffrey was allowed to want his typist, for wanting to stroke his skin and kiss the mole he has where . . . ' She stopped.

There was a silence while he worked out just how much that last phrase had given away. He made a note to observe, should he see Giles again, whether he had any respectably visible mole, for without that information Bridget's slip was valueless. And of course even if he had a mole on the back of his hand or just under his left eye, that would not necessarily be the mole to which Bridget was alluding. He, himself, had a mole at the base of his spine, just above his left buttock: he could not remember Bridget ever having shown herself particularly enamoured of it. He sat on, speculating. After a while, he said, angry at his uncertainty and at caring about it, 'Go on, then. Since that's how you feel. Spell it out. See what it sounds like.'

But she could not. Angrily she said, 'Women of my age can't say some things. I told you. There are words we hear without shock, words we read. But we can't say them. It makes people think we don't feel things – but we do.'

He smiled kindly. 'It'll pass. I'll collect the bill.' He

gestured for a waitress. He was no longer worried, she was retreating.

She felt his patronage. But she could still not use the four-letter words which were the only ones to convey her need. 'I still want love,' she said, 'I'm still human. I want love.'

The phrase was inadequate to her; she did not hear, as Mark did, the raw edge of feeling which led old Graham-Robertson, who had paused by the table to greet Mark, move sharply away, as if she had spoken indecently. He paid and got out of the place as swiftly as possible. The lunch had achieved nothing for either of them.

He talked it over with Rebecca. She was less shocked than he was. He thought perhaps Rebecca's feminine sympathy would bring Bridget to her senses. And Phyllida was Giles's age, about. They would ask Bridget to dinner, and in the domestic atmosphere, sitting at the table with her own daughter, she would surely see how ridiculous it was for her to attempt to enter the young people's social circle in any other role than that of an older woman, a mother, a gracious hostess.

'Perhaps', said Phyllida tartly, 'we should ask Giles too. Since he seems to be almost one of the family.'

But this Mark refused to accept. 'A mere holiday companion,' he said. He had decided to treat the whole affair more lightly. It must be stopped of course, but perhaps he had been a little over-dramatic and thereby driven Bridget to those embarrassing and exaggerated revelations. She must be coaxed back to good sense.

Bridget arrived to a warm welcome. Rebecca looked and felt splendid. Pregnancy suited her: she had become serene, beautiful.

'How well you dress, Rebecca.' Bridget had tried to disguise her own far-off pregnancy, to hide her bulging waist. Now Rebecca, in clinging folds of ivory-coloured velvet, sailed across the room to meet her, leaving a trail of yellow petals from the roses she was wearing, and reminding Bridget of the goddess Ceres, or even Flora. 'What lovely material.'

'Do you like it? I hoped you would.'

There was friendship between these two, Mark realised, relieved but outraged.

'You look splendid.'

'Frieda says I'm carrying it high, it will be a boy.'

'Oh, I hope so, Mark always wanted a son.' This was true, and Bridget's happy acceptance of a fact for so long denied convinced Mark for the first time that her heart was truly elsewhere. Until this moment it had not occurred to him that for years he had half assumed, sadly but complacently, that while Rebecca loved him and he loved her, he was also the centre of his ex-wife's thoughts and longings. He felt a momentary sense of total loss, as if the divorce of years before were only now made absolute.

'A baby for us, a holiday for you, promotion for Phyllida,' he said. 'And we are all together to celebrate. What an unexpected year.'

He tried to adjust to happiness and found it easy. He seemed for once a good man in the middle of his family; nobody had been unbearably hurt after all. Perhaps Bridget should be allowed her fling, her visit to California. She would come back having learned her lesson and willing to settle down in Waddon after all. He beamed round the table as they settled, not even tensing when Bridget asked after Frieda.

'She's out at a party,' he said. 'I took her, a seventy-fifth birthday at Arnie van Blijven's. And I am to fetch her at ten precisely because Arnie's parties are so unintellectual. Her words, not mine, isn't she marvellous?' Even his mother was happy.

'I want to hear about Phyllida's promotion,' said Bridget slowly, 'but first of all, Mark, you said, you mentioned, a holiday, for me.'

'Indeed I did. Obviously it is in our minds. I was a bit . . . a bit unkind when you told me, a bit conventional perhaps. Well, all that fuss over a holiday. So, where are you going? Not just San Francisco, surely? What about San Diego? I can give you an interesting introduction in San Diego . . . Tell us.'

'Mark, it is not a holiday. We are going out for quite a long while. Indeed, I hope for good. Perhaps you and Rebecca will come and visit us there. When the baby's old enough to travel, I mean. Giles and I are going to California for good.'

'For good? You can't go for good.'

'Why not?'

'What will you live on, for God's sake? How will you eat?'

'I am selling the flat. It should keep us for quite a while, I'd think. Long enough to establish ourselves, surely, I hope.'

'You're mad. You're bloody mad. I paid for that flat, I'd remind you, for your old age, and that won't be long let me point out, and not for – all right, all right, so I've spilt the wine – yes, Rebecca, I see – well, sit down blast you, I'll bloody well spill the wine at my own table if I want to, has everyone gone mad?' He made a deliberate sweep across the table with his left arm. 'There, that's the other bottle gone. Fussing about the wine when we've just – ' He pushed his chair back and moved across to the fireplace, resting his arms on the mantelpiece. His shoulders were shaking. Phyllida had never seen him cry before. 'It's anger, blast it,' he said, over his shoulder. 'I'm angry.'

'So am I, rather,' replied Rebecca drily. The wine from the second bottle had jetted across the cloth and left a wild streak, like blood, across her ivory dress. She ignored it and started to mop up the tablecloth, to push together with a napkin the broken pieces of a wine glass. Phyllida said, 'Come up and change, Rebecca, it's nylon velvet, we'll try soaking it,' and put her arm round Rebecca, who looked no longer like Ceres unless in that moment when she realised Proserpina was stolen. She suddenly gave up dabbing at the cloth and said, touching the spoilt dress, 'It's like blood . . . '

'Wine, a libation,' said Phyllida firmly. 'A libation to Lucina, not an omen.'

She had never felt so responsible.

'Mark hasn't even noticed,' said Rebecca on the edge of tears. 'It is all for Bridget, this upset, not me or you or Frieda . . .'

'Yes,' said Phyllida. 'But that doesn't mean he loves her more, only that she is more of a nuisance. And you are too sensible to indulge in hysterics at this very awkward and inconvenient moment, and if you don't want to save that dress you can give it to me and I'll take it in and wear it myself. It is far too pretty to abandon. Besides, daddy may throw something else any moment, and I'd rather it hit mummy than you or me.'

So Bridget was left alone with Mark, and he turned round and looked at her with a defeated air. 'You're buying him. An old woman with her fancy man. And getting him cheap.'

'I know I'm ludicrous in your eyes,' she said, watching him notice every line on her face, every crease on her dress. 'I know it's the traditional comic role. But I don't care. It doesn't matter what it looks like to you, Mark, because it feels happy to me.'

He sat down across the table from her, and felt sadly for her hand.

'Oh my dear, my dear . . . does he love you though, at all, even if you do love him? And for how long?'

'No, I don't think he loves me, how do I know? I don't ask him, it doesn't seem very probable. But he's fond of me. We are happy together. It's enough.'

'For how long?' he repeated.

'Oh, I know the score, Mark. A few days, a few months. The first pretty boy or the twentieth pretty girl. But perhaps not, perhaps somehow something will go on. A friendship. A kind of marriage.'

'It can't.'

'No, I know.'

'Then what's it all about? How can you let yourself in for this? Think of the pain, think of the humiliation. It's a disaster course.' He returned to the old charge he had sworn not to reiterate, but without the earlier contempt. 'You don't love him. You just want him.'

'I'm not sure of the difference, Mark, any more.'

'To begin with, love lasts.'

'Oh, well, that . . . ' She looked at her left hand, where her wedding ring had once been.

'It lasted quite a while,' said Mark defensively. 'I did love you.'

'I know. Still, it's not a good argument, is it?'

'And love . . . one gives things up for it. One risks things.'

'Quite.'

'You know what I'm getting at. To alter your life for a mere boy, a mere fancy.'

'You're probably right, I see that. But it makes no difference. You're talking as if I were trading in something real for something false. Gold bracelets for junk jewellery. If I refuse the junk jewellery, what do you reckon are my chances of finding a gold bracelet? What am I losing, Mark? Because what you're saying is, go back to your Waddon flat and wait for Mr Right to turn up. Well, at my age?'

He was silent.

'Or should I try and become asexual and self-sufficient? Why? And in any case, I've got a taste for junk jewellery, I've gone off the gold standard.'

She was wearing a bright and pretty plastic necklace, and she felt for it for a moment, recalling Roger who had given it to her. 'Though junk jewellery isn't fair as a description of Giles, you know. It was a step in the argument.'

'I know. But he's so young, what can you have in common? He doesn't share anything in your background. And he's making use of you.'

'He doesn't see my background. He doesn't label me. I like him for the reason middle-aged men pick up young girls.'

'A woman at a party told me that was fear of impotence.'

'I used to think that. It's a bit unfair. It's just that young bodies are more sexually attractive than old bodies. Women aren't supposed to notice that. I used to have a special motherly smile for young men I passed in the street, I'd wonder if they were doing well at university or getting promotion in their jobs. Now, I eye them. It isn't done to admit it of course. It rather shocks me. Perhaps I'm corrupted. Do you think . . . but if so . . . and poor Rebecca's meal is all spoilt.'

She moved as if to get up.

'You will be penniless, abandoned, ill and ashamed within a year,' he said desperately. 'I cannot understand, I cannot.'

'Let me tell you a story. There was a French king, a long time ago, in the Middle Ages. I don't know which one, one of the Henries I expect. And King Henri condemned a man, one of his servants, to death, for breaking one of the hunting laws. The man threw himself at the king's feet and begged for mercy. Now King Henri had a favourite horse, a chestnut, a beautiful mare, and the condemned man worked in the stables and knew of the king's love for his horse. He begged for pardon and the king moved away impatiently, but then he begged for a year of life, because in one year, he promised, he could teach the king's favourite horse to talk. And the king granted the delay, adding that if the horse learned to talk the man would be rewarded and allowed to live, but that if it did not the man would be put to death lingeringly with the most terrible tortures. So the man left the king's presence and his friends surrounded him and commiserated, saying he was worse off than if he had been killed immediately and more swiftly, and asking him whether he did not now regret his unwise promise. 'Oh, no,' said the man, 'after all in a year anything may happen. The king may die. Or I may die. Or the horse may talk.'

She paused, and then went on. 'So you see, that's why I'm going. To save my life. I was dying in the Waddon flat. I might as well die as go back to it. And in the end, it's a risk worth taking.'

'The horse may talk?'

'Yes.'

There seemed nothing more to say. He got up and called Phyllida and Rebecca back; they had been busy trying to save the meal and somehow the evening was reconstituted and Giles was not mentioned again.

BOTH JONATHAN AND Serafina had been outraged by Bridget's and Giles's plans when they heard of them. Jonathan, on the verge of proposing to Laura-Lorna, and awaiting any moment promotion to his firm's Paris office, was becoming more conventional. He was beginning to talk about the Company Image and re-opened communications with his family in Switzerland. He used a phrase Mark would have been pleased to hear.

'But, Giles, you are no better than a gigolo.'

'The first "g",' said Giles, spoiling the effect, 'is usually soft. Softer even than in Giles. There is no reference at all to gig, as in pop group. It is amazing that with all your advantages you have so little linguistic knowledge. You mean,' and he corrected the pronunciation ostentatiously, "Giles, you are no better than a gigolo." I'm so glad you didn't use the Washington expression "walker".'

'You're just letting yourself be bought.'

'I shall endeavour to provide value for money. We do after all live in a consumer society. It is usually considered a virtue.'

'It is absolutely repulsive.'

Whereupon Giles astounded Jonathan by saying very quietly, and rather frighteningly, 'And now you've had your fun and expressed your moral superiority, that will be all from you on the topic. I don't mind for me, but I won't have Bridget upset. I am extremely fond of Bridget. I thought you were too.'

'Yes, of course . . . I mean, Bridget . . . '

'Right then. Watch it. I haven't a reputation to keep up any more: you have. Which makes you one hell of a lot more vulnerable and me for once a good deal tougher.'

'I shall be glad to have you out of the flat,' said Jonathan. But the lease was in both their names and he could do nothing about it. In any case, if he were to go to Paris, and it seemed very likely, the friendship would come to an end. As of course it would if Giles carried out this preposterous idea. It was extraordinary as the days wore on how the two of them settled by force of habit into very much their old relationship. Phyllida announced her intention of moving back to her own room if Bridget would only go back to Waddon every night, or instead of odd nights only.

'I could sleep on the sofa for the two or three nights I shall be back in Battersea,' said Bridget. She sounded cheerful.

Serafina looked suspiciously from Bridget to Giles to see whether some conspiratorial glance passed between them at this; she was not comforted by its absence. Phyllida refused Bridget's compromise, but without hostility, and it was clear that negotiations of some kind would proceed. Normality, in some form, was coming back.

'But I can't move back to Waddon for the whole week,' said Bridget, during one such amicable conversation. 'Who will look after Mr Redditch unless I spend quite a while here, checking his medicines and stocking the fridge and doing the laundry?'

'I will,' said Serafina. She had not gone back to work. Official letters arrived from time to time but she did not open them. She threw them in the wastepaper bin and pretended they had not come. Her salary minus the National Health sick pay was still being paid into her bank account. She hoped she would not be expected to pay it back.

'You couldn't bear it. You hate him.'

'Oh, no. I've got quite fond of him, really,' said Serafina. 'And as it is poor Giles has to look after him on the nights you stay in Waddon, after a day at work, and it's all too much. No, it's time I took over. Giles'll help me, won't you Giles? We'll look after Mr Redditch together. After all, he's Giles's grandfather.' She beamed at Giles. Bridget's hold over him had been established largely by her use of Mr Redditch, she thought, and two could play at that game. 'I will try and take him across to the park occasionally now that the summer's come,' she added sweetly.

Although Bridget had no intention of being edged out of the flat entirely, not even for Phyllida's sake, Serafina's offer did enable her to stay in Waddon more often, and so to take prospective purchasers over the flat herself and show it in as good a light as possible, with warmth and fresh flowers and crisply-laundered curtains. It was important that the flat should be sold quickly, or the whole impetus of the plan might vanish. The light of common day might change her mood or Giles's. And it was important also that it should be sold for a good price, for though Giles, as an American citizen, could get work, Bridget foresaw that she herself might finish up illegally washing dishes in San Francisco kitchens alongside equally illegal Haitians and Mexicans.

'Oh, no,' said Giles when she made a studiously unconcerned comment about this. 'I could always marry you, I suppose. That'd give you American citizenship and stop the problem.'

'Would it? Good.'

Neither of them was quite sure about this, and indeed Bridget was almost certain that she had heard of the English wives of U.S. citizens being unable to take paid work. Some girl in Boston had written sadly to a lecturer at the college, and a friend's daughter too, in Philadelphia . . . but she could not recall the details and let it slide. 'We could check at the Embassy,' said Giles, uncertainly, but they preferred not to. Better not to discover bad news. Better not to alert the watchdogs, they thought. Better not to know of legal snags. Better to assume all would be well. And after all one could live for years on £35,000.

'Say it in dollars,' said Giles. 'It's enormous. We might even run a car.'

'Oh, we shall have to run a car,' said Bridget.

'And we'll both find jobs anyway.'

Bridget had had new passport photographs taken, at a proper studio, throwing away the horselike ones from the kiosk with no sense of guilt. The new ones pleased her. She took some time affixing one to her visa application, considering what to put on the form at the point where it asked the purpose of her visit. She did not tell lies on forms. She had been brought up to tell the truth even to officials; she was shocked by people who went through the green channel at Dover even when they had two bottles of cognac instead of one. So the truth it must be. Nevertheless, to announce that she intended to settle in California would obviously be unwise. She paused for a moment and then filled in the form unhesitatingly, in clear block capitals, not needing to think when she reached the difficult space. Purpose of visit, it asked. Pleasure, she wrote firmly and happily. Pleasure.

She told Mark about this and he was a little shocked, listening to her plans with continuing dismay. He had begun one of his lists, but it did not comfort him. 'Listen,' he would say to Rebecca, 'it may work, you know, it may work. Quite a lot of people . . . Anne Thackeray Ritchie and George Eliot and Angela Burdett Coutts all married men twenty or more years younger than they were . . . and there was Colette – I must check to see whether she married him, but the young man was absolutely devoted to her.'

Rebecca tried to help him build up his defences and discovered Gertrude Douglas, Lord Alfred Douglas's sister, in a review. 'Her husband was only a boy,' she said.

'There you are then.'

'Yes. Five and we've hardly started.'

Nevertheless Mark's burden of anxiety was not lifted. Even Erin Pizzey's picture in the paper with her new husband (only twenty-one the paper said but he looked older, people got things wrong) did not lift his spirits. 'Six,' he said.

It was not a very encouraging total.

He decided as a last resort to appeal to Giles's better nature, and asked him out to dinner. He took him neither to the wine bar nor to his club. He avoided the wine bar because he wanted to impress and overawe Giles, and because in any case wine bars were in his view for luncheons only; and he avoided the club in case old Graham-Robertson overheard another embarrassing remark, for it seemed likely to be an embarrassing conversation. He took Giles to Chanterelle's and they sat among the bamboo and greenery and weighed each other up.

'It is quite brave of me to have come,' said Giles thoughtfully, having rejected the elegant soups in favour of smoked salmon mousse. 'You are looking just like a heavy father about to ask a young man if he can support his daughter in the style to which he would like her to become accustomed. And you know perfectly well I can't. Bridget is going to support me.'

'She is not a wealthy woman and she is a very insecure one. I suppose it is no good appealing to your better nature.'

'Oh, none at all. That is what Bridget does. She is very good for me, I feel sure. If you had my interests at heart you would not disapprove at all.'

'Stop posing. It is too serious for that.'

Giles was silent for a while, almost as if he were thinking only of the food which had been placed before him.

'This is really a splendid place. I hadn't been here.'

'It is well spoken of,' said Mark.

'I am here under false pretences though.'

'Why? What do you mean?' Mark found himself distracted: he was wondering whether there was perhaps a mole on the back of Giles's neck. There was, he had just observed, a very small one, hardly worth noticing let alone kissing, on his right wrist. He wrenched his mind back to Giles's statement. 'Why?' he repeated.

'Because of course I can't go to California. Only I don't know how to tell Bridget.'

Mark put his fork down, leaning back in his chair, swept by relief. 'I knew you'd see . . . and it wouldn't be right for you. You couldn't stay fair to Bridget.'

'As to that, sir,' said Giles, suddenly old-fashioned, 'I think it would have worked.'

'You can't seriously have expected to enjoy being tied to an older woman for ever.'

'I think that is a most improper remark for any man to make about his ex-wife. Moreover, Bridget is a delightful woman and I am not prepared to sit here and listen to her being insulted. I think, sir, you owe her an apology. I shall be glad to receive it on her behalf.'

For God's sake, thought Mark, the idiot'll challenge me shortly. The roles he and Giles had been playing were suddenly inverted. He shifted uneasily, peering cautiously across the table for a hint that this righteous indignation was an act, a tease.

'I assure you, sir, that I was looking forward to a good deal of delight and entertainment in Bridget's presence, and I would, too, I hope, have given her . . . ' He paused to consume the last forkful of smoked salmon. A lack of delicacy, thought Mark, eating smoked salmon paid for by a man whom one was berating in these terms. He was comforted, but said nothing. Giles was already being quite pompous enough. Not a lack of delicacy, then, but a welcome sign of humanity and youth. He waited for Giles to continue, as he quickly did, with the words, 'the delight and company which friends do give each other. I strongly object to any suggestion on your part that . . .'

All this, thought Mark, would have been very proper from a middle-aged man to a younger one in 1890. It was amusing but it angered him as well. He was damned if he was going to put up with it in the mid-twentieth century from a young nancy-boy who had ordered the most expensive dish on the menu for his main course; and who was in any case almost certainly just playing games with him, as well as games of a rather different sort with his ex-wife.

'I meant no reflection on Bridget of course,' he said politely. This appeared to satisfy Giles. They sat in silence. The raison d'être for the meal appeared to have gone. They ate their way through the next course, talking of cinema, until Giles raised the topic again.

'It's not that I don't want to go to California, though. You misunderstood me. It's that I can't.'

The waiters came and went. Mark said nothing. He watched Giles eat a raspberry sorbet.

'I can't abandon grandfather, you see. I don't believe Bridget could, actually.'

'Have you only just thought of that?' He had been going to offer the young man a rather good cognac, but angry at his wasted evening, at the general thoughtlessness, at the whole situation, he chose without enquiry a cognac for himself and a Benedictine for Giles, thereby signalling both his own economic status and his contempt for Giles.

'I've only just *realised* it,' said Giles. 'We'd thought of it before, of course we had. In theory it would have solved the problem. Once I'd gone, the Social Services would have had to act. Even social workers couldn't assert that the rest of them had any responsibility for grandfather at all. There wouldn't have been a relative in the country to take care of him. We'd have genned Jonathan up to phone the Area Office as soon as the plane had taken off and some official or other would have had to do something. We were going to give Jonathan a list of the relevant statutes to read over the phone. There might have been a sticky day or two, but eventually grandfather'd have found himself comfortably situated in an old people's home, among lots of company, which is where he really ought to be. Much better for him. It's the logical solution.'

'You make it sound so, certainly. And Bridget agreed?'

Giles lit a cigarette (which made Mark all the gladder that it was Benedictine and not brandy that the waiter now placed before him). He launched his next words through a drift of smoke. 'I don't think you understand how desperate Bridget is to go to America,' he said apologetically.

'I understood it to be your idea.'

'Oh, yes, my idea, entirely. Africa or China would do Bridget just as well. That's hair-splitting. I mean, Bridget has latched on to the whole idea of getting out. You've all sat around letting her sink into a swamp of boredom, it seems to me. How to survive was her problem.'

'It is most people's problem.'

'Really? *You* expected more than survival. You didn't leave her till you'd got your sex-life neatly arranged for. You had a girl, you're awaiting fatherhood, you've got a job you enjoy, you're doing pretty well.'

'Bridget has to solve her own problems, live her own life.'

'That's what I'm saying. Going off with me is the first thing she's wanted to do for years. She's clinging to the idea like a shipwrecked sailor to a liferaft. If she lets go, she'll drown. Right. So then you expect her to say, when I tell her we're not going because of leaving grandfather, 'That's all right, Giles, of course we can't go, there's your dear old grandfather to think of first'. What do you think she is, some kind of saint? No, I gave her a loophole and by God she went through it. She

201

didn't *let* herself think other than that it was a sensible way of getting him into a home.'

'It doesn't sound like Bridget.'

'It sounds like anyone. What right have you to expect Bridget to behave better than anyone else just because she's middle class and middle-aged and ever so well brought up? We both wanted to go and we were both bloody well going.'

'And now you're not?'

'No.'

'Why?'

'I can't do it to the old man. Don't laugh.'

'I wasn't. Would you rather have a brandy?'

'Uh? Oh, no, thanks, I prefer Benedictine.'

'Why can't you do it?'

'Not tough enough I suppose. I don't know. I could murder him, often, nearly have once or twice, but just to walk out and leave him stranded . . . only if I don't, I leave Bridget stranded, don't I? There doesn't seem to be a right course of action.'

It occurred to Mark, looking across the table at Giles's puzzled face, that this might be almost the first time the young man had tried to solve a problem in moral terms.

'But you've decided?'

' "Decided", sounds too deliberate. It's just that I can't walk out on the old man. It isn't an imaginable thing to do. Not to him or to Jonathan and Phyllida and Serafina, come to that. Hell, we're friends. Kind of. Only how am I going to tell Bridget?'

It was some seconds before it dawned on Mark that this was not just an expression of uncertainty but an honest request for information.

'I've no idea.'

'Only I've got to do it soon, I suppose, before she sells the flat.'

'You'd certainly better do it soon.'

'She'll . . . she'll be a bit upset.'

'She'll certainly be upset.'

Mark was unable to offer any help nor did he want to. He found himself as confused as Giles. He was growing extremely angry at the prospect of Bridget's disappointment. He had embarked on the evening in order to persuade Giles that Bridget should not go to America; he found himself determined at the end of it that she should.

'There must be some way of solving the problem.'

'Can you think of one?'

'No.'

'Then I shall tell her tomorrow.' He stared out into the wet summer night. 'How do you think she'll take it?'

'I don't know,' said Mark slowly. 'I don't know her any more. But I'm afraid.'

He had not been afraid, when he told her about Rebecca all those years ago, that she would kill herself, it had not occurred to him as a possibility. Now he did fear that she might well do so, but whether this change in his attitude was a reflection of a real change in Bridget or of a greater sensitivity in himself he did not know. 'There must be a way round it . . . look, she'll have about £40,000 I assume.'

'£30,000 more like. We're hoping for £35,000 but I doubt it.'

'Are you sure? A good flat it was, two bedrooms and a large lounge, thought I'd done rather generously for her, new luxury block and all. Central heating and a garage. Flats are in demand.'

'It's O.K. The heating's warm air, though, expensive to run and inefficient. And then it's not in a good area. Straight on the main road and miles from a station. Well, you remember. And the kitchen's inadequate, you couldn't fit a freezer into it.'

It did not sound like the flat Mark recalled bestowing on Bridget with haste and generosity. 'I remembered radiators,' he said.

'No. Warm air.'

'Oh. All right then. Let's say £30,000 at the worst. Couldn't you use £10,000 to put your grandfather into a good home, a private one, and get him settled before you go? It'd keep him there two years anyway.'

'Do you think I ought to use Bridget's money that way? Because quite honestly, I don't.'

'I think if it's the only way to implement her plans for her future it's perhaps necessary.'

Giles thought this over. 'But I can hardly put it to her. I can ask her for things for me, that's fair enough, but not for the whole bloody family.'

Mark could not follow this morality at all, but was no longer concerned with it. It was some means of getting Bridget and Giles to California after all which had puzzlingly become his main aim. 'Leave it to me,' he said, 'I will suggest it to her. She is probably in a state of great conflict over it herself you know. The Bridget I know would not be happy in California had she left an old man abandoned to officialdom over here. It will still leave you some £20,000 to get started on. I will take her to lunch at a favourite little wine bar of mine and tell her about the Miller Eventide Home.'

He found himself feeling quite parental towards Giles and a little sorry that their relationship must end so soon.

'No,' said Giles. 'I cannot do it. I must tell Bridget we are not going, refrain from handing in my notice, and settle down in some small flat to looking after grandfather. Sod him.'

So they parted, Giles in deep gloom and Mark in a furious temper.

'But I thought you didn't want Bridget to go to America?' asked Rebecca, who had begun to look forward to Bridget's departure since, while she was fond of Bridget, the time had surely come for Mark to be more concerned with her own imminent baby.

'I hadn't really thought, I suppose, how much it must mean

to her, how little alternative she has.'

'It will be a disaster either way it seems.'

'The disappointment will kill her,' said Mark.

SERAFINA WOULD NOT have cared if Bridget did die, though for once she was not thinking of Bridget or death. She spent that evening daydreaming of a future in which she and Giles kept house in a little country cottage. Mr Redditch, transformed by Serafina's loving care into a gentle, wise, and admiring old man, and given to raising cucumbers and tomatoes, pottered about all day in a green-house placed conveniently out of sight at the bottom of the garden, rarely impinging on Serafina and Giles's domesticity other than by proffering baskets of freshly gathered vegetables. Serafina was much respected in the village and Giles was doing well at work. All this had been financed either by Serafina's winning a premium bond or by her mother dying and the consequent sale of her mother's flat. Or by both, in which case old Mr Redditch would spend much of his time in the stables, polishing the riding tack. Once she and Giles had been married for a year or two, old Mr Redditch would tactfully disappear.

Meanwhile, however, Mr Redditch was snoring in the armchair, Giles had left to meet Mark, and Bridget was safely out of thought and mind in Waddon. Bridget was quite an old woman, Serafina had decided, and nobody could ser-iously prefer her to herself. She sat sleepily watching TV and sipping coffee, her peaceful mood lasting until Jonathan's furious demand as to why she hadn't got Mr Redditch to bed yet.

'Get him to bed yourself,' she said.

'I'm going out.'

'Then it can't matter to you.'

'No. But it does somehow. Can you manage to get him in by yourself?'

'I expect so. Otherwise he'll just have to wait till Giles gets back, won't he?'

'And indeed why not? As I'm out. Only I thought I heard you telling Giles you'd see to him if he went out tonight and not to worry that Bridget was in Waddon. Still, as you say, it's Giles's affair really.' He went out.

Serafina hated putting Mr Redditch to bed. Nevertheless, once Jonathan had left, she decided to do it. Then, when Giles got back, there would with luck be a tranquil hour or so before bedtime. The flat would be theirs. He would be grateful that her care had enabled him to go out. Anything might develop.

'Beddie-byes, Mr Redditch,' she cooed, hauling him up from his chair, and manoeuvring him through the door.

He swore at her the whole time he was undressing, until he collapsed breathless on the edge of the bed with his pyjama trousers twisted in his hands. He could not work out how to get them on; could not find out at all how his feet should match up with the holes. When she had sorted this out for him they were both angry, but the struggle to get him sitting up in bed united them by the intensity of physical effort in which it involved them both. Serafina's crossness diverted itself to Jonathan. He had gone out, she felt, with unnecessary speed. 'If Jonathan had still been here', she asserted, 'we'd have got you sitting up in a jiffy.'

'You try putting your arms round me from behind, girl, under my armpits . . . '

'I can't *get* behind you. Not room.'

'Lean over then and reach, and I'll push up with me hands and feet. Now.'

But his arms were not strong enough or his co-ordination was too purposeful. His body slipped in the bed as his arms pushed. They looked at each other in despair.

'I'll get some more pillows', said Serafina, 'and prop you up where you are till Giles gets back.'

So he ate his supper uncomfortably and insecurely propped in a kind of nest in the middle of the bed.

'You, girl,' he called.

She left her television programme unwillingly.

'I spilled my tea.'

It took her almost an hour to change the sheets and his pyjamas and get him back to bed. This time however she managed to get him propped up against the pillows in the usual way. It was a trick, she decided, you had to get him sitting right at the top of the bed, almost against the wall, pushing the pillows out of the way, and then when you lifted his feet into bed, and his bottom slipped down as his body sagged, it would finish up where you wanted it. She felt almost triumphant.

'Bridget gets me comfier,' said the old man. 'She wouldn't have made such a meal out of changing me neither.'

'Well, Bridget's not here.'

'No. How'll I get on when they go to America, girl?'

'I've got a name.'

'I use it when I can remember it. Not a name that sticks in my mind. How'll I get on, girl?'

'I don't think Giles'll go to America. I've been talking to him about you when Bridget's not around. She doesn't know everything. We'll look after you.'

'Not very well, you won't.'

'Better than the Old People's Council Home, so you'd better be grateful.'

'You upset me and I'll wet the bed.'

'You wet the bed and you'll stay wet.'

'I want to do number two.'

'You must want. You should have thought of it sooner. Goodnight.'

'I want my pain-killers. The backs of my heels are agony.'

He would want a glass of water if she gave him his pain-killers, and would drain it, and then he would want to urinate in about ten minutes' time. He always did. He would never use a bottle, it would mean hauling him out of bed.

'Just lie still a minute. See if the pain goes. You've got to have all your other medicines in under a couple of hours, at ten o'clock. You don't want to start drinking now, do you?'

'You're hard.'

'Yes.'

'I'll tell Giles you're hard. Bloody sadist, I'll say. Wouldn't give me my pain-killers. Wouldn't give me a drink of water even. Come to that, I never had my tea, remember? I spilled it. Better make a fresh pot. Make it stronger this time, looked like gnats' piss that last one did. And I'll want something else to eat before I go to sleep anyway, something later.'

'Why can't you just shut up and lie down?'

'Because I haven't had my medicines,' he said.

This puzzled her. It wasn't time for his medicines. 'It's too soon. I want to give them to you a bit later, then perhaps Giles'll be back or Jonathan, and they can help settle you.'

'I've been here ages. My feet hurt. What time is it then?'

'About eight.'

'Never. It must be later. Time to go to sleep.'

'Well, go to sleep.'

'I got to have my pills, haven't I? Want me dead, do you?'

'It isn't time.' Serafina still stood impatiently in the doorway, poised to go. She wondered if he really thought it was late. He might well get confused about time. Old people did. She recalled her grandmother with distaste.

'Hard, that's what you are. I said.'

She came back. 'O.K., if you want them.' It would save her a job later and it did not really matter.

'Pain-killers first, mind.'

That meant two of the long white tablets. She gave them to him together with his two sleeping pills and he swallowed

208

them down. The little bottle of digoxin for his heart was not evident; she would look for it later. She had not been able to find it that morning, she recalled, but the missed dose seemed not to have done any harm. There was also a large jar of brown granules about which he protested regularly. He could not carry the dessertspoonful of them to his mouth himself without spilling them. Serafina now spooned them out and lifted the spoon to his lips, but despite the anxious concentration which both brought to the act, his lips, as always, disturbed the pile before his mouth could close safely around it. A little hail of tiny pellets fell among the bed-clothes. He looked guiltily at Serafina. 'Not many tonight, not as many as some nights. Not enough to bother with really.'

'No.'

They avoided each other's eyes. Both of them knew that the heat of his body would melt the granules and leave disgusting chocolate-coloured stains on the sheets. Time enough to bother about that next day. Bridget could change the sheets if she insisted.

'I don't want one of my heart pills.'

'Two every night.' But she still could not see them. The small bottle of digoxin had vanished.

He watched her search for them. 'We run out.'

'Nonsense.'

'Yes, we have.' He had been sick a few nights earlier, immediately after swallowing them, and had fiercely asserted that they had caused his sickness. It was now a continuing struggle to make him take them.

'Here they are.' She had spotted the bottle where he had hidden it, among his handkerchiefs. She emptied two of the tiny pills into her hand. He shut his mouth firmly. His old man's lips vanished. All she could see was a straight line slashed across his sallow face. Like a rat trap, she thought, a cliché rising to her mind from some childhood reading perhaps. Certainly she had never seen a rat trap nor could she logically see the appropriateness of such an idea. He was looking at her as if he were a rat. She was trapped but he was the rat. She held the pills out to him, together with the glass of water. He struck at the hand holding the pills and they rolled away on to the floor.

'Do without them, then.' She put the glass down and began to take the top pillow away. A greasy smell rose from his hair.

'Got to have my sleepers.'

He liked these, perhaps because they were an attractive pink. They seemed safe, they reminded him of the little pink cachous which his youngest aunt used to give him to suck as a bribe to be good when he was left in her care while his mother went out cleaning. 'I want my sleepers.'

'You've had them,' she reminded him.

'No.'

'Yes, with the pain-killers first of all.'

He screwed up his eyes as if trying to look back into the past through a mist.

'Honest you did.'

'Can't have. I always have my sleepers last.'

'Well, today you had them first.'

'That was pain-killers. You'll see, I won't sleep, I'll lie awake all night. You'll see. I'll call you. I'll show you.'

He was quite capable of it, she thought desperately, capable of fighting to keep awake, of demanding to be taken to the loo, to be given another glass of water, to be given another pillow. He would destroy her.

She said, 'Well, I told you,' and handed him another two sleeping pills.

'I'd been counting, you see,' said the old man complacently after he had swallowed them. 'I always has four pills at night, two different kinds, and then tonight I had my pain-killers too, and that makes six, and I've had six pills now, and that's right. I been counting on my fingers to keep tally.'

'Quite right, Mr Redditch. Goodnight.'

But he had to be taken to the loo and have his bottom wiped and hauled back into bed and the neat little trick to get him sitting against the pillows didn't work as well as she thought. And then he demanded tea.

'I won't sleep without my tea.'

She pushed her hair out of her eyes with the back of her hand.

'Do lie down and . . . please do. Your pills'll begin to work and you'll not get the benefit . . . '

'I'm not sleepy yet. I want something else . . . I want . . . '

She seized the bottle of sleeping pills and emptied three or four into her hand, pushed her hand against his mouth. 'Go to sleep,' she yelled. 'Go to sleep.'

He stretched for a glass of water, swallowing the pills without protest.

'Thought I'd had my pills,' he said, mildly surprised.

'Well, they weren't working then.'

'Naughty, naughty. No need to be so rough with me.' He was not surprised. Just so had his mother lost her temper with him when he was little, pushed rejected food into his mouth, held his nose to make him swallow medicine. People were like that. He'd known a nurse or two like that as well. He closed his eyes, wondering whether he really wanted tea and not milk. Whisky was the thing. While he was considering this, the light was switched out, and he began to doze.

'Goodnight,' said Serafina, closing the door behind her in the happy certainty that tonight at least he would sleep soundly.

NOBODY WAS PARTICULARLY surprised next morning to find that Mr Redditch had slipped away in his sleep. The doctor gave a certificate without hesitation. 'A man of his age, with his heart condition, one had to expect it at any moment. Might have lived for years, might die at any second. One can't tell.' Even Serafina could not believe that the tiny adjustment in his medication, the absence of digoxin over a short period, the slight increase in his sleeping pills, could have been responsible for his death. In any case nobody knew. She had known it was a risk, obviously, but then he had been so insistent . . . She felt very angry with him for dying so inconveniently at a moment when she might, had she been less level-headed about things, have allowed herself to feel guilty. He could just as well have died a day or so later. It was just like Mr Redditch to try to make her feel guilty, to make the worst of her perfectly natural impatience. For the rest of her life she was to remember Mr Redditch's death as an example of the way life treated her unfairly, of how people ganged up on her, of how fate was never in her favour. He had died to spite her and she never forgot it. It shaped her life.

It was not for a couple of days that she realised what Giles realised as soon as he saw his grandfather dead in bed. There was now no need to sacrifice California, no need to hurt Bridget, no need to buy yet another expensive city suit. Which of these three thoughts was strongest in his mind he did not know, but he was not without an ironic self-awareness and decided, unfairly perhaps, that the last was the more immediate emotion. Certainly it dictated his pose to Jonathan, who saw through it but entered upon the game. They had no other way of dealing with a death which

212

came so conveniently yet which, because it was after all death, and because they were young and ordinary, evoked, as death does, terror and compassion and guilt. So they talked wittily about Giles's clothes.

'SO THE OLD man is dead,' said Frieda. 'Very convenient for everybody.'

They were sitting in the garden. The sun was bright enough to dazzle, not quite hot enough to make them seek the shade, but hot enough to make Rebecca pull her flowing cotton dress down to protect her always winter-white legs from burning.

'Bridget will enjoy the sun in California, I suppose. She doesn't burn like me.'

'It's the penalty for your lovely red hair,' said Phyllida kindly.

'She is not though, not really, going to California? Not really, not Bridget?' Frieda's wail floated ineffectively across to Mark. The widely spaced chairs, the sun, the absence of an enclosing wall, drained intimacy and tension from the interchange. He waited a long time before replying: the whole conversation was slow, as open air performances of Shakespeare tend to be, each speaker awaiting the progress of some new arrival to the scene across wide stretches of intervening turf.

'She is going, yes. Quite soon, I believe. Contracts on the flat were exchanged yesterday. Six weeks or so, I think it is. It seems settled.'

'She will be gone before Mouse arrives,' said Rebecca. 'I'd have liked her to see Mouse before she went. But we can send photographs.' She had begun to date all events from the arrival of her baby.

Frieda had been preparing to murder Rebecca for some

213

time, since it was clear that until Rebecca had gone she could have either Bridget or Phyllida but not both. It was not however until this moment, in the sunwarmed Hampstead garden, that a sense of urgency overcame her. Until this moment, the plan, even the latest one kindly revealed to her by God, had been something to hug to herself comfortingly at those moments when she felt most forlorn. Now she could see quite clearly Rebecca's horrid pink enormous baby dressed in Bridget's clothes and occupying Bridget's room. The body grew in her vision until its flesh pressed against the wall, its podgy elbow filled the window frame.

'I shall never see her again if she goes. Never. I shall never see Bridget again.'

Nobody could think of an answer to this likely prophecy.

'I am an old woman. She was my daughter for so many years.'

'We must think of Bridget,' Mark offered.

'She would rather stay here. You are driving her out between you to get rid of her. I wonder you do not kill her, the way someone killed that poor old man.'

'Mother, no one killed Mr Redditch,' said Mark. 'He died of a heart attack or something, he died in his sleep. You must not say such things. You should not think them.'

'Oh, I do not say it was anyone here. You do not really want Bridget to go, and from what I have heard you saying among yourselves his death can only hasten her departure. My little Phyllida has too innocent a heart. As for Rebecca, she is too idle with pregnancy to do any such thing at present, she has not the energy to go creeping into other people's flats, no, not in her present state. I do not accuse you Rebecca, you are too big and clumsy in your present state. But only in England, where people have still no idea about evil, would so convenient a death be allowed to go unexamined. The English are children about the human heart.'

'Once and for all, mother, Mr Redditch was not murdered.'

'If you say so. But it makes murder so easy,' said Frieda, and fell silent, trying yet again to unravel the remaining knots in her plan to dispose of Rebecca. She could see Rebecca's death quite clearly in her mind: Rebecca would run down the stairs from visiting Frieda in her attic flat, running down to greet Mark as he returned from his day's work, would catch her foot in a trip-rope of Frieda's embroidery wool stretched across the stairs, fall the length of the staircase, and break her neck. Her fall would snap the wool which Frieda would gather up on her way down, pulling it loose from the banisters and thrusting it into her pocket. She would arrive at the scene of the accident looking at Mark, whose eyes would be entirely on Rebecca, as if she had rushed from her embroidery on hearing the crash.

On this scenario, lasting in all twenty seconds, Frieda had dwelt with pleasure ever since it had been revealed to her by God at Arnie van Blijven's party. 'No,' she had said to Trudy the next day, 'it was, as I foretold, not an intellectual party, but an alert mind can find some profit everywhere, and I found many interesting points to ponder on.'

'Sermons in stones,' said Trudy.

That Frieda allowed this to pass without completing the quotation showed how preoccupied she was. For at the birthday party, which had taken place in the house proper, in an ordinary civilised room belonging to Arnie van Blijven's son and daughter-in-law, instead of her crowded bedsitter with its one electric ring, Frieda had observed, standing higgledy-piggledy next to each other in a crammed bookshelf, a copy of the *Opie Dictionary of Nursery Rhymes*, a *Larousse Dictionary of Mythology*, and a couple of paperbacks, *Death in the Afternoon* and *Rebecca*. Frieda knew instantly what God's meaning was. He was referring to Jack and Jill falling down the hill, to Jill breaking her crown, and to the Fates which spin the life of every man upon a thread, a thread which He was directing Frieda to snap. He wanted Rebecca to fall downstairs and be killed one afternoon. The message was so obvious to her that she feared when others looked in that direction lest they read it too.

She had wondered since that afternoon whether she should have looked further along the shelf at other titles. Possibly she would then have found solutions to the problems vexing her about how to put the plan into operation. She sat in the garden, apparently dozing, going over and over the difficulties, the same three difficulties, the same three minor difficulties. It was as if some schoolmistress from her childhood were questioning her; there was a determined but patient voice in her head: 'How do you plan to get Rebecca upstairs to your flat and yet arrange it so that when Rebecca goes down again you will have placed the trip-rope in position?' it asked in academic phrasing. 'How will you ensure that Rebecca will in fact run down the stairs, when these days she runs nowhere, but moves about ponderously and carefully? And above all, Frieda, how is the trip-rope to be fixed?'

'I will solve it, Fraulein, I can work it out,' asserted Frieda slipping momentarily into a dream, only to wake with a start as Phyllida slammed a door somewhere or other. The problems however did not slip away with the dream; they remained to anger Frieda with their apparent insolubility. The last question above all perturbed her; she might manipulate Rebecca, she felt; 'After all Rebecca is only a stupid Belgian; one can always control the really stupid,' she told herself.

But how was the rope to be fixed?

For the Hampstead dwelling, though old and commodious, was still not in any way a great or magnificent house. It was a suburban home. Its staircases climbed the walls: they did not sweep grandly down between two sets of wrought iron banisters. On the stairs up to Frieda's flat, there were mean straight banister rails on the right, but only wallpaper stretching smoothly down to the skirting board on the left. God seemed to have forgotten this. There was nothing to hook the rope round, no projections upon which to hang it.

One afternoon when the house was empty Frieda had tried to hammer a nail into the skirting just above the third step from the top, but either the wood was too hard or the angle too awkward, for she made not the least impression upon the board. It was particularly frustrating as she had plenty of embroidery wool the exact shade of the carpet. She sat on a stair looking at strands of it lying against the deep green Wilton. 'She'll never see it. I've only got to get it fixed, half a dozen strands just about here.' She gazed about her crossly. Her hand strayed across along the wall as if she half hoped to find a projection budding strongly forth. 'I shan't miss the wool either, it's a vulgar shade of green. That's why I've got so much of it left, I suppose, not a shade I like. Just the colour that woman would choose to re-carpet with, of course.' The matching of the two shades of wool was, she recognised, a clear sign of God's providence. She therefore felt irritated with God that He had not also thought to ensure that the staircase to her flat had been provided with two sets of banisters.

'Just like a man, of course, no attention to detail,' she admitted, gathering up the embroidery wool and climbing, a little breathlessly, to her flat.

But she should have trusted Him, she realised, as the garden tea-party came to an end, or perhaps He was responding to her reproachful prayers, for when Frieda followed the others inside after tea, carrying in Rebecca's favourite porcelain cake dish, which Rebecca had deliberately left outside to be brought in with care when she had nothing else to carry, she found an argument developing between Mark and Phyllida as to whether the contact-adhesive cup hooks which Phyllida had bought the day before were either pleasing or safe enough to use in the china cupboard. Phyllida had begun to make little domestic additions to the house and Mark was torn between pleasure that she should feel interested enough to do so and anxiety to protect Rebecca from having her house taken over by his organising and insensitive daughter.

As so often Rebecca calmed the storm. 'They're quite plain, absolutely inoffensive. Let's have a month's trial of their safety. We'll put one up and hang this on it.' She produced a heavy Woolworth's mug which had somehow survived from the days of Phyllida's childhood. 'If it'll support this, it'll support anything.'

She had every hope it would not, for she had so far managed to limit the use of plastic in her kitchen. She would loosen the hook or fracture it after a week or so, she decided, and get rid of the hideous mug and the threat of rows of clumsy hooks simultaneously. Though she had to admit, as Phyllida held one against the wall, that they were very inconspicuous.

Frieda also thought it might be a good idea to weaken the hook in some way if it were possible. 'I could put this cake plate under the mug,' she thought, 'and what a lovely crash we should have then, what smithereens of china across the kitchen . . .'

But then she realised that such minor teasing of Rebecca was no longer of importance, since Rebecca would so soon be dead, and then Bridget could use the cake plate, which was valuable and pretty. Rebecca's heart had failed as she saw Frieda standing in the kitchen doorway with the plate in her elderly shaking hands. She was now rather touched to see Frieda place the plate carefully in the middle of the table and to be told to take care of it. 'It is pretty,' said Frieda. 'It should be kept for future people.'

'Of course,' said Rebecca, nodding. She threw the remaining cup hooks into a drawer (for Mark was already fixing one against the cupboard wall) and turned to the washing up.

'See', thought Frieda, 'how difficulties melt away when the right is on one's side. How Bridget will enjoy serving tea on that pretty china.'

And she crept downstairs that night, because Bridget would soon be in California, perhaps irretrievably so once she had gone, so that there was no time to waste if Bridget were to have the cake dish, and filched one of the hooks. It was a horrible white plastic, which would not show against the white paint. Naturally God would not have allowed Phyllida to choose yellow or scarlet. She had a skein of the wool with her, so that she could quickly try the effect when the hook was fixed. The others were watching *The South Bank Show*; she would be wiser she knew to wait until all were in bed, but the nearness of the solution to her problem drove her on and she could not wait. She peeled off the protecting strip of plastic from the hook, stooped down on the third stair from the top, and pressed the sticky base of the hook firmly to the skirting board as she had seen Phyllida press the trial hook downstairs to the wall. She had to crouch. Push hard, she said to herself, feeling the hook slip slightly from its position. Push. Push hard. Keep still, pushing. Her arm began to ache but she did not shift. Push Rebecca out. Push her under. Push the house down. Her hand relaxed, her left was still gripping the long thread of green wool, the house was oddly full of noise, or was it her head, but they would not come now, not now, she could straighten up and move from this awkward corner, so dark it was, for she had not turned the light on, not turned the light on, yet it was dazzling, it was rushing and flashing and dark. And dark.

The noise of Frieda's fall brought Mark and Phyllida and even Rebecca running. She lay at their feet with a broken neck, her feet entangled in a skein of trailing wool. 'But', said the doctor, 'it was probably a heart attack which led her to fall. She might have had the attack as a result of the fall, or it might have caused it. She might not have felt the fall.' He was kinder this time than on his first visit, for it was the same Indian doctor who had visited them before. Mark had hopes that the doctor might not recall the previous unfortunate encounter, but in vain.

'We met previously, I remember,' said the man thoughtfully. 'Your mother was not very good about her heart pills. She had lost them when I saw her before.'

His eyes wandered round the group, and alighted with some puzzlement on Phyllida. 'You were not here then, though, were you? It wasn't you who hit your head, surely? A rather older woman, I thought.' He hesitated.

Mark had a terrible feeling that he was about to ask if Phyllida were the fourth Mrs Mayor.

'This is my daughter,' he explained. 'It was her mother who hit her head. She is quite recovered.'

There was a silence. Mark felt he had still to rehabilitate his family in the doctor's eyes. It seemed terrible to be having this conversation over Frieda's dead body. Surely there were decencies to be observed beyond the quiet closing of the eyelids? 'This is my daughter,' he repeated. 'She has come home, she is helping her stepmother, my wife, you met her before. She should be sitting down.'

'When is the baby due?' asked the doctor. He did not sound interested.

'Not for a little while,' said Rebecca, who disliked physiological intimacies.

'Phyllida is helping her stepmother, she has come home to help her,' lied Mark.

'I wish you well. I suppose Dr Fielding is au fait with all this.'

'Yes,' said Mark. 'I had rather expected him to arrive in answer to my phone call actually. He has been our family G.P. for well over fifteen years.'

'On Sundays I am on duty. Always. It is in our agreement.'

Mark foresaw grimly that his future son would unerringly

choose Sundays to fall off coalshed roofs, break ankles, knock into projecting branches and scald himself with teapots.

'You will think we are very accident prone here,' he said lightly to the doctor. It sounded odd to him; he should have kept quiet. He found he was crying and the doctor was patting his shoulder, which was comforting.

'A mercifully sudden way to go, for an old woman,' said the Indian in his unexpected Oxford accent.

And after that other people took over, funeral directors and solicitors and government clerks. There was no trouble over the death. The inquest was a pure formality, as Frieda had always assumed Rebecca's would be.

So there were two funerals for Bridget to attend in the midst of her departure arrangements. She hoped her own end would come as easily and simply as had Frieda's and Mr Redditch's. She was the only mourner to attend both funerals, and had been the least disturbed. She began to live in the future. 'Death is natural,' she said reassuringly to Phyllida and Giles, 'a simplification of life. As long as we live first.' She did not share their unease at the convenience of these deaths. For it was not only Giles whose life was made easier by his grandparent's death. Phyllida found Frieda's death solved the immediate problem of where she was to live; she moved into the attic flat. The Battersea flat was being vacated; other Londoners, unknown to each other as yet, would occupy it soon and construct a different refuge. Jonathan and Giles had surrendered the lease. Jonathan was already in Paris when Phyllida gave her little housewarming supper in Frieda's flat. Serafina was there, but it was their last sight of her, for she had fled to her father's. She had abandoned Battersea and her mother, and decided to allow her father to spoil her; she had decided to forgive his desertion of his wife and indeed of herself, since he was now growing very rich by selling hard-porn video tapes and opening more and more video rental shops. He had bought a new house with a swimming pool in

Weybridge. It was just her luck, she thought, that he had not grown rich more quickly; or then she might have married Giles. Nevertheless she was not unhappy for a while. They fortified each other's sense of innocence as they discussed again and again the impossibility of putting up with Serafina's mother. Eventually Serafina's father would get tired of these conversations and Serafina would be asked to leave, but of this, and of successive suicide attempts, and of the slow decline before her, Serafina was naturally unaware.

So neither Jonathan nor Serafina was at Heathrow to wave goodbye to Giles and Bridget. Phyllida and Rebecca and Mark made up the farewell party; Phyllida, had she known, might have waved goodbye to Daniel Johnson too, for he was booked on the same flight. He was travelling Club Class, however, for the San Francisco church to which he was retreating, with a sense of defeat which was never to leave him, was prosperous and knew what was due to their new pastor. He was to spend his future in a more settled and middle-class area than that in which Bridget and Giles would find themselves. It was improbable, though not impossible, that they would ever meet. What is certain is that Phyllida did not glimpse him, or ever think of him again, and that even Giles and Bridget, travelling on the same flight, did not notice him, for the jumbo jet was full, and he boarded it early. In any case Bridget had eyes only for Giles, and Giles, as Bridget noted, was watching a family nearby with a good-looking son. Then he shrugged cheerfully and put his arm round her shoulders. 'Manhattans straight up as soon as we're off, I think,' he said, relishing the American turn of phrase. She saw as clearly as any of them what calamities might lie ahead. But she could not wish it different. I am a ridiculous woman embarked on an absurd and disastrous adventure, she thought, but she did not mind.

By now the routines of departure had caught them up. The luggage had been checked in, farewells said. Mark found himself relieved when the two groups separated and he had to peer through the crowds to wave goodbye to them as they turned for a last smile before going through passport control Bridget said something to Giles and they both laughed. Together they waved and turned away, borne away from London on a tide of delighted amusement.

Phyllida wondered what other passengers would guess about them. There seemed no pattern to their behaviour within which this fragile relationship might be understood. They were so clearly not mother and son.

'An aging film star and her secretary?' asked Mark, startling her by the revelation that they were considering the same problem.

'Mummy a film star?' she jeered.

'No, of course not. Though she was quite pretty as a girl, you know. But no confidence at all.' He made a discovery. 'She looks confident enough these days.'

'But not a film star.'

'No.'

Even she and her father did not know, she realised, how close Giles and her mother were, how the equation between desire and money was weighted. And neither Giles nor Bridget could know how long what they were creating would endure, what deserts of fear and resentment might lie ahead of them, how soon they would find themselves enemies or for how many years they would offer each other comfort.

'California, here I come,' her mother had said getting out of the back seat of Mark's Cortina in the Terminal 3 car park.

Phyllida thought of the small Waddon flat, overcrowded with unwanted furniture. She imagined the great and sunny Pacific beaches. She saw unwillingly, as in a vision, her mother lying alone in the middle of a great expanse of sand, but whether she was weeping in terror or blissfully sunbathing she could not discern.

'All the same,' she said insistently to Mark and Rebecca as

they walked away, 'it isn't just silly of her, is it? It is rather a magnificent thing to do, isn't it? Brave? It might just work? Don't you think it's magnificent? A kind of splendid behaviour really. A trusting of the future, a daring kind of love. Isn't it, in a way, splendid?'

But the roar of traffic and planes and people drowned Rebecca's answer and Phyllida dared not ask again.